STILLWATER RISING

Also by Steena Holmes

Finding Emma
Emma's Secret
The Memory Child

STILLWATER RISING

Steena Holmes

LAKE UNION
PUBLISHING

Published by Lake Union Publishing, Seattle

www.apub.com

Amazon, the Amazon logo, and Lake Union Publishing are trademarks of Amazon.com, Inc., or its affiliates.

ISBN-13: 9781477825150
ISBN-10: 1477825150

Cover design by Kimberly Glyder Design

Library of Congress Control Number: 2014937381

Printed in the United States of America

This book is dedicated to the families who have been affected, in one way or another, by an event similar to what has happened to this fictional town. Your loss can never be adequately shared, but I am humbled by your strength.

CHAPTER ONE

JENNIFER CROWNE

The water in the bay rippled with the push of a breeze that wafted in through the open kitchen window. With her eyes closed, Jenn welcomed the morning kiss on her cheeks as the air surrounded her.

She tightened a shaggy brown housecoat around her body and waited for the flow of the coffeepot to slow enough for her to fill her mug. The drip of each drop into the pot of liquid rang in her ears, along with the steady tick of their old grandfather clock down the hall. Every small sound intensified against the morbid stillness in the house, a facade that ate her insides every second there was no noise, no laughter.

She leaned down, planted her elbows on the wood block of her island, and stared out their large bay windows that overlooked Stillwater Bay. Her husband had built their house on the cliff with the bay on one side and the town of Stillwater on the other. Glass windows filled three-quarters of their home. Rob claimed it was so they could see everything around them, but to Jenn, there was no place to hide.

Once she had loved the openness. Now she hated it.

A light fog hugged the waters below as it drifted out with the current. Every day since *that day* a fog had covered the shore. As if the bay itself was in mourning, a thought that comforted Jenn more than she wanted to admit.

A light scuffle and creak from upstairs alerted her that Charity, her thirteen-year-old daughter, was awake. A glance at the clock confirmed it was still early, barely past six in the morning. Jenn sighed at the thought of another long day when she had to be stronger than she was.

She'd been dreading this day since the letter came in the mail.

She checked the chocolate-chip muffins she'd pulled out of the oven earlier to make sure they were cool enough, just as her daughter came down the stairs.

"Good morning." Jenn straightened and held out her arms. Despite the dark circles beneath Charity's eyes, her gaze was bright, almost to the point of feverish.

"Morning," Charity mumbled as Jenn gave her a hug. She pressed her lips against Charity's forehead to test for a fever.

"Can we go in a bit early today?" Charity pulled away and reached for a muffin from the tray.

"I was actually thinking . . . why don't we go into the city for the day? We could go see a movie, do some shopping . . ." Heading into the city was one of the last things she wanted to do, but it was better than the alternative.

"You can't be serious?"

It had been a gradual change, but the sweet, innocent daughter Jenn once knew was gone. She saw glimpses, when Charity didn't think anyone was looking, but gone was the charming little girl Jenn knew, and in her place was a hormonal, surly teenager who didn't seem to remember what it meant to respect her parents.

"Yes, Charity. I'm serious. It could be"—she struggled to find the appropriate wording—"fun?"

"Shopping? Fun? No thanks. I'd rather go to school, Mom." The exasperation was quite clear in Charity's voice.

Jenn's shoulders sagged. The school.

"It's going to be a madhouse, so I'd like to get there a bit early if we could. Mandy and I planned to meet up so we could go in together."

Jenn didn't know how her daughter did it. How she could be ready to head back into *that place* so soon.

Just the thought of the school, the mere mention of its name, brought vivid images to mind, images Jenn knew would haunt her for the rest of her life. Thank God Charity would be going to high school in Midland in the fall.

"Amanda's going? Of course she is." There was no reason she wouldn't. "Well . . . I thought your dad would take you. Didn't he say that? He knows I can't . . . ," Jenn sighed at the dubious look on her daughter's face. Of course he wasn't going to take her.

"Mom, you have to drive me. You can do it."

"I'm sorry. I don't think I can," Jenn managed to whisper before she took a deep breath and fortified herself.

What was it Robert had said to her last night? That people looked up to her, counted on her to be strong. But who would be strong for her? Not her husband. He wanted to pretend it had never happened, burying himself in his work instead of allowing himself to grieve for what they had lost.

Her gaze drifted to the abundance of floral arrangements and cards that littered her house. She wanted to throw them all out, rip up the cards she couldn't bear to read with the well-meaning words written on them, and burn them until she choked on the smoke.

The grief counselor had told her that one day she'd want to read those cards, that the words written would give her the strength to remember, to get past the nightmare she lived. Soon she'd have to throw out the dead arrangements, the ones that had withered, but even those she couldn't touch. Every time the local deliveryman rang her doorbell, she had him place the vases on the foyer table for either Robert or Charity.

"How's the muffin?" Jenn changed the subject as she took another piece of her muffin and nibbled on it.

"Edible," Charity mumbled as she reached for her second one.

Jenn shook her head but kept quiet. *Pick your battles*, her counselor had said.

"Are you ready?"

Charity shook her head as she glanced down at the pajamas she wore.

"No, I mean, are you sure you're ready to go to the school today? I'm sure Amanda or even Principal Stone could gather your things for you."

"Mandy's mom says we can either be the victor or the victim. And if we don't face our fears, then they'll soon control us."

Of course Amanda's mother said that. It wasn't her child who had been gunned down at the public school. It wasn't Amanda's mother who had found her son facedown in his own blood.

"And is that what you're doing? Facing your fears?"

"I'm not afraid of anything." Charity's head popped up, and her chin jutted out.

Jenn sagged against the counter and turned her attention back to the scene outside her windows. The water in the bay beckoned her, soothed her.

"I wish I could say the same thing," she whispered. She was afraid of everything lately, it seemed. Before the shooting, she knew what she wanted in life. In fact, she'd taken steps to change her life, to be more in charge. She thought about the envelope sitting in her desk drawer and wondered if she'd ever get back to the woman she used to be.

"So can we? Mom? Hello-o?"

Jenn shook her head and refocused.

"I'm sorry?"

Throwing her hands up in frustration, Charity just frowned and stood there with her hands on her hips.

"Right. School. No. I don't think you should go." Jenn filled her mug with coffee, grabbed another muffin, and started to head over to the breakfast nook when her daughter's voice stopped her.

"But Dad said . . ."

Jenn turned. "I don't care what your father said. I'm not taking you. If he wanted you to go, then he should have been here to drive you."

She'd had this argument with Robert last night. She'd suggested instead of going into the office in the wee hours like he normally did to get a head start on work, he should stay home and they would have breakfast as a family, then they could deal with this if it came up. Apparently he hadn't believed her when she said she wasn't going to drive Charity to the school.

"That's not fair."

"You should know by now, life isn't fair."

"I'm calling Dad." Charity reached for the phone.

"Yes, great idea."

A letter had been mailed last week to all the families letting them know about the school opening the last Friday before summer vacation officially began. A day for closure and remembrance. The day was going to include games and outdoor activities, but opening the school—for even a short period of time—had nothing to do with supporting their children and everything to do with maintaining the pretense that their town was learning to move forward.

"But Dad—" Charity half turned away from her as she spoke to Robert on the phone.

Jenn watched as her daughter's face crumpled. She breathed a small sigh of relief as her daughter hung up the phone. Jenn didn't say anything, but she was thankful Robert backed her up on this even if he didn't agree with her.

"He can't drive me. He has a bunch of meetings today. Which totally sucks." Charity pushed items around on the island.

"There's no reason to go, Charity, you know that. If it's just to see your friends, then you can do that anytime."

"That's not it."

"Then what is it? Explain it to me. Why are you so insistent to return to that school?"

"You don't understand." Charity lowered her gaze. "Please, Mom, will you just take me?"

Jenn shook her head. "Please don't ask me again."

She never wanted to step foot back in that school. Ever. She doubted there would ever be a day when she didn't drive by without remembering, without the sinking weight of depression and grief hitting her.

Robert had asked her how long she was going to be like this. When she asked him what he meant, he only stared at her. Then he said the words she wasn't ready to hear.

"You've lost yourself. Little by little, and I don't even think you care."

But she did care. She did. But it had only been a month since she'd lost her son. A month. Of course she wasn't going to be her usual self.

A week ago today, the town had held a funeral service for the students who had been murdered in a fit of rage by a local teen. Weeks before, each family had held their own private services. A time to mourn the loss of their children in a senseless act. There were so many questions without answers, so much anger, hurt, and fear.

Jenn wished she were more like Robert, who didn't seem to feel any of that. But she did. She felt all of it, and it was overwhelming. She tried to wear a mask, knowing it was what Robert wanted, especially when they were out in public, but it was hard.

Her ten-year-old son had been one of the last children to be found.

"I'm sorry, Charity. But as far as I'm concerned, you should never have to set foot in that school again."

"I can't believe you. This isn't about you. It's about me going to my school, seeing my friends, and learning to live life again. Unlike you who doesn't want to live at all," Charity mumbled before she ran back up the stairs and slammed her bedroom door.

Jenn winced as the sound echoed through the house.

CHAPTER TWO

CHARLOTTE STONE

Sweat dripped down Charlotte's face as she bent over, hands anchored on her knees while she struggled to breathe. She'd killed it today, and it felt good. Great even. She reached for the towel at her feet and wiped her face and neck before standing up straight and stretching. The sounds of the buff fitness instructor on the television screen congratulated her for an excellent workout as Charlotte reached for her water bottle and gulped it down.

She needed that. She'd let her workouts slide in the past few weeks, and it showed. Her patience was thin, her energy low, and she was starting to get fidgety. But after this workout, she felt good. Sore, but good. Energized even. As if she could handle anything that came her way.

She made her way up the stairs, taking two at a time, not ready to let the burn leave her yet, and poured a cup of freshly brewed coffee. She'd bought new beans yesterday and ground some up before heading down for her workout. The aroma of those beans still filled the air, and she knew it would be a good cup of coffee. Exactly what she needed.

She picked up the mail she'd set to the side yesterday and sorted through the abundance of letters that still came in. Letters from various students and families from Stillwater Public School, and even from people who didn't live in their town but had been moved by the tragedy, as if it had touched them personally. All letters Jordan rarely opened, let alone read.

She flipped through all the envelopes and set aside the three addressed to Jordan with childish lettering. She didn't understand his hesitation when it came to opening them. Stacks of similar letters filled a shoe box in her office, so many letters praising Jordan for his heroic acts and describing how his selflessness saved countless lives. She still teared up when she read the ones from the younger students thanking him and calling him their hero.

He was a hero. She knew it. The town knew it. The world knew it. But sadly, she didn't think Jordan realized it.

The sliding door off the kitchen opened, and a cool breeze wafted around her ankles. Charlotte set the letters down and glanced over her shoulder to see her husband standing at the door, his back to her, while he banged his running shoes together to get rid of the sand. His navy running shirt and shorts were drenched and so was their dog, Buster, who plopped down on their back deck with his tongue hanging out.

"Looks like you two had a good run." Charlotte took a sip of the strong coffee before she set her cup down on the counter and poured some for her husband.

"You should come out sometime with us," Jordan offered his obligatory request, same as he did every morning.

"Maybe next time." The words were automatic, but they both knew she'd never join him. Running was his thing. Not hers.

Jordan grabbed his coffee, placed a kiss on her cheek, and made his way to the guest bathroom where he always showered off.

Charlotte hated to clean a trail of sand throughout the house, so when they built the guest addition to their home a few years ago, she made Jordan start cleaning up in there after his runs.

While he headed downstairs, she went upstairs to their bedroom and had her own shower. Afterward, with her hair still wet, Charlotte took her coffee into her office. She needed to get a head start on today. She planned to go to the public school, where Jordan served as principal, and then spend the day there with the students and any parents unwilling to leave their children alone.

Not that she blamed them. Her hands shook slightly as she sank down in her desk chair and reached for the *Stillwater News*, the weekly paper that was little more than a gossip column for the town. She'd been worried about the front-page article and even asked Arnold Lewery, the editor of the paper, to let her take a peek at what he'd written, but ever since the media had swarmed their town and refused to leave, Arnold had become tight-lipped about what he featured in the paper.

In the beginning, almost every article he wrote, whether it was a piece about one of the families affected by *the event* or a new development, he'd been scooped by one means or another. Their town had become overrun with media within hours of the shooting, and they still couldn't walk down Main Street without a microphone being stuck in their faces or the knowledge they might see themselves on the evening news.

They'd managed to hold a few special town meetings without alerting the media presence, and it became quite evident that everyone, including Arnold, expected her to fix the mess they were in with the media and to shelter them from prying eyes.

"Staying Strong" read the title on the front page. Charlotte was pleased to see the image she'd submitted via e-mail to Arnold last week. She was glad he used it. There'd been too many images of the school ensconced with police tape, memorial flowers, and weeping parents. This photo, taken last year right before the annual summer parade, featured welcome banners, balloons, and children's play centers set up at the school for the summer party. Starting at Stillwater Public, the parade always made its way down Second Bridge, across Main Street, and then up First Bridge until everyone joined together back at the school for the festivities. She hoped the image would help the town remember the good things about Stillwater Bay and not the sad, horrific event that had torn them apart.

She knew not everyone was on board with the school reopening. She'd had more than enough parents complain and demand that the school stay closed, and while she attempted to understand their pain and knew they only spoke out of fear, she had to look past the emotional impact of the school shooting back in May and look to their future.

She was determined that today would be the first of many steps their town needed to take to move forward past the ugliness of what had happened.

Charlotte flipped through the paper, reading the letters to the editor and the small-town gossip, and almost missed the short article written about Julia Berry, the mother of the shooter. She set the paper down on her desk and leaned back in her chair. Her heart went out to Julia. If anything, what had happened was as much Charlotte's fault as anyone else's, including the mother of the sixteen-year-old shooter.

From day one, everyone knew Gabriel Berry had bad blood in him. He was that boy who was always in trouble. The moment he stepped foot into a store, all shop owners knew to keep their gaze on him. She'd lost track of the number of times she learned from the town sheriff's weekly updates that Gabe Berry had been escorted home in the middle of the night after deputies found him hanging around the local cemetery. Who lurked around a graveyard in the middle of the night? It wasn't *natural,* people said. No matter what anyone did, how they reached out to him, it never seemed to matter.

Since the shooting, Charlotte couldn't shake the feeling that all of them shared responsibility for failing to help Gabriel. The blame couldn't be directed at any one person, no matter how much the media tried to do just that.

She glanced down at the article again: "One Bullet, One Boy and One Mother."

A shiver ran down her spine as she read the lie in that headline over and over and over.

CHAPTER THREE

JENNIFER

Jenn tugged the edges of her housecoat tighter as she sat outside on her back deck.

She felt guilty for not taking Charity to school. Not enough for her to change her decision, but enough that she knew she'd handled the situation wrong. Jenn couldn't imagine she was the only parent not okay with the school being opened; no doubt there must be others. What were they doing this morning? Had they argued with their kids as well, or had it been a mutual decision?

It was the beginning of summer. Thanks to the spring rain, the grass was a vibrant green, flowers were blooming, and the trees were full of chirping from the birds nested there. Where had the time gone? Maybe she could talk Charity into helping her with some baking today. They could watch a movie together, eat ice cream, and then meet Robert after work for dinner at Fred's Tavern. No doubt her daughter was up in her room, headphones over her ears as the music blared, anything to pretend her mother wasn't around. She knew this because it's how Charity had acted the past few weeks.

She would either be at her best friend's home or in her room. Anywhere and everywhere, except with her mom.

It hurt, but Jenn was trying to give Charity the space she needed. And, if she were to be completely honest, Jenn hadn't minded the space herself. It meant her life was quiet without any expectations, other than when Robert needed her.

Hiding, withdrawing inside herself, that was how she was coping. If coping was the right word to use.

A lone sailboat sat out in the bay today. Alone, engulfed in silence. Jenn wished she could do that, jump on a boat and set sail, away from all the prying eyes, all the mundane words that meant nothing to her. Alone with her thoughts, with the ability to remain numb without the condemnation from her family and friends.

Life wasn't fair. God was cruel. And yet, none of that mattered. She was still expected to place one foot in front of the other, to move forward with her life, even when all she wanted to do was bury herself in grief beside the son she'd lost.

Robert's voice whispered in her head. *You're still a mother.*

Jenn pushed herself up from her chair and headed back into the house. She refilled her coffee mug, adding an extra shot of Baileys, and noticed that the bottle she had bought only last week was almost empty. She stood there in her kitchen, unsure of which direction to go. Back to bed? Watch a movie? Have a bath?

Or talk to her daughter.

Her feet moved toward the steps as her decision was made.

Her counselor had told her to take it one moment at a time. And in this moment, she needed to be a mother to Charity.

As she slowly climbed the stairs she thought about what she'd say when she opened the door. How would Charity respond? Would she still be upset? She was a thirteen-year-old with mood swings; for all Jenn knew, she could be asleep already.

She knocked on Charity's door and waited. She couldn't hear anything from behind the closed door, so either she had her headphones on or she was asleep. Jenn knocked again, this time louder, but there was still no response. So she opened the door and peered inside.

The room was empty. Charity wasn't in the bathroom either.

Jenn ran down the stairs and looked through the house, walking through the rooms, but she was alone. At the front door she realized Charity's running shoes and schoolbag were gone.

Her fists clenched at her side as the sudden onslaught of anger filled her. How dare she!

Jenn grabbed her cell phone and purse, reached for her keys, and called Robert as she made her way to their garage.

"Do you know what she's done?" Jenn said the moment Robert answered his phone.

He sighed on the other end.

"I had a feeling she would."

"You had a feeling?" Jenn's words were clipped as she held the phone up to her ear and backed out of her garage. "You had a feeling but didn't bother to say anything to me about it?"

"Why should I? You're the one who is home. I told her not to go to school today, that I'd come home early this afternoon and we could do something together." Robert's voice heated in anger. But she didn't care.

Then his words hit her.

"I'm the one who's home? What do you mean by that? I asked you to stay home this morning." She paused as something down the street caught her attention. "Crap. I can't handle this right now."

"What's wrong?" The Bluetooth function took over, and her husband's voice filled the SUV. Jenn set the phone down and shook her head. She wasn't ready for this. Not yet.

Stillwater Bay was a small town. Nine months of the year the population maxed out at just under three thousand, but in the summer months, from June to the Labor Day weekend, their numbers doubled and sometimes tripled in size, thanks to their proximity to the bay and premium real estate. The landscape on top of the cliffs held million-dollar summer cottages with billion-dollar views.

"The Andersons are here. I don't have their basket made up or anything," Jenn muttered as she drove past their house. There were only five houses on their street, with two facing the bay, one facing the island the town of Stillwater sat on, and two backing onto the golf course. Out of all those houses, Jenn and her family were the only ones who lived there year-round.

"Are they early?"

"Of course they're early." She turned left and headed down First Bridge Street. Two bridges led into their town. The double bridges not only added to the quaintness of their town but also made it special. Ahead of her, in the distance, was her daughter, walking on the sidewalk.

"Found her." The tight band across her chest loosened, and she felt like she could breathe again. Her anger drained as she drove toward Charity.

"You'll take the basket over later, right?"

Robert's words didn't click at first. Baskets. Andersons. Keeping face despite their mourning.

"Of course I'll take over their precious basket. Why wouldn't I?"

"I overheard your talk with Charity the other night regarding the baskets." There was doubt in his voice.

"Then you would have heard my answer." She hoped the exasperation in her voice was loud and clear.

Every word she'd spoken that night to Charity about the baskets was for Robert's benefit. She'd already had this discussion with him and even suggested having someone else do the baskets, someone like his secretary for instance, but he wouldn't hear of it. It wouldn't be the same, he'd argued. People would think we aren't coping, he'd said.

"People expect the baskets. It's a tradition. From our home to theirs. It's a small way to let them know they are wanted in this community, that they matter—"

"It's your way of saving face," Jenn had mumbled. But Robert had heard.

He'd turned to her, placed his hands on her shoulders, and squeezed. "We can either let what happened destroy us or strengthen us." He had then placed a kiss on her forehead and walked away.

The other night she'd been in her office going over her lists, making sure she had enough supplies on hand for these baskets. Charity had stood there, in the doorway, not wanting to come in and help.

"Why do *you* have to do the baskets? Why can't someone else?" Charity muttered as Jenn counted the baskets in her cupboard.

"Like who?" Jenn had responded. "Everyone in this town has been affected by what happened. It wouldn't be fair of me to ask someone else to take on something I love doing." *Or used to love.* She wasn't ready to be social, to put on her happy face.

She drove up close to Charity and, with a push of a button, rolled down the passenger window.

"Need a lift?" The anger she'd felt earlier when she realized Charity had disobeyed her paled thanks to Robert's inquiry regarding the baskets. Which was probably a good thing since this really wasn't a battle she needed to fight with her daughter.

"Are you mad?" Charity stepped toward the SUV but didn't open the door. She hefted her schoolbag over her shoulder and looked around.

"More like disappointed. Come on, I'll drop you off."

"I'm sorry," Charity apologized as she got in. She dropped her schoolbag down between her legs and buckled up.

"It's not okay to take off without telling me," Jenn sighed but didn't drive forward. She wanted to have a talk with Charity about this, and the drive to the school would only take two minutes at the most.

Thankfully, her daughter had the decency to look contrite.

"I know. It's just that Amanda and I had plans, and we promised Principal Stone that we would help out with the younger grades."

"I see." Jenn wasn't too happy to hear that last bit. "When did you talk to Principal Stone about this?"

Charity fiddled with her fingers. "Well, I didn't, but Amanda did. I think." She shrugged. "We talked about the idea at least."

"Why didn't you tell me this earlier? When I asked?"

"Would it have mattered?"

Silence was Jenn's only reply.

As they made their way over the bridge and passed through the downtown area, Jenn kept her attention focused on the road ahead of her and not on the small crowds of people who lined the sidewalks, waving at the vehicles as they passed with banners and signs.

"Why are they doing that?" Charity scrunched down in her seat as if to hide herself. Jenn understood the feeling. She noticed Samantha Hill, the lone reporter left from the outside world, in the crowd. For over a month, massive throngs of media had swarmed their town. Once the funerals were held and things quieted down, most of the media had left. All but the one reporter from UCN.

"Mom?"

"I think they just want to offer you guys support."

"That's kind of nice, right?"

Jenn nodded. Sure, it was nice.

"I didn't expect so many people to be here." She glanced over at the school parking lot, on the corner of First Bridge Street and Pelican Street, where the only school in town was located.

"There's Amanda. Can you drop me off here?"

Jenn pulled over to the curb and turned her blinker on. She was thankful she didn't have to drive closer.

"I'm going to hang with Mandy after school, okay?" Charity unhooked her seat belt and opened the passenger door.

"That's fine. Love you," Jenn called out. She wasn't sure if Charity had heard her since she slammed the door, but she did give her a small wave. Jenn watched her daughter link arms with her best friend and walk toward the school together.

That day had started out like any other. She'd made the kids breakfast and they'd rushed to school, running a little late due to Charity having to change her outfit three or four times that morning.

On the drive down to school, the kids fought, with Bobby upset about being late and worried that he'd have to get a late slip and stay after school. Jenn had gone in with the kids and signed them in at school; said hello to Jordan, the school principal, as he walked with the kids down the hallway to their class; and waved at the kindergarten teacher, who hustled her kids from the cloakroom into their class. She remembered the sound of her cell phone ringing and the feel of her keys digging into her palm as she searched her purse for the phone. She'd pushed the school doors open with her hip as she answered her phone and bumped into *him*, Gabriel Berry, on her way out.

Those next few seconds were forever etched in her mind. If she'd been paying attention, if she hadn't been on the phone, if she'd actually stopped to think about why that boy—especially that boy—was at the public school and not at his own school, maybe things would have been different.

She pictured Gabriel as they bumped into one another, the scowl on his face, the frantic, wide-eyed look. She should have known; she should have noticed. But instead, she'd been on the phone with her lawyer, who'd called to make sure she'd received the documents.

It wasn't until she'd made her way to the parking lot, almost at her SUV, before she heard the first shot. And then the screams through the open windows.

Jenn covered her ears as the screams replayed in her mind, over and over and over. For days afterward she thought if she could just concentrate hard enough, she'd be able to pick out the different voices from those screams and maybe, just maybe, hear her son.

Lost in thought, she screamed herself as someone knocked on the passenger door window.

•   •   •

The door opened and her best friend, Charlotte Stone, the mayor and wife of Principal Jordan Stone, popped her head in.

"What's wrong? Are you okay?" She held the door open wide and stood there, a look of concern on her face.

"You scared me." Jenn waited for her heartbeat to return to normal while Charlotte opened the door farther and sat down in the passenger seat.

"Sorry." She reached across and grabbed Jenn's hand. "How are you doing?"

Jenn leaned her head back against the headrest and rubbed her forehead. She stared out the open sunroof at the dark-gray clouds as they rolled in and had the sudden desire to drive down to North Beach and view the bay as the turbulent wind rolled in.

"Char, I love you, but would you please stop asking me how I'm doing?" She kept her gaze upward, counting how long it took for the massive cloud to pass over her. "Isn't there something else you could ask that doesn't start with needing to know how my mental state is?"

"Jenn . . ."

"No. Seriously. Can we just agree not to ever ask each other how we're doing? Ever? If I need to talk, trust me that I'll talk, and I'll do the same for you. Okay?" She turned her attention from the clouds to her friend and caught the wariness in her gaze.

"I'm okay. I promise."

"Fake it till you make it," isn't that what they always say? She doubted she'd ever be okay from losing her little boy, but she wasn't the only one in town who had suffered a loss that day. She needed to focus on that.

She could tell from her best friend's gaze that she didn't believe her.

"Do you have time for coffee later? There's something I want to discuss with you."

Jenn's brow rose. All she wanted to do was head back home and bury herself under mounds of covers while the storm rolled in. And maybe make herself a drink.

"I'm not really dressed for coffee." She wasn't in the mood to socialize, even if it was with her best friend.

"Just meet me for coffee at Gina's in about an hour. That should give you enough time to freshen up, right?"

The school bell rang, and Charlotte opened the door.

"Please?"

"What are you doing here at the school?"

"Supporting Jordan. He's not as tough as he appears to be. This has shaken him more than I'd like to admit."

"So why open the school even if for a few hours? Why allow our children to relive the horrors? Don't you think they've gone through enough?"

"They need closure. All the psychologists I've spoken to say the same thing." She reached for the door and closed it before sitting back in the seat with a dejected air. "There's not much I can do, but this . . . this I can. Give closure, help others to heal." She pointed toward the school yard. "Besides, you know we closed off all the main areas where . . . only the gym and the front of the school are open, and we have outdoor activities planned for the morning."

Jenn shook her head.

"Not good enough, Charlotte. I'm telling you, as a parent, the worst thing you could have done was open that school, even for half a day. We need to put this behind us, to move on . . . this isn't the closure our kids need."

This wasn't the first time she'd voiced her opinion about this whole issue to her friend. She'd been open about it from the very beginning.

As far as Jenn was concerned, the school should be torn down and a memorial put in its place. Another school could always be built elsewhere.

CHAPTER FOUR

CHARLOTTE

A swell of pride filled Charlotte's heart as she watched the parents and children make their way onto the school grounds. She thought for sure more parents would feel the same as Jenn, and if truth be told, she had doubted many would show up today. Never had she been happier to have been proved wrong.

"Hi, Mayor Stone," the cheerful voices of a group of girls called out to her as they passed her. The four girls all had their arms linked together as they headed toward the front doors.

The resiliency of children amazed her. To experience something so horrific, to have their innocence stolen at such an early age and in such a terrifying way and still be able to smile, it stole her heart. It made her to want to be a better person, to look at life differently, to stop looking at the future and enjoy the moment.

Jordan stood at the front door, in his suit, and welcomed each student into the school. Some he shook their hands, others he gave a side hug, but not one student managed to slide past him without a greeting. That's the one thing she loved about him so much, his gentle heart. He had been the perfect principal and the perfect partner

and husband during the aftermath of the shooting. The perfect hero
to the children in that school.

"Mrs. Stone?" A tiny hand tugged at hers. Charlotte knelt down
to face little Ellie Thomlin.

"Hi, Ellie, I love your dress." Charlotte fingered the hem of the
pink dress Ellie wore. The material was so soft, and she knew her
mother, Lauren, had made the dress herself.

"My mommy made it." Ellie wore a proud smile on her face as
she swayed her dress so it billowed out.

"It's beautiful, just like you." Charlotte smiled up at Lauren,
who gave her a small nod. Lauren's face was tense despite the smile
she gave her daughter. It was the same look on Jenn's face earlier.
Lauren's blond hair was pulled back into a tight braid, and she
looked like she'd lost some weight, which wasn't a good thing since
Lauren was in the middle of battling breast cancer.

"Will you come with me into the school?" Ellie's soft voice
whispered.

Charlotte reached her hand out and waited for Ellie to take it.
"Of course."

Ellie had been one of the children hidden in a closet on that
fateful day. Lauren had mentioned over coffee that Ellie was still
afraid of the dark and close spaces. No doubt she always would be.

"Are you looking forward to the Teddy Bear Picnic next week?"
Charlotte asked as they slowly made their way toward Jordan. She
noticed the way Ellie tried to hold back, making her steps smaller
and smaller the closer they got to the front doors.

Ellie nodded.

"I think we might need more teddy bears, though, would you
like to help me pick some out?" Charlotte glanced over at Lauren
as she said this. She knew she should have asked first and hoped she
hadn't overstepped.

"Really?" Ellie's eyes brightened.

"If it's okay with your mom," Charlotte added.

"Please, please?" Ellie begged.

Lauren swung Ellie's hand, which was clasped tight in hers, and smiled down at her daughter. "Of course."

Charlotte winked at her before she wrinkled her nose at Ellie. "It's a date then. How about I pick you up Sunday after breakfast? We can walk downtown and go through all the stores looking for the best teddy bears they have, okay?"

Ellie gave a deep nod of her head but then stopped dead in her tracks. They'd reached the end of the grass and were only feet away from Jordan and the front doors.

"It's going to be okay." Charlotte stroked Ellie's hair and wanted to cry as her little body trembled. "You're very brave, Ellie."

The little girl shook her head. "No I'm not."

Charlotte caught Jordan's gaze as he waited for them. She squared down in front of Ellie and gently touched her chin. "But you are. You're here and you even dressed up. Do you know what that tells me?" She paused. "That tells me that you are a very strong little girl who is determined to conquer anything that comes her way."

Ellie's lip quivered before she took in a deep breath and looked up toward her mom.

"Today is going to be a good day, Ellie. I promise." Lauren bent down and placed a kiss on the top of her daughter's head. "We get to choose to have a good or bad day, and today is going to be good. I know it."

Ellie took the first step, from grass to pavement, and Charlotte noticed the way Lauren's shoulder relaxed.

"She's been so scared to come back today," Lauren murmured.

Charlotte reached for her hand. "I'm so glad she did, though. I know it must be hard."

"No, you have no idea how hard." She shook off Charlotte's hand and wrapped her arms tight around her body. "Her nightmares came back earlier this week, and last night she hardly slept. Every time she closed her eyes she could hear the screams. I almost didn't bring her."

A moment of guilt filled Charlotte before she shook it off. No, she wasn't going to go there. The psychologist she'd spoken to had confirmed that the children needed closure and that while today would be difficult, for most it would be a step toward facing their nightmare.

"I'm sorry. Is there anything I can do?"

"You've already done it. She'll have something to look forward to this weekend." She squeezed her hand. "Thank you."

"Miss Thomlin, don't you look like a ray of sunshine." Jordan stepped away from the front door and stopped in front of Ellie. "I think Mary is inside waiting for you." He winked at her.

"Mary's here?" Her voice notched in excitement, Ellie let go of Charlotte's hand and turned to her mom.

"Can I go in now? Can I go find Mary?"

"Let's go find her together, okay?" Lauren mouthed *thank you* to Jordan before she left to trail after Ellie.

Charlotte walked beside Jordan as he returned to his station at the front door. Some stragglers still lingered on the front lawn or in the parking lot.

"Are you ready?" she asked him.

Jordan nodded before he stopped and turned to stare out on the grounds. "Last year this front yard was full of parade floats that parents were getting ready, do you remember?"

"Do you think I made the right decision?" Not just for reopening the school for one day, but also for canceling the annual school parade. She pushed it back to coincide with their July Fourth events.

He shrugged. "Change, no matter the reason, is hard. We should have done something, though, anything to help cement today as a good memory."

She laid her hand on his shoulder. "But you did." The back grounds of the school were covered with obstacle courses, water balloons, and games for the kids to enjoy.

"Will a little bit of fun in the school playground wipe away the nightmares? You can still see it in the kids' eyes." Jordan rubbed his eye and sighed. "I wish there was more I could have done . . ." His voice drifted off.

"You were there, protecting them when you could have lost your own life. You saved children's lives, Jordan. I'm not sure what more you could have done."

A shadow of . . . something, regret maybe, crossed over his features.

"Principal Stone?"

They both turned and faced the school where Pamela Holden, one of the teachers who taught sixth grade, stood holding one of the doors open.

"Could you come inside, please?"

Anyone passing by wouldn't have been concerned by her words, but with one look at her face, both Charlotte and her husband knew something was wrong. Jordan jogged back toward the doors while Charlotte followed.

In the few seconds it took to make it inside, Charlotte imagined all the worst-case scenarios she could think of, but standing in the school foyer, there was nothing to see. In fact, the area was empty.

"What's going on?" Jordan asked.

"It's Molly." Pamela pointed toward the staff lunchroom while she walked ahead. When she entered the room, she stood to the side and waited for Jordan and Charlotte to join her.

"She's hiding in the closet." Pamela kept her voice low.

Jordan headed toward the closet and sank down to rest on his heels. He didn't open the door, instead leaned toward the small opening and spoke quietly to the little girl inside.

Charlotte sat down on one of the chairs in the room and watched as Jordan attempted to coax the seven-year-old out of the closet.

While Charlotte couldn't hear what was being said, she did sigh in relief as the door slowly opened and a hand reached out. She wondered how many times this scene would play out with other children.

CHAPTER FIVE

JULIA BERRY

A tiny stream of sunshine pierced the darkness in her room, illuminating dust particles in the air and tempting her to crawl out of bed and open the curtains. Instead, she burrowed deeper beneath her blankets and turned her face toward the wall where a photo of Gabe sat on her small dresser.

Her son's face shone with happiness and joy as they stood together, on the beach a few years ago. Gabe would have been around thirteen then. That was the beginning of the end.

A thud, clatter, and then another thud had the walls in her room shaking.

Julia burrowed deeper in her covers. She knew what those thuds meant.

Right now, outside her bedroom wall and soon on her front porch, the ground would be covered with broken eggs and smashed glass bottles. On the outside walls of her home, the words *Murderer*, *Monster*, and even *Slut* or *Whore* would be graffitied across the whitewashed boards of her cottage home she rented.

She expected an eviction notice anytime. Legally, she wasn't sure if they could force her to move, but morally, she probably should. It's what would be best for the town.

She wasn't the murderer. She wasn't the monster. But she had given birth to one. Somehow, somewhere, something had changed within Gabriel. It was her job as his mother to notice this, to see it, and then do whatever needed to be done to help.

But she hadn't done enough. That much was obvious.

Gabe's smile in that photo taunted her. Had he known, back then, what he would become? He had been a smart kid, blowing her away most days with his knowledge, level of understanding, and ability to read people so easily. She often wondered if he'd learned to manipulate those around him as well.

Her heart squeezed tight as she realized what was happening to her. She was slowly starting to see her son in the same way everyone else did. A monster.

With a groan, she flung the tattered cover of her handmade quilt off and slid her legs from beneath its warmth. She couldn't do this. Not again. She needed to force herself up and move, do something. Her home was a mess; she hadn't cleaned it in weeks. Dishes needed to be done, laundry washed, floors swept . . . but the idea of doing all of that exhausted her.

She reached for her long sweater and dragged it across the bed until she wrapped it around her shoulders and slowly stood, her one hand firm on the small bedside table as the room spun. The room always spun nowadays whenever she got out of bed.

She could hear Lacie's voice in her head, scolding her. *You need to eat.*

Every time she ate something, her stomach rebelled. She wasn't sure if it was the drugs her doctor had prescribed or just her body revolting against being healthy. With the way she was losing weight, maybe she carried her own death wish.

With slow steps, she made her way into the kitchen, her slippers shuffling against the hardwood floor, and she blinked at the image of Lacie standing at her messy kitchen counter.

"I hope I didn't wake you." Lacie glanced over her shoulder and smiled.

"What . . ." Julia moistened her cracked lips. "What are you doing here?" She rubbed the back of her neck and wished she'd pulled her oily hair back into a ponytail.

"Sit down before you fall down," Lacie ordered. "I just wanted to make you some fresh coffee and bring you something to eat for breakfast."

"I don't need to be mothered," Julia mumbled but did as she was told.

"Are you sleeping?"

Julia shrugged.

"But you're taking the pills, right?" Lacie turned on the coffee machine.

Julia shrugged again. "I am. I just . . . I don't like how they make me feel."

Lacie grabbed a container and brought it over to the table. She opened the lid and set it in front of Julia.

Homemade double-chocolate muffins. Julia breathed in deep and found herself reaching for a muffin.

"How do they make you feel?"

"Numb."

"I would give anything to feel that way. Anything." Lacie's eyes watered before she blinked repeatedly.

Oh God. "I'm sorry. I'm so . . . so sorry." How could she be so selfish?

"Don't. I can't . . . We promised, right?"

Julia nodded.

"You are not to blame. If you want to feel . . ." Lacie shook her head. "Then feel. But you have to promise me that it won't destroy you."

"I promise."

"You've lost way too much weight. You haven't been out of your house in days and"—her nose scrunched up—"you could really use a shower and some clean clothes."

"I didn't ask you to come here." Julia leaned back in her chair and placed her hands in her lap.

"I'm not leaving until you finish that muffin and drink some coffee."

Julia stared at her dirty kitchen floor and couldn't believe she'd let things go like she had. She'd always taken such pride in her clean home, happy that despite its small size, she'd been able to make it feel cozy and clean. Gabe would be embarrassed to see things now.

"How can you"—she hesitated—"how can you get through each day and not feel like giving up?"

Weary lines covered Lacie's face, and for the first time, Julia noticed how tired her friend looked. Maybe she wasn't handling it well either.

"I have my family to think about. What I want to do and what I have to do are two different things."

"I wish I had done something," said Julia. "Seen something. I feel like it's all my fault, and I need to fix it somehow, and yet . . . I can't."

"So that's why you let people egg your house and spray paint horrible words on the siding? Why you let them treat you like garbage?"

Julia didn't say anything. Yes, that was the reason. Because she felt she deserved it. If it helped them feel better, if it helped them to deal with their grief in a small way . . . then she would take whatever they threw at her.

She didn't think she said that out loud, but she must have because Lacie stood up and gave her a hug, holding on tight.

"Here's what I'm learning. Grief demands an answer, and sadly, sometimes there isn't one. But that's not your fault and it doesn't mean that people can take out their anger on you."

Julia didn't know what to say.

"How people are treating you, it's not okay. This isn't how this town should be reacting. You're not at fault." She sat back down in her chair and pushed the container of muffins forward. "I don't blame you, Julia, for what your son did." Her eyes closed as she paused. "I can't let my grief overwhelm me to the point where I don't recognize myself. I can't do that. And neither should you."

Julia watched as Lacie stood up and busied herself with cleaning her kitchen. Julia finished her muffin and then went over and wrapped her arms around her friend, leaning her cheek against Lacie's back. She could feel the sobs shake Lacie's body as she stood there, crying, but there was nothing she could do. No words she could say to take back the fact that Lacie's child was now gone.

How does one go about apologizing for that?

She didn't know. She made her way back toward her bedroom, where she tossed her dirty clothes into a laundry basket and then headed into the bathroom to shower.

CHAPTER SIX

JENNIFER

After heading back home and changing into something a bit more presentable, Jenn made her way downtown, parking just outside Sweet Bakes, the local bake shop. The sky was still dark, the clouds slowly gathering together. She grabbed her umbrella, just in case the heavens decided to open like she thought they would. A good thunderstorm would do her soul well today.

Gina's was just down the street, but the downtown area of Stillwater was so small that you could walk the length of the downtown in fifteen minutes. It was one of the things Jenn loved about her town.

Robert's real estate office was located next to the bakery, the perfect location, especially for the summer tourists who flocked to Sweet Bakes for Anne Marie's confections.

Jenn's favorite treat was Anne Marie's *pain au chocolat* and her macaroons. All French inspired from her time spent there as a pastry chef.

Before stepping out of her SUV, she caught sight of Samantha Hill, the reporter from UCN in her rearview mirror. Why was the woman still in town?

Jenn hated the reporters and how they focused on the killer and not the killed.

"Go away." She hissed into the microphone shoved into her face.

"Mrs. Crowne, just one question, please?"

"Really, Ms. Hill? One question? You said that on the day of my son's funeral as well, didn't you?"

Their son's funeral had made front-page news, a fact Jenn would never forgive. The image of her standing off to the side as she stared at her son's casket, the haunted look in her eyes, she'd never forget it. How could they memorialize something like that? Why did they have to focus on her, on her grief?

She knew why. Robert. Her husband was the reason, and parts of her heart hated him for that.

She understood the deal made between the reporters, Charlotte, and Robert, who believed it was better for the town if the news focused on only one family while the others mourned in private, but she doubted she'd ever forgive Robert sharing something so private with a world that had no true understanding of the devastation they experienced.

"Mrs. Crowne, please, I promise." Samantha followed her to the sidewalk and then sneaked around her to block her way into the bakery.

"Fine." Jenn refused to smile, be polite, or offer anything in the way of kindness to this woman, no matter what Robert said.

"It's about the school reopening today. What are your thoughts?" The microphone held steady in her face.

Jenn tossed her hair back and gripped the handles of her purse.

"I think it's horrible and unfair to the children and parents of Stillwater to expose them to a place where so many lives were lost."

A gleam appeared in the reporter's gaze as she struggled to keep the smile off her face.

"Mayor Stone believes it will help the students move forward, do you not agree?"

Jenn snorted. A tiny part of her knew she should keep her mouth shut, that she should hold back her anger and tactfully agree with whatever Charlotte had said, but she couldn't. Not this time.

"Move forward? By what? Forcing them to face the horrors of their past? Is this the closure my daughter needs, is that what you are asking? In order for her to deal with her brother's death, does she need to revisit the scene, to see the area where her brother and fellow students were gunned down to death? No. She doesn't. None of them do." Jenn clenched her hands tighter as she struggled to keep her voice down.

"But it was my understanding that portion of the school was closed off."

"Just because flowers cover my son's grave doesn't hide the fact that there is still a grave. It doesn't matter what section of the school the children are in today, they won't forget. They will never forget."

"Does the mayor know how you feel?"

"Of course she does. But she doesn't have children. She wouldn't understand. I'm sure I'm not the only parent who feels this way." Jenn shrugged.

"And yet, your daughter is at the school, right this very minute, isn't she?"

Jenn took a step back, her mind a whirl with how to respond. Yes, Charity was there; she chose to be.

"My daughter is a victor, not a victim. This is her way of proving this to herself. As a mother, I want to protect her from the world, but apparently I can't. If I could, I would have been able to protect my son too." Jenn took another step back, ready to flee, but was stopped by the reporter.

"Just one more question, I promise. There's a rumor that the school might close, forcing the students to attend a school in Midland. What do you think of this?" The conniving gleam in Ms. Hill's eyes burned brighter, as if the anticipation of Jenn's outburst would be the fuel to her already burning fire.

Jenn didn't disappoint.

"I'd like to see the school torn down and something else built in its place, a memorial of sorts for the lives lost. The children of Stillwater do not need to be subjected to the reminder that we couldn't protect them. This town should never have to relive the horror of what we experienced. Absolutely." Conviction filled Jenn to the core. Yes, this was the right thing to do. "Shut it down. It's the best idea I've heard all day."

· · ·

Jennifer pushed open the bakery door and took in the delicious aroma of chocolate and freshly baked bread. She breathed in deep, hoping that the anger coursing through her body would dissipate.

"I don't know how you do it." Anne Marie stood at her front window. "The way you smile and appear all gracious. Some days I wish I were more like you." Anne Marie turned and held out her arms to give Jenn a hug.

Jenn shuddered. "And most days, I wish I were more like you." She gave Anne Marie a small smile before they both turned to stare out the window and watched as Samantha Hill stuffed her equipment in the back of her UCN car. "Besides, I wasn't all that gracious out there. I probably said more than I should have."

"You? I find that hard to believe," Anne Marie laughed. "Oh honey, don't be so hard on yourself. You know what you need?" Anne Marie reached for a tray that sat on a small table beside her and held it out for Jenn to see. "Try one. It's a new recipe."

Jenn's eyes widened at the display of small chocolate squares. The top of the squares were all drizzled with chocolate and covered with a light dust of icing sugar in the shape of a heart.

"What are they?"

"My version of a chocolate kiss. Just try one. I promise it will make everything else in your life disappear the moment you take a bite."

Jenn eyed the chocolate. "If that were true, you'd be my personal fairy godmother." She winked at Anne Marie, who pretended to look upset.

"I thought I already was." Anne Marie replaced the tray on the table and took a square for herself. "Can you believe this is my second batch? I almost ate half of the first one I made before boxing it up and sending it up to the school for the teachers."

Jenn eyed the other half of her square. "These are delicious! I might need to take a few more, as samples." She loved to bake, but her level of baking was nowhere near where Anne Marie was. She'd tried to talk the woman into holding classes, but she'd yet to be successful.

"I think I can do better than that. I have a box with your name on it in the back."

"And this is why I love you." Jenn smiled as she bit into the last piece of her chocolate and let it sit on her tongue. The soft chocolate with a hint of strawberry was exactly what she needed today.

"I added some extra cookies as well. I made some for the kids who went to school today, but I figured Charity would be at home, so I didn't want her to miss out." Anne Marie walked past Jenn and headed to the back of her store.

Jenn shook her head. "She went to school."

Anne Marie paused. "I see . . ."

Jenn snorted. "Do you? Cause I don't. She snuck out of the house to go. I caught up with her just before she hit Main Street."

"She snuck out? Why that sly little . . ."

Jenn gave her a look. "It's not funny. She knew I didn't want her to go."

There was a light in Anne Marie's eyes, a twinkle that Jenn knew too well. "Seems to me, I remember a young girl who used to sneak out of her parents' home all the time as a teen." She smiled.

Jenn wagged her finger at the woman. "That was a long time ago, and things were different back then. This is the first time Charity has snuck out."

Anne Marie rested her hip on the edge of her counter. "I'm sure it won't be the last. She's a teenager. She's learning to spread her wings and figure out if she's ready to fly yet or not."

"Well, I'm not ready."

Anne Marie chuckled. "Of course you're not. I doubt you ever will be." She sobered. "Does Rob know?"

Jenn shrugged. "He wasn't surprised. Seems I'm the only one in our home who thought the school opening today was a bad idea." Words Samantha had said earlier hit her and she gazed out the window. "Have you heard the rumor that the school may be closing, permanently?" She watched Anne Marie's reflection from the window.

"I have. Not sure if it's serious or not, but there seem to be a few families in the area who feel the same way you do."

This caught Jenn off guard. "There are?"

"Haven't you been going to that small group at the church? The one Pastor Scott set up for the victims and their families?"

Jenn shook her head. She wasn't quite ready to share her grief, not like that, and since Robert hadn't pushed the issue, she'd left it alone.

"Robert went to a few . . ."

Anne Marie's brow rose. "Robert? Your husband? The man who shows no emotions and can weather anything that comes his way? He went?"

Jenn nodded. Anne Marie knew her husband better than most others. They were siblings after all.

"A couple of times, to show support, when it first started."

"But not you?"

Jenn's lips thinned. "I'm not . . . ready. It's only been a month. I don't . . . I don't want to be told I need to say good-bye or be fed some line about how this was all in God's great big plans."

"If you're not ready, then you're not ready." Anne Marie walked over to her and gave her a big hug. "When you are, then I'll be there for you every step of the way, okay?"

"Okay." The relationship between brother and sister was a tense one at the best of times, but Jenn was very thankful to call Anne Marie a friend.

"Our summer families have started to arrive." Jenn wanted to change the subject.

"I know. Trust me, I know. I had the pleasure of finding a few messages from the wonderful Carla Anderson on my phone this morning when I arrived." Anne Marie reached for her order book and pointed out the list of items Carla had requested. Freshly baked buns, dozen cookies, squares, coconut cream pie, and *pain au chocolates*.

Jenn cringed at the list. She saw the words *Welcome Basket* underlined a few times.

"I wasn't expecting them so soon," Jenn tried to explain, but Anne Marie waved her away.

"Seriously? Don't even bother. I told that woman a thing or two this morning when I spoke with her."

Jenn gasped. "You did not!"

With a twinkle in her eye, Anne Marie laughed. "Trust me, Mrs. High and Mighty should have been knocked down a peg or two a long time ago." She held up her hand. "I know, I know . . . they are important to Robbie, but seriously, since when did I start caring about my older brother's feelings?"

Mortified, Jenn could think only about Robert's reaction when Carla's husband, Shawn, told him. Which he would. No doubt a golf game had already been scheduled, along with a weekly barbecue where Jenn would have to act as hostess, once again.

"Listen, sweetheart, you're not going to be so involved with the events this summer, are you? If there's anyone who deserves a break, it's you. Robert's had you and your family front and center throughout all of this, and it's been a darn shame." Anne Marie patted Jenn on the shoulder before she made her way through the store, straightening up shelves.

Jenn sighed. She wanted to defend Robert, but what was the point? Anne Marie knew too much, saw too much, and had a bad habit of saying too much. She'd see right through Jenn's false protests.

"I need to keep my mind busy," she said instead.

"Uh-huh."

Jenn grabbed a loaf of bread off a shelf. "I feel like I'm going crazy. If he's forced me to do anything, it's because he knows I need it."

"What you need is to let yourself grieve. You haven't yet, have you?"

Grieve? Of course she'd grieved. What she hadn't done was accept her son's death. That's something she would never do.

"I'm not the only mother in this town who lost a child."

Anne Marie stared at her, and she blushed under her gaze.

"Oh honey, you might not be the only mother, but you are a mother. A mother who lost a child."

Jenn held up her hand. "No. Not now, okay?"

"What are you so afraid of?"

Jenn tore her gaze away from her friend and stared out the front window and onto the street. There was a reason she was here. Focus on that.

"Has Robert had his daily croissant yet?"

Anne Marie's eyes narrowed before she shook her head and reached down into the display case and pulled out the tray of chocolate croissants. "You know I love you, right?"

Jenn focused on pulling out her wallet. "I know. But I'm just not ready for this. Not yet, okay?"

"You know where to find me when you need me." She pulled out two croissants and placed them in a bag.

"Oh Anne Marie. I always need you."

"Good. I'm glad to hear you say that because I've got an idea, and you're not going to say no." Anne Marie leaned forward and rested her arms on the top of her display case.

"Really? And what is this idea of yours?"

"You'll let me help you with the baskets."

"You do help me. Three-quarters of the baked goods in every basket are from you."

She had a standing order with Anne Marie for her welcoming baskets she always handed out to the families who had their summer homes on Marina Drive. Cookies, croissants, and the bakery's famous cinnamon buns. Jenn added her own homemade jams, muffins, and other homemade treats before she dropped the baskets off.

"Not just with the baking this year. With everything. I'll stop by Sunday and grab your supplies. Maybe Charity can even help. Between the two of us, I'm sure we've helped you with enough baskets to know what we're doing. Okay?"

A weight Jenn hadn't been sure she carried lifted off. It would be nice not to deal with the baskets this year. To not have to face each person and listen to their platitudes and pretend everything was okay. She wouldn't say no.

"Why don't you come for dinner?"

Anne Marie shook her head. "No way. I love you, but being in the same room as Robbie right now would lead to dire consequences. I'd hate to be banned from your home altogether. Again." She shrugged. "I'll just pop over later this afternoon, before he comes home."

Jenn reached out to grab her sister-in-law's hand. "He does love you, you know that, right?"

"Oh, I know. But sometimes, honey, love isn't always enough."

Anne Marie held out the bag with the croissants and then headed toward the back where no doubt she had some loaves or cinnamon buns rising.

Jenn stepped out of the door and stood on the sidewalk. The street was practically empty, but a soft breeze wafted in off the bay.

She pushed opened the door to her husband's real estate office next door and smiled hello at Brenda, the receptionist who worked part-time, but searched the small space for her husband.

"He's just in the back grabbing coffee," Brenda said.

Jenn headed that way but stopped when she heard Robert's voice. The door to the back room was slightly ajar, and she caught sight of her husband leaning against the wall with his cell phone up to his ear.

"Listen, now is not a good time." He caught sight of her and waved her in. "No, I understand but the season is just starting and . . . yes, I understand how you might feel that way but . . . it's still her home . . . listen, I'll call you later, okay?" His shoulders stooped as he hung up the phone, and it took him a moment before he pushed himself away from the wall.

Jenn held up the bag with the croissants. "Looks like you might need this."

Rob rubbed his face, but the worry lines didn't disappear. "You have no idea." He reached for the bag but let it drop on the counter beside him.

"What's going on?" He held the look of someone defeated, and that wasn't like Rob at all.

He turned and rested the palms of his hands on the counter and placed his weight on his straight arms while his head hung low. She placed her hand on his back and felt the ripple of his muscles tense beneath her touch.

"The Robertsons, owners of the beach cottages, want Julia Berry to be evicted." Weariness laced his voice.

Jenn shrugged. She didn't see the issue. Julia Berry wasn't someone high on her list of favorite people. In fact, if truth be told, that woman deserved whatever life dealt her.

"The faster she leaves town, the better," Jenn muttered beneath her breath. Robert heard her, though; she knew he did by the way he rolled his shoulders and shook his head.

"You don't believe that," he said to her.

Jenn said nothing.

"God, Jenn, when did you become so cold?" Rob turned and faced her. "It wasn't her finger that pulled the trigger; it wasn't her who entered that school." Robert crossed his arms as his eyes blazed with fire. "You can't blame her."

Jenn snorted. "I can and will blame her. I'll never forgive her, Robert, never." Her nostrils flared as she drew in breath. Anger ignited through her veins, and she couldn't believe her husband didn't feel the same way.

"She lost her son too." Robert's voice dropped along with his gaze.

"Do you honestly think I care about that? Her son killed himself. After he shot our son and countless other children." A shiver ran down her body at the despair on her husband's face. She couldn't understand him. How could he sympathize with *that* woman? "I'm more concerned about this town and the other parents who are struggling to survive just one more hour without their children than I am for the mother who raised a monster. If that makes me cold and angry, then so be it. I'd rather be angry than . . ." Her voice drifted as Robert's gaze lifted off the floor and met hers.

"Than what? Than be the woman who mourns for her child? No, you'd rather just ignore it and pretend like it never happened. It's easier that way, right?" Robert demanded.

"I'm not ignoring it. And pretend? Is that what you think I'm doing? Pretending?"

She'd thought—no, she'd hoped—that they'd be able to be the anchors for one another while they grieved and that perhaps their marriage would somehow survive, but it wasn't working out that way.

"Was there something you wanted to talk to me about?" Robert sighed. "Otherwise, I should get back to work."

"No, nothing else to talk about of course." Sarcasm dripped from her voice, but she doubted he heard it. "I'm on my way to meet Charlotte for coffee, but that UCN reporter distracted me and I ended up next door. Sorry for bothering you." She turned to leave and then stopped. "Will you be home for dinner tonight, or should I leave you a plate in the microwave again?"

"What did Samantha want?" There was an edge to Rob's voice she'd grown accustomed to whenever he mentioned the reporter. From the very beginning the two of them hadn't seen eye to eye, for obvious reasons.

"She wanted to know how I felt about sending Charity back to school."

"What did you tell her?"

"The truth." Jenn turned to face him.

"What did you say?" Robert straightened, and instantly she caught how his whole demeanor changed. Gone was the man at war with his wife and exhausted because there was no end in sight, and instead here stood the Robert Crowne everyone knew, the man in charge.

"That I think the school should close."

"Please tell me that was off the record." Rob rubbed the back of his neck and groaned.

"Probably not." Jenn shrugged. "It seems I'm not the only one that feels that way either." The school shouldn't have opened today. There were other things they could have done, ways to help the children grieve and move on, rather than forcing them to relive their nightmares up close.

"Jenn, you can't go off spouting things like that. Not without talking to me first." His shoulders bunched beneath his shirt. "If that makes it to the news, once word gets out that you want teachers to lose their jobs . . ."

She shook her head. "No, that's not what I said."

"But that's how it will sound. Think about it, Jenn. For heaven's sake, think with your head before you speak from your heart. Please."

She wanted to argue with him, to demand he stop telling her what to do, but it was pointless. He wouldn't listen.

"Where are you going?" she asked instead.

"To see if I can clean up this mess before it's too late," Robert called over his shoulder.

Brenda, the receptionist, looked up as he stormed out the door and looked to Jenn, who'd stepped out into the main office, for answers. Except she had none.

What had just happened? How were they so off the mark as a couple? At one point in their lives, they'd been in sync with almost everything. They once had the same goals, the same ideals, the same vision.

CHAPTER SEVEN

CHARLOTTE

Charlotte marched into Gina's, her favorite coffee shop in Stillwater Bay, needing a large mug of the strongest brew Gina had. The last hour at the school . . . she was just glad it was over.

After coaxing Molly out of the closet, Jordan had walked her into the gymnasium where her teacher waited for her, then took the stage, where he spent some time talking with the students about coming back to their school and not allowing the evil that had happened to win.

Charlotte had stood there, along with a group of parents who refused to leave, and was proud of her husband. He didn't talk down to the students but rather spoke on their level, something they'd both agreed was the smartest move he could make today. There was no hiding from what had happened; they could face it and move forward.

There had been some low murmurs behind her back as Jordan spoke, and when she'd turned to face those who'd been speaking, she'd been greeted with frosty glares. She'd glared back.

Maybe having the students return to their school for half a day before summer vacation started hadn't been the smartest decision on her part. But she'd honestly believed it had been the right one.

She still did and she wasn't about to apologize for it. She'd learned a long time ago being the mayor of a small town meant sometimes friendships would get tested, but she'd accepted that part of the job.

Despite some of the parents' objections, the children had banded together, comforting one another and holding hands or arms tight, and she'd known then that there was a future for them, as a school, as a town, as a small community.

"Charlie, I didn't expect to see you in until later." Gina, the owner, came to the door and gave her a hug.

Charlotte forced a smile on her face. "I got away earlier than I expected." She glanced around the room and noticed Jenn waiting for her. "She's here already, that's great."

"She's been here a few minutes, and I just put on a fresh pot of the new bold brew that arrived." Gina smiled. "I also left some extra goodies on the table with Jenn. You both look like you could use a treat today."

It was hard to miss the frown on Jenn's face as she approached the table.

"What's wrong?" she asked.

Jenn shook her head but bit her lip before she raised her coffee mug and took a drink.

Charlotte let it slide as she sat down and reached for a shortbread cookie. "Have you been waiting long?"

"Not really. This is only my second cup." Her attempt at a smile was weak. "And my third cookie. I had to sweet-talk Gina into bringing more."

Silence settled over them while Charlotte ate her cookie and waited for her coffee. She looked around the empty room and sighed. Normally this place was busy, all the tables would be full and you'd have to raise your voice just to be heard. Out of the eight tables, only two were full, including her own.

"It's quiet in here," she said.

"Too quiet. Gina said it's been like this for a while now. I think people have just gotten used to the reporters taking over and they've stayed away, not wanting to be interviewed over and over again." Jenn frowned as she stared down at her cup.

Charlotte twisted in her seat and glanced out the window. "But they're almost gone. Samantha is the only one left, right?"

"I don't think it matters." Jenn shrugged.

"Here you go, sugar." Gina set the coffee cup down and then refilled Jenn's.

"Are you ready for our summer families to arrive?" Charlotte asked Gina.

A smile settled over the woman's face. "I can't wait. I'm ready for the hustle and bustle to begin. I have some summer students that need the hours too. It's the summer season that helps us out through the winter ones."

Charlotte studied Jenn once Gina left. "What happened after you left the school? You seem . . ."

"I ran into Samantha."

"So?" She liked the woman. Yes, she could come across as abrasive and nosy, but compared to the other reporters that had come, she was the kindest.

"Rob had to do some damage control afterward." She grimaced.

Charlotte didn't like the sound of that. She knew the mood Jenn had been in after she dropped off Charity and could only imagine what she'd said to the reporter.

"I thought Samantha agreed to back off after the funerals?" At least, that was the agreement she and Robert had been able to make with the reporter. They'd agreed to some exclusive interviews if Samantha would give the families of Stillwater a break. They needed time to heal, but that wasn't possible when every time they stepped out their front door, a reporter was there asking them questions.

Jenn shrugged. "I was just in the wrong place at the wrong time."

"What did you say?" She reached across and placed her fingers on the top of Jenn's hand. Jenn withdrew and leaned back in her chair.

"She asked how I felt about the kids going back to school." Jenn's voice petered off, and she wouldn't look Charlotte in the eye.

Charlotte rubbed at the back of her neck. *Great.*

"Let me guess, you told her you didn't agree with my decision." She really didn't expect to be told anything else. If there was one thing about their friendship, it was that it was based on honesty and trust. Jenn wouldn't shy away from expressing how she felt, but she wouldn't backstab Charlotte either.

"I told her the school should be closed," Jenn whispered.

Charlotte sat back in shock. "You said what?"

Jenn's eyes closed and her shoulders slumped for a moment before she took in a deep breath, straightened her back, and opened her eyes.

"I said that the school should be closed. Forever." Strength gripped Jenn's voice, and Charlotte was confused by the sudden change.

"Close the school? And what would happen to the two hundred students who attend there? Where are they supposed to go?"

Jenn shrugged.

"No, I'm serious, Jenn. You were one of the parents who fought to keep the school open in the first place a few years ago. You said the bus drive was too long for the younger ones. That's the only reason why we still have a public school—because of parents like you."

"It was. But things are different now." Jenn wouldn't look at her, and she knew that was a bad sign.

"If we close the school, you do realize what would happen, right? Most of those families with small children would move, and what about the teachers and support staff? What are they supposed to do for work? Because you know they won't find positions in the other schools . . . there's no funding for that. So all those people would be out of jobs . . . or have to move to find a job. Really, Jenn? Is that what you want?"

Did her friend not realize the damage that would occur if the school closed? Did she not realize the fractures that would occur throughout the town at the mere suggestion?

"It's not a matter of what I want anymore. It's a matter of what's best for our children. Something you obviously don't care about."

That hurt. "You don't mean that."

"Why wouldn't I?" A hint of anger laced Jenn's words. Charlotte caught the way her fingers tightened around her coffee mug. "How could you possibly think it was okay to send my child back into the place where her brother died? They're only children. They need to be protected, and today, it had nothing to do with protecting our children and all about your image as the mayor."

Charlotte recoiled as if she'd been struck. "That's not true," she whispered.

"Really? You're so concerned about this town moving forward that you've forgotten we all need time to grieve. We can't heal until that happens."

"But we have grieved." The moment Charlotte said it, she wished she could take those words back.

"How about I pretend I didn't hear that."

Charlotte winced. "I'm sorry. I should never have said that, I—"

"Have a different focus than the rest of us. I get that. But just because you don't have to deal with an empty bedroom where your child should be sleeping at night, doesn't negate what everyone else is going through."

"You're right. I'm sorry." Charlotte nodded. She couldn't pretend to understand what Jenn and other families were going through.

"I'm sorry for what I said, by the way." Jenn toyed with her coffee mug.

"When?"

"To Samantha. It was out of line, even if it was the truth. Robert realized that before I did." Jenn's gaze had turned inward, and she could only imagine the conversation that had occurred between the two.

Sitting on the council, Robert understood how important it was to show that their small town was strong, that it would recover from what had happened. In the past weeks, Robert had sat in her office and they'd discussed various strategies, rearranged the calendar for the summer season, and created a plan to appear united and whole to outsiders.

Robert was a rock of strength, and sometimes Charlotte forgot that he was also one of the families who had lost a child.

But it only took one look at Jenn to remind her. She knew her friend tried to stand strong next to Robert and hide her grief, but Charlotte could see the pain in her eyes and the wobble of her smile.

"It's okay," Charlotte said. "You can't always appear to be unshakeable. Samantha just played on your weakness. She knew today would be hard for many families. I just hope she doesn't attack anyone else." She'd talk to Robert later this afternoon to see how he'd handled it.

"How was it at the school?"

Charlotte took a sip of her coffee. "It was hard. A lot of parents stayed close, which is completely understandable." She closed her eyes, remembering Molly. "And some of the kids had a hard time. But Charity . . ." She smiled as she remembered how Charity and her friend Mandy had stepped up to help the younger kids. "Charity was amazing today. You would have been proud of her. We paired up the older grades with the younger ones throughout the activities, but Charity was all over the place. She brought smiles to a lot of faces this morning."

Jenn nodded. "I think that's why she wanted to go."

Charlotte leaned forward. "Maybe this is her way of learning to heal."

Jenn's head shook. "Maybe. I wish she didn't have to, though. She's not the same girl, and I don't think she ever will be. That innocence children have, she lost hers and there's nothing I can do to help bring it back." Her lips tightened and when she looked at Charlotte, anger and hatred were etched on her face. "She faced a monster, and something inside of her changed forever."

Monster. There was something in Jenn's voice as she said that word that bothered Charlotte. It was one thing for the media and the world to call Gabriel Berry a monster, but another for those in Stillwater to label him the same. Yes, what he did was horrible, but he was one of their own, a child they all knew.

"I don't think . . ." Charlotte's voice trailed off as she caught the way Jenn's face froze.

Charlotte turned in her seat and couldn't stop the smile that spread. She pushed her chair from the table and opened her arms for a hug she couldn't wait to get.

"I didn't know you girls were in here today." Lacie Helman's eyes twinkled as she walked into Charlotte's open arms and hugged her back.

"I was going to pop by later today," Charlotte whispered in her ear. Lacie was her rock.

"Can I join you?" Lacie asked. Charlotte grabbed a chair from the unoccupied table beside them and pulled it close. This was perfect. She had an idea she'd wanted to talk to both of them about.

"How are you doing, honey?" Lacie asked, her focus turned toward Jenn.

"Why does everyone keep asking me that?" Jenn's lips pursed.

"I'm sorry . . . did I hit on a nerve?" Lacie glanced over at Charlotte. "Did I say something I shouldn't have?"

Charlotte shook her head.

"I'm fine. I'm the same today as I was the last time you asked. I'm okay. I'm not falling apart; I'm not a piece of glass that will break if you say the wrong words." Jenn leaned back in her chair, a determined look on her face. "I'm fine. You, of all people, should understand that."

Lacie's brow rose.

"And, if I need a counseling session, I'll be sure to call your husband," Jenn muttered. "Better yet, I would attend those group sessions he has going on."

Charlotte and Lacie blinked in surprise.

"He's the last person you would want to talk to right now, Jenn. Trust me on that." Her gaze clouded over before they were interrupted by Gina with a pot of coffee. Without asking, she filled up Lacie's cup, then dropped off a handful of creamers into the middle of the table. She laid her free hand on Lacie's shoulder and squeezed.

"Good to see you," she said.

Lacie glanced up and attempted to smile. Charlotte was perplexed at the sudden change.

"Come see me afterward, okay?" Gina said softly, to which Lacie nodded.

"Are *you* okay?" Charlotte placed a bit of emphasis on the word *you*. She was starting to feel a little bit worried. Out of anyone, Lacie was the last person she would have thought to be anything but okay.

Lacie Helman was a pastor's wife. Actually, she was *the* pastor's wife in Stillwater Bay. Lacie was the type of woman who placed everyone's needs above her own and was more than happy to do so.

Lacie was also a mother who had lost her child during the Stillwater school shooting.

"I'm"—she glanced over at Jenn and gave a soft smile—"fine." She took a sip of her coffee. "Scott and I had a bit of a . . . disagreement . . . and I just needed to get out for a bit."

"Where's Liam?" Jenn asked.

Lacie and Scott had three children. Liam was their youngest, seven years old with Down syndrome.

"Scott took him out fishing." She shrugged. "That boy is fascinated with fishing rods and worms lately. I found him trying to sneak some into bed with him last night."

Charlotte tried not to laugh. She loved Liam. His heart was so pure and full of joy.

"I didn't see Kylie this morning."

Lacie's chin rose a notch. "You wouldn't have. She stayed home."

Charlotte caught the subtle way Jenn leaned forward at this statement.

"Was that her choice?" She couldn't imagine it being Lacie's decision. Lacie had been one of the people Charlotte had consulted with before she made the decision to open the school today. Lacie had been supportive.

"It was . . . a mutual choice. I don't think Kylie realized how much the idea of going to school today stressed her. What about Charity?" She turned to Jenn. "Did she go?"

Jenn nodded. "She insisted. Even snuck out of the house when I told her I wouldn't drive her."

"You caught her?"

"About halfway across the bridge before the island. Said she wanted to be a victor and not the victim."

Lacie's brows rose. "Really? I keep hearing that term over and over, but I wonder if we're taking it out of context."

"How? You choose to either be a victim or not, right?" Charlotte asked.

"Sometimes you don't have the choice. We're all victims right now. All of us. That choice, of not being a victim, was taken from us." Lacie's voice mellowed, any evidence of a smile from earlier gone. "How we move on, that's the choice ahead of us. But we'll always be a victim."

"I'd rather be a victor," Charlotte stated.

Lacie lips twirled. "Wouldn't we all. But to be a victor . . . you must first know what you're fighting for, right? I'm just worried that we're moving ahead too fast. We're not giving ourselves time to adequately—"

"Grieve," Jenn and Charlotte said together.

"Exactly."

Charlotte mulled this over. It was very similar to what Jenn had said earlier. Was she not being sensitive enough? Was she trying to push everyone past the grieving process before they were ready? It was impossible, though, for her not to see how this was affecting the town as a whole. It was her job to ensure they made it through, that the local businesses didn't suffer, especially with the summer season at their door. Charlotte rubbed her eyes, suddenly weary.

"Listen," she said, "there's something I wanted to talk with you both about. Did you read the paper today?"

Jenn shook her head, but Lacie nodded.

"Did you read that article about Julia?" she asked Lacie.

"I did. She's not doing well, and I'm not sure what to do anymore."

"I wish Arnold would censor some of what he puts in the paper." Charlotte thinned her lips as she thought about the constant barrage toward Julia in the paper.

"Why?" Jenn spoke up.

"Because she doesn't deserve it. Not this. When I spoke to her last week, she'd mentioned the death threats haven't stopped." She still couldn't believe that someone like Julia would get death threats. That didn't happen to people in her town. The city, maybe. But not Stillwater. But then, she would have said the same thing about children taking guns into schools as well until it had happened.

"The poor girl. It's not fair, how she's being treated. It's time this town rallied behind her, more than we have, and show everyone she's not to blame." Lacie met Charlotte's gaze and nodded.

"Exactly." Charlotte couldn't be happier that Lacie had brought this up. "She's a victim in all this as well. It hurts my heart that it's our own citizens who are caught up in the hatred and tearing her apart like this."

"It's time to erase the evil in this town."

Startled, Jenn leaned her body forward. "Evil? Erase it? Do you even know what you're talking about? How can you spiritualize this? How? Your own son was murdered by her son. *Her. Son.*" Jenn's body trembled until the table shook beneath her elbows she'd leaned on the table.

"Jenn—"

Charlotte was cut off by the snarl on Jenn's face.

"Don't," she said to her. "Don't try to tell me how I should be feeling or what I should be doing. And don't"—Jenn pushed her chair back, and Charlotte cringed at the scraping noise on the floor—"tell me that I need to start showing some love to the woman I hold responsible for taking my son away from me." Jenn's nostrils flared as a deep flush covered the skin on her face and neck.

"I would suggest, Mayor," Jenn spat, "that you start concentrating on this town and its survival this summer season rather than focusing on the emotional impact to those who are grieving. Obviously you have no idea how we are feeling, and it's time you stop pretending like you do."

Charlotte's heart dropped as she watched Jenn leave the coffee shop.

"You've got a good heart, Charlie." Lacie reached forward and grabbed her hand. She held on tight. "A good heart. That girl is breaking apart, and it scares her. She loves you. You're safe for her to lash out at."

"But I've hurt her."

Lacie nodded. "Maybe. But she's hurt herself as well. There's nothing you can do to make it better. Not for Jenn." Lacie looked to the ceiling. "Sometimes it's hard to look past our own fears. But if we don't, then we tend to get lost in them. Let's go see if maybe we can stand by Julia, shall we?" She gathered her purse and stood.

Charlotte felt like she'd just been punched in the stomach and then told it was for the best, but she followed after Lacie, making sure she'd left more than enough money on the table to cover their coffees and treats.

She wished she could follow after Jenn and talk to her, apologize, and try to understand, but she knew—better than anyone—that forcing Jenn to confront an issue wasn't the way to go about it.

CHAPTER EIGHT

JENNIFER

A ray of sun appeared through an opening in the clouds and glistened off the water like tiny diamonds dancing to a rhythm she couldn't hear or understand. The water slapped the sand as it boiled in, angry or disgruntled and in sync with the way she felt.

The way her emotions were rolling inside, she hadn't waited for the storm to break before she made her way to the beach, relishing the way the water crashed upon the rocks off to the side. If she were to head to the lighthouse and climb down to the rocks, she could feel the heavy spray on her face and let it soak her. Cleanse her.

When she'd stormed out of Gina's, she'd rushed down the sidewalk to the water, not really thinking about where she was going, just knowing she needed to be someplace where she would be alone.

Jenn dropped down to the sand and toed off her shoes, digging her feet deep down until she couldn't dig any further. She needed to feel anchored, and the weight of the heavy sand on her foot helped.

Her heart was heavy, almost too heavy for her to carry right now.

The overwhelming feeling of failure threatened to carry her off, like the pebbles tumbling about in the gentle waves. With each surge the pebble pushed forward and then rolled back until it was too far away to reach the shoreline again.

Jenn couldn't help but admit to herself that she would be okay if she were to be swept too far away, as horrible as that sounded.

There were a few children, down by the play park, and their squeals of laughter drifted with the wind down to where she sat. Her eyes closed as she listened to their happiness, and though the tight band around her heart squeezed until she thought she couldn't handle more pain, a slight smile played with her lips. One of the voices sounded like her son's.

Bobby loved the beach. *Had* loved the beach. She used to bring Bobby down to the sand, armed with buckets and shovels, and together they'd build forts and castles surrounded by moats. Just like the kids down the way were doing now.

Jenn hugged her knees close to her chest, rested her chin in between, and listened to the noise around her. She needed to find some sense of peace, some stillness that she could grab ahold of, before she headed back home.

Nothing about today had started off the way she expected. Perhaps that's what had her in a tailspin. She should have realized Charity wouldn't have stayed home, that she'd want to be at the school. She should have been prepared, and she hadn't been.

"Look what I found."

Jenn raised her head and squinted. The sun shining behind a head of blond curls created a halo effect. It was the little girl who had been laughing earlier.

"What did you find?" she asked.

The little girl had her hands behind her back, and she shifted from one foot to the other. She brought one hand out and opened her palm, as if offering the gift nestled in between her fingers to Jenn.

"Isn't that pretty." Jenn smiled as she studied the pastel-colored shell. Charity used to do the same thing, comb the shore for seashells and colored rocks. A few pieces still sat on the shelves in her room.

"Would you like it?" A dimple appeared in the little girl's cheek.

Jenn caught movement to the side of her and noticed a woman walking toward them.

"Is that your mom?"

The little girl nodded.

"Does she have any of your special shells yet?" Jenn asked.

The little head with blond curls shook her head.

"I'm sure she would love one, don't you think?"

The little girl pursed her lips as she glanced over to her mother. "But you look sad," she said. "I know this will make you happy."

Jenn's heart skipped a beat. *I know this will make you happy.* Bobby used to say the same thing to her. He would always bring her things he found, whether it was a smooth stone, a pink seashell, a furry caterpillar, or even a dandelion weed . . . he always knew how to make her happy.

Jenn blinked past the tears that formed and took the small shell from the waiting palm.

"It's perfect," she managed to whisper before the mother called her daughter away.

Her finger traced the raised edges on the shell, wiping away some of the sand, and Jenn gave into the tears she'd held at bay. The tears scalded her as they trickled down, over her cheeks and then down her throat.

She missed her son. Her arms ached constantly to hold him. She listened for his voice at all times, and she'd never be able to tuck him in at night or kiss his cheek or see the twinkle in his eye. It killed her every time she realized he was gone.

Having Robert and Charity wasn't enough. She wasn't enough. Something was missing inside of her, something that was destroyed the moment she knew he was gone.

She knew, deep in her heart, that it was her fault. Hers. She'd seen that boy walk into the school. She could have stopped him; she should have realized something was wrong. And yet, she'd been too focused on herself and on the phone call with the lawyer.

CHAPTER NINE

SAMANTHA

Out of all the towns Samantha Hill had visited throughout her career as a reporter, Stillwater Bay had to be the most obscure, quaint little town she'd ever visited. She could have sworn she'd seen some of the old Victorian homes here in a Thomas Kinkade painting. Everywhere she went, there were white picket fences, flowering shrubs, and welcome mats on every doorstep.

Only the puppy dogs trailing after running children in the fields were missing from the scene.

It was hard to believe that something as horrific as a school shooting could ever happen in an idyllic town like Stillwater Bay. When she'd first been given the assignment, she'd pictured the town full of bicycles, worn boardwalks that stretched along the beach, and young girls skipping in white frocks. This town was known as a hard-to-get-to vacation spot in the middle of nowhere on the West Coast, a place bypassed by many on their way to more popular destinations, unless they were into antique shopping, bed-and-breakfasts, and sand riddled with seashells.

Small-town girl, Samantha Hill was not. And yet, something about this town appealed to her.

Her day hadn't exactly gone as planned. She had intended to be at the school when it opened, talk to the parents, ask the principal more questions, and get some shots with the kids walking in . . . but Charlotte had stopped her. So she'd stayed downtown and spun her wheels.

"Coming in for dessert?" Shelley, her landlady and owner of the Seaglass B&B, poked her head out the screen door.

"Would love to. I just need to make a phone call first."

"Don't be long; the pie is still hot."

The smell of freshly baked apple pie drifted out the open door.

"I'll be fast. I just need to call my—"

"Editor. I know. He's been calling here all day, worried since he couldn't reach you on your phone," Shelley said.

"Sorry." Samantha frowned. She'd told him not to call the residence. Plus, he should have seen that she'd read his million text messages throughout the day. He'd expected her to send in her piece from the school. Instead, she'd sent in a piece about how the town was handling the reopening. Not exactly what he wanted, and yet, he didn't turn it down. She was the only reporter left in Stillwater.

She still had nightmares of the scene at the public school. She'd been one of the first reporters there, which meant she'd seen the aftermath of the murders and witnessed the stretchers coming out of the school with cloth-covered bodies of small children and teachers who had been murdered by a teenage boy.

Sam pulled out her cell phone and checked for any new messages. Half a dozen in the last hour. They all said basically the same thing.

Come home.

She didn't want to. She wasn't ready to. There was something about this town, about the people here, that made her want to stay. And that was so unlike her to feel that way. She loved Seattle. So what was it about this town that compelled her to linger?

Her phone rang, and she knew she couldn't avoid him forever.

"Yes, Alex?" she sighed into the phone, leaning back on the lounger, and smiled at an older couple who waved to her on their daily evening walk.

"I was starting to think you were avoiding me."

"Never," she said. "I just . . . got busy."

There was a pause on the phone. "Please tell me you managed to talk to the principal at least."

"Just in passing."

"You talked to him, though, right?"

She heard the expectation in his voice and wished she had the answers he wanted to hear.

"Not yet." She made sure to add that last bit. "I know he's hiding something; I'm just not sure what."

Alex groaned. "You can't get anyone to say anything about him? I need something to back this doubt of yours."

"I know. Trust me, I know. Give me a few more days, please. A week. There's a story here; I just need to find my sources." She bit her lip while she waited for Alex to tell her to take all the time she needed. That's what she really wanted. There was so much here, so much she could soak in, take advantage of. She had been tired, bone tired, but the air here, it reenergized her. Made her feel alive again. A feeling she hadn't experienced in a long, long time.

"I can give you a few days, Sam, but that's it. If you've got nothing, then it's time to move on. I can use you here."

"There's more here, Alex. I know it. There's something off about"—she hesitated to say the name—"well, there's something

he's not saying. And I can give you stories. This town isn't as . . .
cohesive . . . as Mayor Stone wants everyone to think it is. There
are fractures all over the place." She hated using people's grief to her
advantage like this, but she knew Alex would eat it up. It's what he
thrived on. And having a shooting like the one that occurred in
such an obscure town, it rocked the country.

She was no stranger to murder. She'd earned a reputation early
on in her career for finding the heart where there was none. When
she reported the grisly details of a gang shooting, a domestic vio-
lence case, or needless accidents, she didn't just report the facts, she
dug deep to bring heart to the events, sharing not only the details,
but the people behind it. Her goal was to help her readers become
invested in the news.

It's why Alex sent her here. Not to just report the details that
every other station would focus on, but to go behind the scenes,
find the stories others deemed unimportant, and grab readers' and
viewers' attention.

So far, it had worked. They boasted some of the highest ratings
in the country, but they were losing their edge. Because she wasn't
ready to head home yet, she had thrown Alex a bone, the principal and her doubts about him. She'd focused on the mayor and
the Crowne family; she'd interviewed the different teachers at the
school and reported on how the shooting decimated a town determined to remain strong, especially with the tourist season on them.

"Days, Samantha. Then I want you home," Alex clipped his
words before he hung up.

Samantha set her phone down on the seat beside her while letting out a deep breath. The thought of leaving, of being forced to
leave in a few days, bothered her. Set her heart racing. She couldn't
leave yet. She wasn't ready.

"If you want that pie before it goes cold, now would be the time." Shelley poked her head out from the screen door.

"I thought you were different." Shelley held the door open for her.

Sam's skin prickled as a breeze followed her inside.

"I am," she said.

When Shelley shook her head, Sam knew she must have overheard part of her conversation. Now what? Did she explain her words and hope that Shelley understood why she was trying to linger in her town or just leave things alone? Sam wasn't one for caring what others thought of her; she'd learned to develop a thick skin years ago, but . . .

"Nothing good comes out of digging in closets. Some things need to remain buried."

"But at what cost?"

"The price tag is always too high, Samantha. You should know that by now."

CHAPTER TEN

CHARLOTTE

Charlotte loved her town, especially on a weekend morning. There was a time, growing up, all she longed for was to move away, but a few years in the city during college and she knew she wanted to come back. Needed to.

Some people found hobbies, such as knitting or baking or swimming, to complete them, but for her, it was this town. Her town. Stillwater Bay was more than just a community to her; it was her family. She cared deeply about what happened to this town and the families who lived here. She looked forward to their summer families who arrived and filled their small town with their busyness and excitement. Knowing that her town thrived filled her with a deep contentment, but when it hurt, she hurt.

Like now.

Even a casual stranger who came for a day visit would see this was a town in mourning. She knew Jenn was right—there was no time limit on the process of mourning—but it was Charlotte's job as mayor to look beyond the emotional aspect, wasn't it? Her biggest fear was the town would get lost in their grief, but how do you ensure that doesn't happen without negating what the families of Stillwater were going through?

She didn't have the answers, but she knew, as she walked down Main Street and noticed the lack of activity in many of the stores, that she needed to find them. Summer was on their doorstep. It was a weekend, but it could have been a Monday morning for all she could tell. There was very little traffic on the street and hardly anyone on the sidewalks.

This town needed the summer tourists and revenue to help them stay afloat during the winter months. She knew many businesses would close and families would go bankrupt if it weren't for the money they made during the warmer months. Without the summer industry, would they survive? Charlotte hoped so, but the innate belief she held close to her heart, that they could face anything as long as they did it together as a community, was disappearing.

With her gaze downward, she almost didn't notice Camille Bloomin squatting down in front of a pail full of floral arrangements.

"Those are beautiful." Charlotte stopped and admired the bouquets of gerbera daisies.

"They just came in." Camille stood up and wiped her hands on her pink apron that matched the bright awning above her store. "My favorites are the pink and orange so far. They scream summer and happiness."

"They do. Can you make an arrangement for the office? I'll pick it up when I get back." Charlotte liked to have a fresh bouquet from Camille greet anyone who came to town hall. She put the flowers in a vase made from lightning glass, crafted by Blake Casser, a local artist. He now had a workshop up by the lighthouse.

"Already made. I noticed last week's arrangement didn't fare as well, so I added extra to make up for it." She scrunched up her nose. "Sorry about that."

Charlotte shook her head. She thought last week's arrangement had been quite nice and hadn't noticed how they held up, but leave it to Camille to see it.

"How are things?"

Camille rearranged signage she'd placed out front and flashed Charlotte a smile. "Not too bad. A few families have already arrived and placed their weekly orders for flowers, so things are looking up."

"And the clubhouse?" There had been talk from the local golf club of hiring a full-time florist this year, and Charlotte had made it her mission to ensure they didn't.

"They agreed to keep Paige on part-time, so we'll work her schedule here at the store to accommodate that, which is a relief."

Paige was Camille's younger sister, in her midtwenties. Together, the sisters ran Still Blooming.

"Did someone call my name?" Paige stood in the doorway with a pail of flowers by her feet. She nudged it forward for Camille. "Here you go."

Charlotte watched as a frown graced Camille's face for a brief second before it disappeared. She reached for the pail and set it beside the one holding the daisies. "I told you I would get it," she muttered.

Paige shrugged her shoulder. "Hi, Mayor," she said before she used her cane to head back into the store.

"Everything okay?" Charlotte caught the tension between the sisters.

Camille sighed as she watched her sister maneuver between the tables before she sat down on a stool behind the front counter. "She was here when the truck pulled in this morning and helped unload it. She twisted her knee and refuses to go to the clinic."

"Are you sure this isn't a case of big sister worry?" Since their parents' death just before she turned twenty, Camille had taken care of her younger sister. Four years ago, Paige had shattered her knee-cap while training for the Olympic US Volleyball team, and the close relationship between the sisters had been altered. The money they'd received from their parents' estate had gone to the countless surgeries Paige had needed and into the floral shop to keep it afloat. Charlotte tried to help in any way she could, and ordering weekly floral arrangements was part of her support.

"I have no idea." Camille threw her hands up in the air.

Charlotte laid her hand on the woman's shoulder. "She knows her body and what she can handle. Trust her."

"How can I trust her when she skipped her last doctor's appointment? When I catch her taking her meds more than she should?" Camille's lips thinned as worry clouded her gaze. "She has another surgery scheduled in six months but . . ." Her voice trailed off as she turned her attention away from her store and up toward North Beach.

Charlotte's heart sank at the news. She had no idea Paige needed yet another surgery.

"Where are you headed today?" Camille asked, trying to cover her anxiety with a lighter tone in her voice.

"First, I have to go fetch a little girl and buy some teddy bears, but then I thought I'd head toward Julia Berry's home and see how she is."

Camille turned to look down toward South Beach, where Julia lived in the cottages by the shore. "I read that article in the paper Friday. I hope she's okay."

Charlotte sighed. Something she'd been doing a lot today. "I hope so too, but something tells me she's not."

"Wait here." Camille briefly touched Charlotte's arm before she headed into the store. Charlotte watched her stop in front of her sister and talk with her before she reached into the small freezer and pulled out a basket of cut flowers.

Charlotte wondered if that were one of the many arrangements Julia had refused to accept from kindhearted strangers throughout the country. Camille had told her that for weeks after Julia's son had shot himself, orders had poured into the floral shop for the mother, some nice and some . . . not so nice. But no matter what, Julia would refuse to take the flowers, forcing Camille to leave them on her doorstep and eventually take them back to the shop. Julia now requested that the money people would have spent on the arrangements be donated to the many charities or funds set up for the families after the shooting.

"Can you give this to her?" Camille carried the basket out and placed it in Charlotte's hands.

"Is this another order?" she asked.

Camille shook her head. "No, tell her it's from us. Today is her birthday."

A lump formed in Charlotte's throat as she could only nod before she walked away. Her birthday? Had Lacie known? She'd called her friend this morning to come with her today, but Lacie said she didn't think it would be a good idea. She had stopped by Julia's house earlier but had left when it had become obvious Julia didn't want any company.

Julia was alone now. How would she spend her birthday? Would she be curled up in bed or on the couch watching sad movies? Would she pretend today was just another day?

Charlotte paused in front of the gift shop located next door to the flower shop. The door was locked with brown wrapping paper covering the windows. She wondered if it would ever open again. This was Julia's store. A small gift shop with handmade items from local artists around the county. It was a local favorite, and in previous summers, Julia usually ran out of items to sell thanks to their summer families. What would happen this year? She knew this was a staple of the town. Somehow she needed to convince Julia to open it up again.

. . .

Charlotte pulled up in front of Lauren Thomlin's home, and the first thing she saw was the overgrown yard and weedy garden. Jordan had asked her before she left to let him know if any yard work needed to be done, so she quickly sent him a text and a picture of what she saw. When Lauren's husband died while serving in Iraq, the community had stepped up and tried to help out as much as they could. Jordan was responsible for the yard work and had set up a schedule for others to cut the grass, weed the flower beds, fix and repaint the front porch, and handle other general maintenance, but it didn't look as if it had been done for a while.

As she walked up the front walkway the door flew open and out ran Ellie, straight into her arms.

"Hi to you too." Charlotte gave Ellie a long hug.

"Are we going to buy lots and lots of teddy bears today?" Ellie's eyes were bright, but she caught sight of a tiny sheen in them.

"Lots and lots." Ellie's hand nestled in hers as they made their way to the front door where Lauren stood.

She looked horrible. Her hair was stringy, dark bags hung beneath her eyes, and her face was pale. She'd wrapped a cardigan around her thin frame, and her knuckles were white from clutching the edges together.

"I was thinking, maybe I could keep Ellie for the day? I believe there's a tea party happening at the bed-and-breakfast today." One phone call to Shelley Peterson, owner of Seaglass B&B, and there would be a tea party if there wasn't one already. Maybe she could even see about setting up a pajama party at Shelley's to give Lauren the night off too.

The weariness in Lauren's gaze abated for a brief moment. But then she straightened from her position of leaning against the entryway and shook her head.

"You don't need to do that. I'm okay."

Charlotte hoped Lauren could read the message in her eyes. *Liar.*

"You're not okay. Maybe you should go in to see the doctor?"

"I'm just tired." Lauren hugged herself tighter.

"Jordan will be by in a bit to clean up your yard, and Gina has some homemade chicken soup on the burner. I'll get her to bring it by later as well."

And if she didn't, Charlotte would beg her to make some. Lauren really didn't look well.

"Charlotte . . ." Lauren's voice wavered as she blinked away the tears that pooled.

Charlotte's heart broke to see this woman, this stubborn, opinionated, and obviously sick woman, struggle to accept the help she needed. But she wasn't going to give her an option.

"I'm not taking no for an answer, Lauren."

"Please, please, please?" Ellie stood there, her voice quiet as she gripped Charlotte's hand.

Lauren looked at her daughter and attempted to smile. "Sounds like it could be a fun day."

Ellie beamed a huge smile up at Charlotte then wrapped her arms around her mom.

Thank you, Lauren mouthed.

Charlotte smiled.

"Why don't you go and get yourself buckled in while I talk to your mom for a minute, okay?"

They both watched as Ellie skipped her way to the car and climbed in.

"Go see the doctor." She left little room in her voice for disagreement.

Lauren shook her head. "I'll be fine."

"Jordan will take you. Don't argue."

Lauren's body sagged, as if the weight of having to take care of herself was lifted.

"Thank you."

"How about I keep her for the night and bring her home tomorrow?" She caught the brief flicker of hope in Lauren's eyes before she was about to say no. Charlotte didn't give her the chance, though.

"Don't worry about her pajamas or anything. I'll get her to pick out a pair today while we're shopping. She'll have a blast, and it will give you time to rest." Charlotte leaned forward and gave Lauren a soft hug.

"She would love that," Lauren murmured.

"I know. It'll be a treat for her. And for you I'm thinking."

"I could use the sleep."

Charlotte was relieved that Lauren gave in. "Yes, yes, you do. I'll send you a text to let you know what is going on and where she is, okay? I might convince Shelley to have a slumber party with her grandkids. They're in Ellie's class, right?"

As Charlotte made her way to the car and to the little girl who was literally vibrating in her seat from excitement, she glanced back toward the house. Lauren sacrificed so much for her daughter, but she wondered if it was too much, for both of them. She needed to see about getting Ellie in some programs this summer.

"All right, you, where to first? I was thinking maybe a trip to Gina's for some waffles?"

"With strawberries and whipped cream?" Ellie's eyes lit up.

"With extra whipped cream and maybe even some chocolate sprinkles."

"It's a deal!"

As she drove away from Ellie's home, she realized she needed to make some adjustments to today's plans.

She still wanted to check in on Julia, but right now, this little girl needed to have a day of happiness.

CHAPTER ELEVEN

JENNIFER

Weekends were usually packed with activities in the Crowne household. Robert had his weekly breakfast meetings with other local business owners and then went to the clubhouse and played a round of golf or worked out in the gym there. Jenn used to get up and make a large breakfast for her and the kids, but in the past month, her morning ritual consisted of sleeping in, making a pot of coffee to help with the massive headache she'd wake up with, and then sit out on her back deck staring out into the bay while Charity was either up in her room or at a friend's house.

This morning, when she woke up, it was to the smell of coffee and bacon wafting through her opened bedroom door. There was a dull throb behind her eyes, and the last thing she wanted to do was get out of bed, but the aroma of bitter coffee pulled at her too strongly. Half in a daze, she wrapped her housecoat around her and shuffled down the hallway to the stairs.

She wasn't quite prepared for the sight in front of her when she stepped into her kitchen.

"What are you doing?" She should have known, expected, that Charity would be home, but seeing her there surprised her.

Charity glanced up from where she was. A large smile filled her face as she motioned to the catastrophe of what was once Jenn's neat and organized kitchen.

"I'm helping to get the baskets ready." Charity had a piece of tissue paper in her hand and was attempting to arrange it in the bottom of a basket.

"I see that," Jenn said, puzzled. "Why?"

Charity shrugged. "Anne Marie called and said she would be here shortly to put together some baskets. I thought I'd get a head start and get everything out," Charity said. "She also asked if I could help this year, and I said yes." She reached for another piece of tissue paper and paused. "That's okay, right? That I'm helping? Cause I want to."

Jenn sighed, "Of course it's all right. I really appreciate your aunt for offering to do this and the fact that you want to help."

She glanced around at the mess. She thought Anne Marie was only going to pick up the supplies, not actually create the baskets here.

"Which basket are you working on right now?"

Charity reached across the counter and grabbed a sheet of paper.

"I made a list of all the families who were returning. I wasn't sure when they would all be here, so I figured I'd start with the Andersons since I know they're here already and just down the street."

Jenn nodded while she glanced at the list her daughter had attempted to make.

"If you grab the pink book off my desk, there's a list of dates and other notes I keep. We can work off that, if you'd like," Jenn suggested. "That way we won't get anything mixed up. For instance"—she reached for a bottle of honey that sat beside the basket—"Sam, the youngest boy, is allergic to honey, so we'll give them some blackberry jam, which also happens to be his favorite."

Charity's smile faltered a bit before she ducked her head and left the kitchen.

She perused the items her daughter had collected and nodded. Charity had managed to retrieve most of the items she'd stored away; she was impressed. She set the list down and poured herself a cup of coffee, making sure to leave enough room to add double the Baileys. She needed it.

"Are you kidding me?" Charity dropped the book on the counter and walked away.

"Hey, where are you going?"

Charity stopped but didn't turn. "To my room to listen to music," she said.

"But . . ." Jenn held up a jar of jam. "I thought you were going to help with the baskets?"

"You've got it all under control. You don't need me. But you might want to hide the recycling with all your liquor bottles before Anne Marie comes."

Jenn slowly set the jar down on the counter while her daughter walked up the stairs.

She glanced down at the recycling box filled with bottles beneath the counter. Wine and Baileys. More than she thought there would be.

A good mom would have gone over to her daughter and hugged her, reaffirming that she was always needed. A great mom would have watched her words before she even said them. But Jenn was neither a great nor a good mom. Lately her daughter would probably say she was the worst mother around.

Sadly, Jenn wouldn't have argued with that statement.

Raising a teenager was more than she thought she could handle sometimes. How much was hormonal adjustments, and how much was real offense? It didn't matter either way; her feelings were valid regardless. Isn't that basically what she had been trying to get Charlotte to understand as well?

She stepped over to the stairs and glanced up, managing to hide her surprise, she hoped, when she realized Charity sat halfway up with her head in her hands.

"Charity, honey?" She climbed up and sat a few steps down but rested her hand on her daughter's knee. "I'm sorry."

Charity peeked through her fingers. It hurt Jenn's heart to see the blank look on her daughter's face.

"Honey, I do need you." She let out a long breath. "I think I need you more now than ever before."

"I just wanted to help," she said.

Jenn nodded. "I know, and I can't tell you how much that means to me."

They sat there, quiet, and Jenn realized it had been a long time since she'd done this with Charity—just be, together. It was nice. Reminiscent of how things used to be, back when . . .

"How about we make some homemade iced tea and wait for Anne Marie to arrive? Once the Andersons' basket is ready, we'll take it to them and maybe afterward go for a walk down to the harbor?"

Her heart stopped the moment she uttered those words. What was she thinking? They couldn't do that. Not there. Not now. Not yet. She was about to suggest another idea when Charity grabbed her hand. She glanced up and knew she wouldn't be able to say anything.

Charity's eyes brightened at the suggestion. "Maybe we can get some ice cream. The truck should be there, right?"

"It's possible." She forced those words out. Everything inside of her wanted to lie, to find an excuse not to go to the harbor, but she couldn't, not after the way Charity's eyes lit up. "I saw some boats out in the bay earlier, so you never know."

Last summer, heading to the small harbor had been one of their favorite things to do. The three of them, Charity, Bobby, and Jenn, would spend hours there, watching the boats come in and out, playing in the sand, and eating ice cream, while they walked along the shoreline that encircled their town.

She didn't know how she could do this today. So far she'd avoided a lot of things that would remind her of Bobby.

"Oh, let's add some raspberries to the tea." Charity jumped up and grabbed for Jenn's hand before pulling her down the stairs. Jenn followed along, her body now chilled.

The kettle on the stove was boiling by the time Anne Marie arrived. She walked in the door, her arms full of boxes from her bakery, without even knocking. Jenn rushed over to help her with the boxes, inhaling the sweet aroma that came from inside them, while Anne Marie went back out to her vehicle.

The moment Jenn set the boxes down, Charity was into them, opening each lid and peering inside.

"Think she'll mind if I taste test?" Charity asked, her eyes alight with mischief.

"Why do you think I brought extra?" Anne Marie answered behind her. She held a larger box with its lid opened, and when Jenn looked inside she found some neat baskets.

"These are adorable," she said as she lifted a few out. She could tell they were handwoven and knew immediately where Anne Marie had gotten them. Only one weaver in town made baskets like this.

"Hey, those are Amanda's mom's baskets." Charity grabbed one from the box and turned it over to find the stamp Sandra Sommerlay added to each basket.

"Sandra came into the bakery this morning and mentioned she had a pile of baskets stacked up and needed them out of the house. I guess with the Treasure Chest being closed, she's been unable to sell most of her stuff."

"Yeah, Mandy and I were talking about setting up an Etsy shop for her mom," Charity said.

"That's a great idea. She's not the only one in town, though. We really need to get Julia's shop opened up again."

Jenn didn't say much; she just looked through the baskets.

"Don't you agree?" Anne Marie asked.

"It's not something I've really thought about," Jenn said. "Using these baskets is a great idea, though. How much do I owe for them?"

Anne Marie tsked. "Nothing. She just asked that we include her business card, which I said wouldn't be a problem. Have you thought about asking for more business donations like that? I bet you'd have tons of products for the baskets, and it's a great way to promote the unique finds in Stillwater."

"It *is* a good idea."

"I thought so too. Which is why I already asked around to a couple places. I brought a few items with me that I thought would be nice to add. They're out in the trunk of my car."

While Charity went out to grab them, Jenn sat down at the kitchen table.

"Thanks for doing this," she said to Anne Marie.

Her sister-in-law only smiled while she rearranged items on the kitchen island.

"I mean it. Not just for helping with this, but for thinking about how to make them better. I really appreciate it."

Anne Marie pulled out a chocolate croissant from a box and handed it to her. "It's okay to let others help, you know. You don't have to do everything yourself. In fact, I think you should give yourself a break and let others take care of things for a bit."

Jenn thought about that. The idea of not having to do it all, not being responsible for something, sounded really good. She once had thought being a stay-at-home mother would be the highlight of her life, but she was a person who needed to be busy, so as Bobby grew older, she had started to fill her days with more and more volunteer events. Whether it was helping out at the school, or organizing the Welcome Wagon committee, or . . .

"I wish. I still have the planning committee for the fair next week. That's not something I can step back from, not at this stage anyways."

"Right." Anne Marie began to assemble a basket together. "But, you can get someone to help man the booth you always do, right?"

Jenn nodded.

"I'm glad you agree. Because Shelley is interested in helping. She's the perfect person to be there to greet people."

Times like this reminded Jenn of how much alike sister and brother were. Anne Marie might complain about the way Robert took over, but she did the exact same thing. Any other time Jenn would have said something, but not today.

"Anne Marie, I think you are my guardian angel."

. . .

Silence reigned between Charity and Jenn as they exited the house. Anne Marie stood by her vehicle, her arms crossed over her chest, watching them. Jenn could almost feel the glare drilling holes into the back of her head as they walked away. In Jenn's arms was a basket full of items for the Andersons.

A basket Anne Marie argued Jenn didn't need to take.

But Jenn felt responsible at least for this basket.

The Andersons were important to Robert. Not only were they their summer neighbors, but Shawn Anderson held a lot of influence, both in this town and in the city. He was a real estate mogul, and Robert needed him as his ally, or so he professed. She knew Robert expected her to take this basket, the one that weighed heavier in her arms with each step she took.

"You should have let her take it," Charity muttered beside her.

Shawn's wife, Carla, wasn't known for her tact, and normally by the end of summer, Jenn was happy to see her pack up their family SUV and leave for their home in the city.

Please let this go well.

Charity reached for her hand and squeezed, and Jenn realized her daughter probably had the same concerns. Carla had three children, two were twins and Charity's age, and their youngest used to have regular playdates with Bobby. If this had been a regular summer, Charity would already have been over here to see Reagan.

"Are you looking forward to seeing Reagan again?"

Charity shrugged. "Are you going to ring the doorbell?"

"Are you going to answer my question?"

Charity stared down at her feet. "Things are different now," she muttered before she leaned forward and rang the doorbell herself.

The yap of a small dog filled the house the moment the doorbell rang. Jenn and Charity looked at each other in surprise—the dog must be a new addition.

"Sh. Not so loud, Lily."

Jenn took a step back as Carla opened the front door.

Carla Anderson was one of those women who could star in any housewives' reality television show. Her husband came from money, and they had no qualms about showing it. They'd bought their summer home five years ago, and in that time they'd transformed it into a picture-perfect beach house that had been featured in at least two home design magazines.

"Well, hello neighbor. I wondered when you would drop by." She stood in the doorway, her manicured fingers stroking the soft white fur of the yappy dog she held in her arms. "You know, I was saying to the kids that it's not officially summer until Jenn Crowne pops over with her gorgeous welcome basket."

Jenn pasted a fake smile on her face as she reached for the basket Charity held.

"Welcome home." She held out the basket and then realized how awkward that looked since there was no way Carla could take it from her, not while she held the dog in her arms. She adjusted her grip on the basket handle instead.

"I told the kids not to expect it to be waiting for us this year, and I was right. Wasn't I, Lily?" She leaned down and placed a kiss on the top of her dog's head.

"I didn't expect you to be here so soon." She tried to sound apologetic, but there was something to Carla's tone that bothered her.

"Oh, I should have called you, I guess." Carla readjusted her dog in her arms. "We thought we would come and support the town for the annual parade and festivities, but I guess you-all decided to forgo that this year, which is perfectly understandable. It's hard to celebrate during such a tragic time." She shook her head as if saddened by the thought.

"Oh, we're still having the parade," Charity piped up.

Carla's brows rose. "You are?" Disbelief flooded her voice. Or was it disdain? Jenn wasn't sure how to read the woman today.

"It's just being postponed to coincide with the July Fourth celebration," Jenn explained. "We decided to start a new tradition this year."

Carla nodded. "Of course, that makes sense."

The basket grew heavy in her arms as they stood there.

"Well." Jenn cleared her throat. "Welcome home." She held out the basket, but Carla just stared at her.

"I'm sorry about Bobby," she said.

Jenn just nodded. "Thank you," she said by rote. That's all she ever said. *Thank you.* Not for the first time, she wondered why she said that. Why was she thanking someone for acknowledging that she'd lost her only son?

"Did you get our flowers?"

She sent flowers? Jenn glanced over at Charity, who nodded.

"Yes, that was very kind." Jenn wondered which arrangement was theirs. Would it be the overly ornate mixed basket that sat on the corner table, or was it one of the many that cluttered their mantel over the fireplace?

"It was so tragic. I cried when I heard on the news that your son had been shot. How dreadful. But look at you, you look great. I'm not sure how you do it. I'd be an absolute mess if one of my children had been killed like that."

Jenn's stomach filled with acid at Carla's words. The acid rose up her throat and coated her tongue, and it was all she could do not to spew the hatred and anger that welled up within her onto the woman who dared to judge her.

"Mom's been amazing." Charity stepped up and placed her hand over Jenn's and took the basket from her. "She's been my rock through all of this."

It took Jenn a moment to hear her daughter's words. Had Charity actually defended her?

"Well, I'm just amazed. I'm here if you ever need someone to talk to." Carla reached over and placed her hand on Jenn's arm.

By now, Jenn's body was stone cold. She had no words, so she just stood there and blinked.

"Jenn?"

"Of course. Thank you." Again with the thanks. "We should do coffee, once you've settled in."

Last year, things had been very different. Jenn would have left the basket on Carla's front porch to greet her when they arrived and then would have been over to schedule a lunch at the golf club for the following day. They would have hugged and shared how the past year had been for both of them, and then Carla would have handed Jenn a small gift, normally a scarf or handbag she'd picked up in the city.

Jenn had a box she normally placed Carla's gifts in. She made sure to drag that box out in the summer and have the items handy, just in case.

"Yes, coffee. Let's do that. I know Reagan has been looking forward to seeing you, Charity, but she's up having a nap. The poor girl is exhausted, with it being that time of the month and all." Carla's dainty shoulder lifted in a shrug.

"No worries. I'm sure we'll bump into one another." Charity kept the smile on her face, but they all heard the false tone in her voice.

Charity set the basket down on the ground, and it was habit for Jenn to reach down to grab it, intending to place it on the small table by the front door, but Charity stopped her.

"We really need to get going, Mom," she said. "Welcome home, Mrs. Anderson."

Jenn kept her mouth shut as she allowed Charity to drag her back down the walkway. She couldn't believe what had just happened back there.

"Oh. My. God," Charity spat out in disbelief. "Please tell me you're not having coffee with her." Charity glared back at the house.

"It's unavoidable, I'm afraid. They are our neighbors after all." Robert would no doubt be inviting Shawn over for a beer within the next day or so.

"They don't deserve our awesome basket. Not after that." Charity's back stiffened as they walked. *I'm here if you ever need someone to talk to,"* she mimicked Carla's voice perfectly but with added sarcasm.

"That's enough, Charity. She means well."

"You're kidding me, right? I'm surprised you didn't rip a strip off of her. I would have."

Jenn stopped in her tracks at her daughter's words, but Charity didn't notice.

"No you wouldn't. That's not how we deal with"—she searched for the word—"people like that."

Charity's hands settled on her hips. "No, because that would make you look bad, right? Well, I'm not like you. I wouldn't have just let her walk all over me like that."

"I didn't." Jenn bit her lip. Had she?

"Yes, you did. You're the one who lost a child. You. Not her." A look of confusion crossed over Charity's face. "She . . . she treated you like you were beneath her." Charity's hands left her hips and crossed over her chest, and she stared down at her feet. "It should have been the other way around," she mumbled. Jenn didn't know what to say or even what to do. "She should have been thanking you for the basket instead of chastising you for being late with it. And being here to *support*"—her face screwed up as she raised her gaze—"our little town during this time. That's hogwash. Those flowers she sent? They died two days after we got them."

Jenn didn't pay attention to any of those arrangements, so she just shrugged. "At least she sent them."

"We don't need people like her here to support us. We'll be fine on our own. Stillwater will be fine." Confidence filled Charity's voice while she continued to glare at the Andersons' home.

"Really? You sound so sure of that."

Charity nodded. "Yep. It's all under control. Don't worry, Mom. We'll be fine."

CHAPTER TWELVE

CHARLOTTE

After a few hours of waffles and shopping for teddy bears, Charlotte had safely dropped off Ellie at Shelley's bed-and-breakfast for an impromptu tea party with her grandchildren. Ellie had been so excited and couldn't wait to help decorate and make cucumber sandwiches. Shelley hadn't minded the intrusion, not when Charlotte mentioned the reason. She'd even suggested keeping Ellie for dinner and doing a slumber party in one of the guest rooms with some of the other girls. Gina had offered to come by and help keep the girls entertained, and Charlotte had promised to return and bring a movie with her. Thankfully, Shelley had ignored Charlotte's offer to stay the night.

One could walk from North Beach to South Beach in a matter of fifteen to twenty minutes. North Beach was the most popular amongst their summer families as it led into the bay. The beach was sandier, there were more rocks for the teenagers to hang out on, and it was close to the family part of the beach. South Beach had more of a rocky shoreline and was closer to the harbor and was home to the summer cottages.

The summer cottages were just around the corner from where Shelley's bed-and-breakfast stood, and it only took a matter of minutes for Charlotte to walk down the sandy path. The cottages were more than what their name implied. While three-quarters of the homes were reserved for the summer tourists or summer workers, a few of the homes were rented out to local families. The cottages were quaint, with wraparound porches and white picket fences, and more often than not, there was quite the waiting list for the summer rentals.

Charlotte's heart sank as the sight she'd feared she'd see became evident. The graffiti that marked Julia's home was brass and ugly. *Killer. Murderer. Die.*

The walkway from Julia's front gate to her door was littered with cartons of broken eggs, broken bags of garbage, and glass.

Charlotte's muscles tensed as she was overwhelmed with anger. She sidestepped some of the glass and broken eggs, placed the flower basket on a clean area of the porch, and took stock of what she saw. Julia's home was visible from Main Street. Surely others had seen this.

Lacie hadn't mentioned any of the vandalism.

Charlotte pulled her phone out of her pocket and called her assistant at home.

"Sheila, there's a mess at Julia Berry's home. Graffiti and garbage. Can you send the crew over here to clean it up?" she barked at her, not bothering to say hello or any other niceties.

"Again?" Sheila sighed.

"What do you mean, again?" She picked out a bag that looked the sturdiest and bent down.

"I send someone over there at least twice a week if not more."

This was news to Charlotte. "Why haven't you told me?"

"My job is to lighten your load. When I see something I know would bother you, I take care of it. This is just as much my town as yours." Sheila was an older woman, at least fifteen years older than Charlotte.

"I know that," Charlotte said. "But this is still stuff I need to know. I could have done something about it before now."

"Like what?"

"Like maybe find out who is doing this and put a stop to it." How could she do her job if she didn't know what to fix?

"Oh Charlotte. We already know who is doing this. Julia refuses to do anything about it." Resignation filled Sheila's voice.

"Really?" Why was she not surprised? Of course Julia wouldn't do anything. But that didn't mean Charlotte couldn't.

"Hopefully you can get someone down today, with it being the weekend. Thank you." She pushed her phone back in her pocket and sighed. She dropped the bag from her hand and climbed the steps to Julia's front door.

She knew Julia was home, the front window curtain flickered as she stood at the door.

"Julia, it's Charlotte," she called out.

She was met with silence.

"Julia, honey, I know you're in there. Please open the door."

Charlotte leaned her hip against the door frame and listened carefully. Small noises came from the other side of the door, like feet sliding on the tile and the light thud of a body touching the wall.

"I have someone coming over today to clean up your yard. I'm sorry it keeps happening." Charlotte decided to make conversation, even if it were only one-sided. Maybe if she talked enough, Julia would open the door, or at least talk back to her.

"And I have something for you, from Paige and Camille. They said it was your birthday." She couldn't imagine Julia was feeling anything remotely similar to happiness today.

"Please take it back." Julia's voice was muffled.

Charlotte shook her head, even though she knew it wasn't seen. "Can't. It's from them personally. They miss you."

"Just put it down then. I'll . . . I'll grab it later."

"Why not open the door and I can give it to you." When was the last time Julia had stepped out of her home?

From the neglected wither of her front gardens, Charlotte would guess it had been quite a while since Julia had ventured outside. Was she eating okay? Was anyone looking out for her, trying to help her through this time?

"I'd rather not."

Charlotte glanced behind her and noticed there were a few people watching her, not being bashful about it at all. It was a small town, and unfortunately, Julia didn't live in a secluded part of it. People would always be around. "Julia"—an idea just came to her— "how about if I meet you at your back door?" There would be more privacy then.

She was prepared for Julia to disagree or even just to walk away. "Okay."

She made her way toward the back, ducking under the tall hedges between the properties that needed to be trimmed, and stepped into Julia's tiny oasis. With large hedges all around, Charlotte was thankful that at least this part hadn't been touched. There were two white wicker chairs in the middle of the yard and some small flower beds that still held blooms. A small table between the chairs held a partially empty coffee cup and a ball of yarn with two needles sticking out of it.

A soft smile spread across Charlotte's face. Knowing that Julia wasn't holed up in her home in depression eased her heart until the woman opened the screen door, and Charlotte saw firsthand how well Julia was, or rather was not, doing.

She set the basket down on the table and crossed the few steps that separated her from Julia and placed her arms around her. The woman was flesh and bones, her skin tone a soft gray, and her stringy hair trailed down her back in a loose ponytail. This wasn't the woman she was used to seeing.

"Oh honey," she whispered. Julia stood straight, her arms tight against her sides, but Charlotte didn't let go. She couldn't.

"I'm so sorry," Charlotte whispered. She found herself rubbing Julia's back and stopped. Julia's body language told her she didn't want to be held, so she dropped her arms and took a step back and almost gasped at the deadness in her gaze.

"For what?" Julia sidestepped her and sat down on one white chair. She sagged back and stared down at her hands.

Charlotte sat down in the other chair but leaned forward and took Julia's hands in hers. They were cold to the touch.

"For not coming sooner." She angled her head to gain Julia's attention, but the woman wouldn't look at her. "For not realizing you needed . . ." Her voice drifted off. What did Julia need? A shoulder to cry on? Someone who would listen and not condemn? "A friend," she said.

"You don't need to apologize to me." Julia looked at her for a second before looking away. She tried to tug her hands away, but Charlotte wouldn't let her.

"Of course I do. What kind of friend have I been to you lately? I should have been here for you." The guilt weighed heavy on her shoulders as she struggled with the small understanding that she'd once again failed.

"Should have been there for me? You were." Tears rimmed Julia's eyes. "You were the only one who was in the beginning."

It obviously hadn't been enough. She knew it hadn't been enough. Charlotte thought back to the few times she had visited Julia. The day after the shooting had been the first. She would never forget that day, when police cars and media had swarmed Julia's home and wouldn't leave her in peace.

"I'm sorry that all this is happening to you. I have people coming to clean it up," Charlotte said.

Julia shook her head in denial. "And it'll only happen again tomorrow. And the next day. And the day after that. There's no sense in cleaning it."

"Of course there is. It shouldn't be happening, and I'll make sure it doesn't happen again." She let go of Julia's hands and leaned back. "You should have told me."

"I don't need you to fight my battles for me, Mayor. I'm a big girl. I can handle it."

Julia must have read the disbelief on Charlotte's face because a slight flush colored her cheeks.

"I'm here as your friend. And as your friend, I'm telling you, you don't have to handle this alone." Charlotte gazed around the yard and noticed things she'd missed earlier. Like the overgrown weeds in the flower gardens, the stray pieces of garbage, and the fact that a lot of the handmade wooden signs or figurines that normally dotted the gardens were missing.

"But I am alone," Julia mumbled.

"Not anymore. If you won't take care of yourself, then let us. When was the last time you had a shower? Are you even eating the things Lacie leaves for you? Since when did you become so selfish?"

Julia threw herself back as if slapped. Charlotte knew she'd been harsh, especially that last bit, but there was something in Julia's expression, the way she'd reacted, that confirmed the woman didn't want or need to be coddled.

"I'm not," Julia whispered. "I'm trying to make life easier for everyone here. I've even thought of moving away, but . . ." Her voice trailed off as she drew up her knees close to her chest and hugged them tight.

"But this is where Gabe is," Charlotte completed her sentence.

Julia nodded.

"When was the last time you left the house?"

Julia shrugged. "A few weeks ago maybe. I tried to go to the cemetery, but there was a large crowd already there."

There had been a few funeral services earlier in the month, private ones for each of the families. Charlotte tried to be at each one if she were welcomed.

"Would you like to go see Gabe? Spend some time with him?"

A small light of hope filled Julia's gaze before it was quickly extinguished. "I can't. There might be others there . . . I don't want to make things uncomfortable for anyone."

Charlotte stood and reached out her hand. "Why don't you go get dressed, have a shower, and I'll take you. You need to spend time with your son, and I'm not taking no for an answer."

She wasn't sure what did it, maybe it was the tone of voice she'd used or the fact she offered Julia something she couldn't seem to do herself, but when Julia stood, it was all Charlotte could do to keep the smile off her face.

●　　●　　●

There was a quiet hush to the air as Charlotte walked alongside Julia as they made their way toward Gabriel's grave marker.

The cemetery was quiet and they were alone, something Charlotte was thankful for. She'd sent her assistant an e-mail asking her to cancel any appointments for the rest of the day. Julia needed time with her son, and Charlotte wanted to ensure that happened. She'd also asked Sheila to send someone over to clean up Julia's home while they were gone and perhaps take out one of the many casseroles Lacie had left and have it ready for when she brought Julia back home.

From the way Julia shook the whole ride here, Charlotte knew this was a much-needed visit and that it wouldn't be quick. And that was okay. Charlotte would sit on a bench and enjoy the stillness while watching over her friend to ensure she wasn't disturbed.

Every grieving mother deserves the time to mourn and say good-bye, and Charlotte didn't think Julia had done that yet.

"Are you sure it's going to be okay?" Julia asked. She carried a bouquet of flowers Charlotte had picked up on their way in her hands.

"Of course it's okay. You have every right to be here as much as anyone else." Charlotte lightly touched Julia's back. Julia seemed to crave touch, and it made Charlotte realize just how much pain this woman was in.

Charlotte led the way to the simple white cross where Gabriel Berry was laid to rest. There were no flowers, nothing to mark the grave, but at least it hadn't been desecrated like Charlotte had feared.

Apparently Julia had worried about the same thing. The moment she saw the small cross, she stumbled and almost tripped. Charlotte grabbed her arm to steady her.

"I thought . . ." Choked up, Julia covered her mouth with her hand and just stood there.

"I'm going to walk around for a bit. If you need me, I'll be over on that bench." She pointed to the black wrought-iron fence a few feet away. Far enough to give Julia her privacy, but close enough to keep an eye on her as well.

Julia's eyes widened as she looked around the empty grounds.

"No one else is here, you'll be okay." Charlotte kept her voice low and gentle, hoping to soothe her friend's fears.

It seemed to work. Julia nodded and then sank down on the ground beside her son's grave. Charlotte watched as she gently placed the flowers beneath the cross before resting her hand on the grass.

Knowing that giving Julia time was all she needed right now, Charlotte made her way through the park. She'd bought extra flowers and wanted to visit each grave of the victims while they were there.

It was hard not to let the emotional impact of seeing all the small white crosses hit her. There were too many children at rest in this cemetery and too many of them unnecessary deaths. Deaths she should have stopped from happening if only she'd seen the signs.

No matter what anyone said, no matter how many times Jordan told her it wasn't her fault, she knew it was. Maybe not all of it, but she held partial blame.

She was pleased to see small arrangements on all of the graves she visited, signs of love and remembrance. There was a small park bench close to Bobby Crowne's grave, and it brought tears to see the assortment of small toy cars, trucks, and boats. She'd seen similar ensembles at other graves, some with little horse figurines, others with hand-drawn pictures or framed letters. These little touches, things so personal to the children, touched her heart.

Why couldn't Arnold Lewery, the newspaper editor, write up stories about these types of things, small memorials to the families, perhaps some stories from the children for the children? Rather than harping on Julia and her son's mental health issues. She made a note to set up a meeting with Arnold and discuss how they could work together to focus on the small victories rather than their past defeats. Maybe that's all their town needed, a little push in the right direction . . .

"Charlotte?"

Charlotte glanced up at Samantha Hill. Sam stood there holding a bag in her hands.

"Of all the places we've run into one another, I would never have thought to add the cemetery to that list." Charlotte scooted over on the bench and tapped the spot beside her. She liked Sam, had found the woman to be both down-to-earth and sensitive. Of all the reporters that had swarmed their town, Sam was the only one who had been able to look past the tragedy and see the town as a cohesive community.

"I like how quiet it is here." Sam sat down and placed the bag she'd been holding between her feet.

"I noticed Julia Berry over by her son's grave," Sam said.

Charlotte nodded. She kept an eye on Julia and was thankful the woman's back was to them.

"I haven't seen her here before." Sam's voice was filled with curiosity.

"How often do you come here?" Charlotte found it hard to believe that Sam would keep tabs on those who visited here. It was morbid and . . . wrong.

"Enough. Like I said, it's quiet. I usually sit over there." She pointed to a bench set on the far outskirts of the cemetery. There were a few older grave markers there and then a small wooded area with a path that led down toward the lighthouse.

"But why? Of all the places where you could seek quiet, why come here?"

Samantha glanced down at the bag between her legs and shrugged.

"What's in the bag?" Charlotte leaned forward while Sam pushed the bag farther beneath their seat.

"Nothing important." She crossed her arms over her chest. "So, are you babysitting or just visiting?" She glanced over at Julia.

Charlotte sighed, "She just needed time with her son."

Sam's brow rose. "You don't need to defend her, not to me. Did you bring her?"

Charlotte nodded.

"I'm glad. I haven't seen her out in weeks and was starting to get worried. Is she doing okay?"

Charlotte's eyes narrowed. "Are you asking as a—"

"As a woman who understands grief. Not as a reporter." She gave her head a small shake. "You should know me better by now."

Charlotte noticed the bags under Samantha's eyes. "Are you okay?" Every other time she'd seen the reporter, she looked refreshed, alive as if ready to meet whatever came her way. Today she looked . . . old, tired, defeated.

Sam shrugged. "I'm fine."

Charlotte didn't believe her, but she didn't pry.

"Julia didn't feel . . . welcome . . . to visit Gabe's grave. She was worried other people would be here and be upset by her presence."

"But that's her son. She should be able to visit his grave whenever she wants. With no ramifications." Sam's lips thinned.

"Have you seen her home lately? The way people are treating her?"

"The graffiti, you mean?"

Charlotte nodded.

"I have. You know, I thought this town would be different. You're all so close-knit, it's almost as if you function as a family. I expected you to close ranks on Julia and shelter her from all of this, but . . . it's like she's your black sheep and it's easier for you to ignore her. It's sad, really."

"She's not our black sheep." Even as Charlotte denied the accusation, she knew it to be true. That's exactly how Julia had been treated, and it was shameful.

"I call it like it is."

"Then help me change it."

Samantha looked over at Julia and smiled. "Is that a challenge?"

"The media has vilified her since day one instead of seeing her for who she really is. Why not tell the whole story?"

"And what about you? How are you going to help?"

Charlotte set her shoulders back. "I don't need to do anything. We'll be doing this together, because I want to. Because . . . you're right. Stillwater Bay is a community, a family, and it's time we started acting like one."

"Why don't I come by your office on Monday and we can discuss this? I already have some ideas."

This surprised Charlotte. Did that mean Sam had been thinking of this before now?

"Come by in the morning. I'm free after ten o'clock." Charlotte pulled out her phone and added in the appointment. "We can talk about your short interview with Jenn regarding the school as well," Charlotte added.

"I kept my promise. You asked me to stay away from the school, and I did."

"I know. And thank you." Charlotte had to give her credit for that.

Sam reached for the bag beneath her and stood. "I'll see you on Monday. If you provide the coffee, I'll bring the croissants."

Charlotte nodded in agreement. She'd never say no to a pastry from Sweet Bakes, and Samantha knew it.

Charlotte turned her attention to Julia once Sam walked away. She was glad Julia had this time, and she'd do everything she could to ensure Julia knew she could visit her son's grave anytime she wished. As Jenn had reminded her this morning, the grieving process was complicated.

CHAPTER THIRTEEN

JENNIFER

Jennifer quickly sent Robert a text explaining dinner was in the oven and that she'd forgotten about a committee meeting for the July Fourth festivities.

It was partially true.

She had forgotten, and dinner was in the oven, but the meeting wasn't for another few hours. She needed some time alone, time to think about everything that had happened today. Her emotions had been all over the place, inconsistent, and she didn't like it. Where had the old Jenn gone? The one who could handle whatever life threw her and plan accordingly? Where had the woman who could take the hard times and figure out a way to make them good gone?

It was as if that part of her heart had died along with Bobby. And as a wife? Did the life they lived together as man and wife even count anymore? They were roommates at best. Yes, Robert had been her strength during the first few weeks after Bobby's death, but that closeness, that . . . togetherness, wasn't there like it had been.

She shouldn't be so surprised, though. Their marriage had been falling apart, piece by piece, until it seemed like all that was left was a shell constructed for Robert's business needs. Back in March, Jenn had met with a family lawyer in the city to discuss drawing up divorce papers, but something had held her back from giving them to Robert.

She'd always wanted the fairy-tale life, the happily-ever-after. Admitting their marriage had crumbled was admitting defeat, and there was something deep inside Jenn, preventing her from doing that.

She wasn't a defeatist. At least, she hadn't been. So what had changed?

She was the one who had changed, but why?

There were broken pieces inside her, deep inside her heart and soul, that she wasn't sure would, or even could, ever be repaired. But after today, first the way she'd shut down with Carla and then at the harbor with Charity, she knew she needed to piece her life back together.

What did it say that her first thought of dealing with her grief was opening a bottle of wine or starting the morning with Baileys in her coffee?

The outing to the harbor with Charity after dropping off the basket to the Andersons' had been a disaster. The closer they'd come to the path leading down to the boat dock, the tenser she'd become. Charity on the other hand . . . it was like she was being set free, unable or unwilling to see that the chains she shed were being cast on her own mother. Jenn's chest tightened, her fingers tingled, and little black dots swam ahead of her with each step she took. She didn't understand what was happening to her, didn't grasp the full extent of her panic attack . . . and she wished she had. Between Marina Drive and Second Bridge Street was a gravel drive that led down toward the dock. It was here that she lost her composure. Her sanity.

The last time she'd come this way had been with Bobby. They'd waited at the top of the drive for someone to drive his boat down and unload it, a process that could sometimes be lengthy. While they waited, Bobby had built a miniature boat dock right up against the wood fence so that his boats would go up and over the first board.

That little ramp was still there when she and Charity walked up, but now small toy boats and single white carnations decorated it.

Jenn froze, unable to move. It didn't matter that she blocked the drive and that cars were lined up waiting for her to cross. It didn't matter that Charity stood unaware next to the impromptu memorial for her brother. But Jenn knew. And the knowledge crushed her to the ground until she became a bumbling mess.

It had been Pastor Scott Helman who came to her, lifted her off the ground, and sat with her beside Bobby's ramp. She couldn't recall in detail what had happened afterward, other than someone had driven them home and Charity had covered her with a blanket while she sat in her large rocker.

She was ashamed by her reaction. What if someone told Robert?

Truth be told, another reason why she had left the house before her husband came home was to avoid the look of reproach in Robert's gaze when he walked through the door.

"What am I doing?" she whispered to herself.

She'd driven out to the lighthouse and down the rocky path as far as she could, then climbed over the fence so she could sit on the large rock face that hung over the water. It used to be her favorite place as a teen to hide, to think, to daydream. The rock wall had crumbled thanks to the weather, but she was safe enough as long as she didn't sit on the edge.

She needed a game plan, a focus, to help her out of this pit she was losing herself in. Yes, she was mourning. She wasn't just mourning for her son, but for the life she'd had. Last summer, she'd never have let Carla talk to her like that. Yes, she would have been polite, but she would have stood her ground. Not like today. She didn't like the woman she'd been today. Weak. Downtrodden. Empty.

The counselor she'd been seeing had told her to look within herself and see who she was in that exact moment—whether it be a mother, a wife, or a volunteer. Whoever she was in that moment, she should be that person to the full extent, with everything inside of her.

But she hadn't followed the counselor's advice. Instead, she'd taken all the many facets of who she was and lumped them together in a pile of worthlessness. She couldn't do it all, so she couldn't do it at all. Perhaps that was the wrong way to look at it. Maybe her counselor had been right.

Right now, she wasn't a mother, a wife, or a volunteer . . . she was Jenn. A woman with dreams, goals, and desires. In this moment, as she sat gazing out on the bay, she could be that woman. A woman with a dream of being fulfilled. A woman with a goal of being someone others could look up to. A woman with the desire to change her town for the better.

Having a goal gave her a purpose. And with a purpose, she knew she could get out of the hole she was mired in.

An idea bubbled up, bringing a small shimmer of excitement, before she squashed it down. The one thing she wanted to do, she couldn't. She knew that. It would be viewed as betrayal, not just by her husband but by her best friend as well.

A best friend who obviously had no idea what she was going through.

Something clicked inside her heart. Like her marriage, had her relationship with Charlotte all been a charade? Was it based on what

Jenn could do for her as the mayor instead of as a friend? It was starting to look that way.

She knew it wasn't fair to expect Charlotte to understand completely what she was going through, but she wasn't the only one grieving. Dozens of families in Stillwater had lost a child; dozens more had children who'd been hurt, terrorized, and traumatized beyond comprehension.

But what about Robert? If she went through with this idea, Robert would be angry. No, he'd be more than angry, he'd be furious, because it would go against everything he'd been trying to do since the shootings occurred.

Everything he'd worked so hard on with Charlotte.

Jenn wasn't ready to face that issue yet.

But it did help to make up her mind.

Feeling more relaxed, Jenn leaned back on her hands and stretched out. A warm breeze played with her hair. She let her head fall back, exposed her throat, and fell into the sensation of being set free, like a bird. She imagined herself drifting upward, toward the clouds, with the wind beneath her. She smiled as the heaviness she'd carried earlier let go.

She could do this. In this time and in this moment, she knew she could do this. Nothing and no one would stop her. And if it meant betraying those around her, then it begged the question, who was the first betrayer?

.   .   .

Jenn parked her SUV outside the town hall and made her way in. It wasn't until she stood in the main hallway that she realized she'd come empty-handed. She hoped nobody would comment on it.

A small buzz came from the committee room off to the side of the building's entrance. She was the last one to arrive. Her cheeks heated up, and she quickly ducked her head, with the hope that no one would notice her.

"There you are," a voice called out.

Jenn plastered a smile on her face and lifted her hand in a small wave.

"Sorry for being late," she said.

A table had been set up with coffee, and someone else had brought a plate of baked goods. She filled a Stryofoam cup with coffee but bypassed the slightly burnt cookies before heading over to the round table set up in the middle.

One empty seat remained, and it was right beside Lacie. Jenn gave her a small smile but kept quiet as Charlie Monroe was speaking. Charlie owned the local hardware store and was head of the fair committee.

"Jenn, we were just discussing the new parade route." Charlie leaned forward and looked at her from the other side of Lacie. "We're going to start at the lighthouse this year and go down First and end at South Beach. The route is quite a bit shorter, but we want to bypass the school this year."

Jenn nodded in agreement. She was the one who had first suggested the reroute when they'd met earlier to discuss postponing the annual summer parade.

"We're running into a bit of a snag, though," Lacie mentioned.

"What kind of snag?" Jenn leaned forward and placed her elbow on the table.

"Well, we normally end with the children's activities that would be set up in the school parking lot. We don't have that venue now."

The fun activities were an important part of the parade. They usually had stalls for face painting, clown lessons, water tanks where kids could dunk their teachers, and other fun things for families to do.

"What about the community center?"

Charlie shook his head. "That's where the midway is being set up."

The midway included the carnival rides, games, and entertainment.

"Surely there is room?" While the parking lot wasn't that large, she did remember that they'd rented only a few rides and booths, making sure to leave plenty of room for other things. "Why can't we move some of the booths down to North Beach and set up some activities there? Sure, things will be a bit different this year, but that's to be expected, right?"

Jenn caught the way others in the committee nodded and jotted down notes on the pads of paper laid out at every seat.

"Merille, you okay with reorganizing the fixtures?" Charlie looked at the woman across the table from him.

"And, Arnold, can you restructure the notice for the paper to ensure folks are aware of the route change?"

"Already done," Arnold mumbled before he took a sip of his coffee.

While talk continued around the table of tasks that were under way for the July Fourth festivities, including a large fireworks display out in the bay, Jenn mulled over thoughts she wanted to bring up and jotted down some key points. She waited for the lull that announced the ending of their meeting before she spoke up.

"Before we all go, there's something I'd like to . . . suggest to everyone here." She leaned forward, planted her elbows on the table, and linked her fingers together.

"This isn't about the parade or anything linked to these festivities. Rather, they are about the school, and I bring it up now because, frankly, everyone here is on the school board." She glanced around the table and met the gaze of each person. She wasn't sure how the next few words she uttered would be taken, but she knew, deep inside, that they were the right words.

"I'd like to propose a discussion regarding the closure of Stillwater Public before the start of the new school year in September."

There. She'd said it. Without thinking of the ramifications or any of the minute details that would go into closing the school. She spoke what was in her heart. Living in the moment, as her counselor would say, and it felt right.

She was met with silence and bewildered glances.

"Why would we do that?" Charlie asked.

That moment of clarity, of feeling the rightness of what she was about to say, dissipated. She wished she could take her words back, rewind and press Delete on these last few moments.

Lacie laid her hand on Jenn's arm. "I'm not sure that is the best plan, not for our small community."

"Why not? It's not a large school. We ship our high school students off to larger schools. Why can't we do that with our younger children? Why force them to remain in a school where they lived a nightmare? How many of you were at the school Friday? Did you not see the reactions from our children as they faced their fears? Why would you want to do that to them?"

"And what would we do with the building? Let it sit empty as a monument to the worst day in Stillwater's history?" Arnold wheezed, in between a coughing fit.

That gave Jenn pause. "We could create a lasting monument," she suggested.

"No." Charlie stood up. "Jenn, we all understand where you are coming from, but the answer has to be no. This isn't something we'll table at our next meeting. It's not even something we'll bring up in our minutes as discussed."

Jenn twisted in her chair to look at Charlie directly. "But I think it should be discussed."

Charlie's gaze remained firm. "Closing the school isn't what is best for this town. Our children are resilient. They will heal. We all will heal." He stepped away from his chair and placed his hand on her shoulder. "I'm sorry. I really am. If you need some time . . . well, we all understand if you decide to step down for a bit."

Jenn shook her head. Stepping down admitted defeat, and that was something she wouldn't do. She looked at the other members around the table and focused on Shelley Peterson. The owner of the Seaglass B&B had lost her nephew in the shooting that day. Perhaps she would understand and sympathize. And Lacie, she knew Lacie had to feel the same way.

"I understand, Jenn. Trust me, I do," Lacie said quietly.

Jenn turned toward her. "Then why didn't you support me, back me up?"

"Because I'm not sure that's the right way to go about it. There are too many ramifications to closing the school. Trust me, I've thought about it. But do you want to be responsible for all our teachers losing their jobs?"

Jenn picked up a pen and played with it. "I'm sure they could find positions elsewhere."

Lacie's brow rose. "Really? In our economy?"

Okay, so she should have thought this through a little more. "So what do we do then? Because we need to do something."

"I'm all for sheltering our kids from the bad world outside our front doors, but sometimes we can't. But what we can do is what we have been doing. Teach them coping methods. Help them face their fears—"

"By forcing them?" Jenn interrupted. She would never agree that pushing the children to face this fear was the best thing for any of them, including her child. Never. And she couldn't believe Lacie was.

"I think we're looking at it a bit differently," Lacie sighed. "We can't hide from this and pretend it never happened. That's not the way to help our children or even our community."

"I'm not hiding." But Jenn knew by the look on Lacie's face that she'd been caught in a lie. "I'm not. I wake up every morning, knowing my son is gone. I wish I could pretend otherwise, but . . ."

"But have you accepted it?"

"Of course not." Jenn jerked back at the thought. "How could I possibly accept it?" Just the thought of being at peace with her child's death tore her already tattered heart into a million pieces.

"That's the only way to heal, as hard as it is." Lacie's soft voice was filled with something other than her own acceptance, and Jenn could hear it.

"Have you?" she asked. "Have you accepted your son's death? Has Pastor Scott? Have you forgiven God for taking your child away like that? Have you accepted the pain and fear he must have been in just before he died?"

Lacie winced.

"I didn't think so." A small level of satisfaction filled Jenn. At least she wasn't the only one still hurting. Still angry. "So don't lecture me when you haven't done it yourself."

Lacie stood up, gathered her belongings, and looked down. Jenn could read the sadness in her gaze and see how her words had hit hard and hurt. She was about to apologize, but Lacie spoke first.

"I'll never understand nor will I be able to forgive something so senseless. But if I don't learn to accept that my son is gone, that he will never sit at my kitchen table again, never argue with me about the clothes he wants to wear or the music he was listening to, then I'll never be able to move on with my life. I'll miss him every moment of every day, but I have two other children to raise, to love, to teach that when life hammers you into the ground, you can still get back up."

The room was empty now; the others had left while the two were talking. Jenn stood up and gathered her own purse. In silence they exited the room and made their way outside. They stopped at the small round water fountain beneath the stairs, and Jenn trailed her fingers in the shallow water.

"Have you gotten back up yet?" Jenn asked the one question circling her mind.

Lacie shook her head. She glanced up at the sky, her shoulders back, and a small tear slid down her cheek. "I'm afraid I never will."

Jenn didn't know how to respond or what to say, so she remained quiet as Lacie walked away from her. She stood there, unsure of what to do or where to go, when she heard her name called.

"Merille, I thought you'd gone home." She eyed the woman with curiosity. Merille wasn't someone she normally stopped and chatted with. Although she should. Merille was a mother who understood the pain of losing a child. Her son had been another victim of Gabriel Berry's rampage.

"I wanted to talk to you, without others around." Merille's voice was low, quiet, and she stood with her head bowed. It took a few moments, but when she lifted her head, there was fire blazing through her gaze, a fire that Jenn understood. "I wanted you to know that you're not alone. There's a group of us that agree with you. We feel the school needs to be closed too."

CHAPTER FOURTEEN

CHARLOTTE

Charlotte parked her car in their driveway and then followed the walkway to the side of their house. The gate was latched but not locked, and the hinges squeaked as she pushed it open. Buster barked in greeting while she locked the gate behind her and met Jordan in the back.

He held out a glass of wine to her.

"How did you know I needed this?" She took a sip and sighed at the blissful quiet of their yard.

Jordan's brow rose. "You were with children all night after spending the day with Julia," he said matter-of-factly. "I'm surprised you didn't come home sooner."

She slipped off her shoes and wiggled her toes against the grass. "Ellie was having a lot of fun but didn't want me to leave her."

"Was this her first sleepover?"

Charlotte nodded. "I think so. Shelley worked her magic, though, and had the kids making cookies by the time I left. I promised we would be by in the morning for breakfast." She smiled as Jordan's eyes lit up. "I figured you wouldn't mind."

Knowing Shelley, she'd have freshly baked muffins, omelets, and waffles complete with homemade whipped cream and cut fruit.

"Did you see Lauren this morning?" She'd sent Lauren texts throughout the day to let her know how Ellie was and what was going on, but she'd only received one text back—*thank you.* Hopefully that meant that she had slept all day.

Jordan sat down on the edge of their deck, and Charlotte joined him. Buster grabbed a bright orange ball and brought it to Jordan, who promptly threw it, and Buster went running after it.

"I knocked to let her know I was there, but she must have been asleep already. Although I'm not sure how she could have slept with the mower going." Buster ran back with the ball and dropped it into Jordan's outstretched palm. He threw it again and then wiped his hand on his shorts. "I tried to cut her lawn as fast as I could."

"She didn't look good, Jordan. I'm worried about her."

His lips thinned before he reached over and placed his hand on her thigh. "Some people have to take care of themselves. You can't do it for everyone."

"She has no one to help her, though."

He shook his head. "She has a lot of people. This whole town, in fact. I think it's just hard for her to accept the help."

Charlotte thought back to how Lauren had almost said no when she'd offered to keep Ellie longer than originally planned. He was right. Lauren did have a hard time accepting the help. But she needed it. Why couldn't she see that?

"How's Julia?"

There was a look on his face as he asked the question, but Charlotte couldn't quite read him. They hadn't really talked about Julia much; Jordan's focus was on his students, and hers was on the town. It was almost as if they had an unspoken agreement to not bring her up in case they disagreed with one another.

Samantha's comment about the town's view of Julia hit a little closer to home than she thought it had.

"Did you know her house has been vandalized on a regular basis? And that she hasn't been to visit her son's grave at all? Or that she's barely eating?"

"Are you trying to save her as well?" There was a note of resignation in his voice.

"What do you mean by that?" She turned to look at him and quickly looked away when she saw the message in his eyes. Pity. Why would he pity her?

"Ever since I've known you, you've always felt it was your responsibility to help people. It's like you don't trust them to do it themselves."

"Sometimes they can't."

"Not if you're the one always doing it for them." He threw the ball again for Buster.

Charlotte let out a long breath. He didn't understand. He never had.

"The only one you've never tried to fix is me. Why is that, I wonder?"

This caught her attention.

"You've never needed it. That's what drew me to you. You were solid, always have been."

Jordan nodded but got to his feet and stepped away from her. Buster ran up toward them and dropped the ball at his feet and then lay down.

"I've always wondered if that's what you thought."

She set her glass of wine down on the ledge and went to stand beside her husband.

"What am I missing, Jordan? Is there something going on that I don't know about?"

He turned toward her, and sadness hit her hard. Something was wrong. She could feel it.

"Nothing I can't handle," he said.

She didn't like the sound of that. He never handled anything alone. She was always there beside him. Like a team. The media had labeled them as a powerhouse team holding their town together. It's what worked for them.

"What happened after you left Lauren's?" In all of their texts today, he never did tell her what he'd done. Now that she thought about it, the conversation had really been one-way. She'd texted him to let him know where she was, and he'd replied back with one word. *Okay.*

"What do you mean, what happened?"

"Just that. What happened today? What did you do?"

He shrugged. "Had a few meetings regarding the new security measures at the school for the new year."

"That was today?" She didn't have that meeting in her calendar.

"You don't need to be present at every meeting I hold. The school is my responsibility. Not yours." His scowl deepened.

Oh, no he didn't. He wasn't going to play this game with her. She straightened her back, prepared for a discussion that went beyond their roles of husband and wife.

"As mayor of this town, the school is my responsibility, and you know it. Everything that happens in this town is my responsibility. And yes, I do need to be at those meetings. What did I miss?"

There was a fire in his eyes, as if he was going to argue, but she stood firm. She couldn't believe he was being like this.

"We're looking into metal detectors at the entrances and lanyards for everyone to wear in the school."

"To distinguish visitors from staff?"

He nodded. "We also discussed making that one wall as you walk in all glass."

The front office was directly to the left of the entrance with one small windowpane. Making that wall all glass made sense; the office staff could see who walked in at all times.

"I like that idea. I'd support it if you needed my vote."

"I don't. It was a unanimous decision."

"Okay, what's going on here? What have I done, because obviously it was something."

He stared at her, as if willing her to read his thoughts, before he glanced away and stared out at the water.

Charlotte glanced up at the sky, at the twinkling lights shining down on them. She loved looking up at the stars. She used to lie on the grass in the middle of the night and count the stars, for as long as she could, until they all blurred together.

"Nothing. Sorry, it wasn't an easy day. I met with the carpenters to go over the interior remodeling that needs to be done and then spent the rest of the day in town making myself available to families. The beach crowd wasn't too bad for this time of year and a few parents approached me looking for some reassurances. Some even asked what they could do to help other families."

"Anyone ask about Julia?"

"Why would they?" His voice had chilled.

Charlotte shrugged. She knew she needed to play this safe, to not go full throttle on this new idea, but it was hard. Jordan was her husband. He should understand and see things the same way. They had the same goal after all.

"Because she's a member of our community, of our family, and she's hurting just as much as everyone else."

Jordan's brow arched and the oh-so-famous principal look he was known for was now turned on her.

"Really, Charlotte? Is this the message you're now going to try to get across? You can't expect others to embrace her, bring her back into the fold, so to speak. She's forever part of the one memory everyone wants to forget."

"I know, I know." Charlotte reached out and laid her hand on his arm. "But she's not the one who shot the students. She's just a mother who also lost her child." She raised her hand to stop whatever argument he was about to throw at her. "I know it's not the same, but it kind of is, isn't it? Gabe killed himself. Her grief is no different than the others'."

Jordan's lips thinned at her response. "There is a difference. But I doubt we're going to see eye to eye on this one."

At his words, a sword pierced her heart. They hurt. Each word he spoke hurt. Was it his goal tonight to tear her apart, to break their bond? To make her doubt herself or what she believed?

"Are we okay?" she asked.

"What kind of question is that?"

She blinked and stared upward. "Will you support me in public regarding Julia?"

"Charlotte . . ." There was an edge to her husband's voice, as if warning her to drop the subject. But she couldn't.

Since the day Julia Berry had moved to Stillwater, Jordan had kept her at arm's length, no matter how Charlotte felt about her. He always left the room when she was there; his words and attitude toward her were . . . not condescending but not welcoming either. He'd claimed there was something *off* about her, something he couldn't put his finger on. He'd never liked her, and so it was no surprise that he felt this way.

"I need you to support me in this, Jordan. Please."

Jordan's hands fisted at his sides as he stood there beside her. "You don't understand what you're asking," he said. The muscle in his cheek flared as he clenched his jaw.

"I'm not asking anything I haven't in the past. We support each other, Jordan. That's what we do. That's who we are." Her muscles tensed, and she couldn't believe this was happening between them.

"Not in this. You can't ask me to support you in this." He turned and walked down toward the beach. Buster climbed to his feet and followed after him.

"I'm going for a run," he said over his shoulder. He didn't bother to wait for her reply.

What was it about Julia that set him off? It didn't make sense—not that kind of reaction.

She puzzled over it while she headed back to the deck and grabbed her wineglass. She took a sip and thought about how Jordan had always been distant with Julia and even with her son. If she remembered correctly, Jordan used to come home in foul moods over how he'd had to deal with Gabe when he was at Stillwater Public. He'd been the only problem child in the school to get beneath Jordan's skin, which was saying something since Jordan had a knack for handling most kids with attitudes.

She was content to sit there on their deck until Jordan came back from his late run, but the sound of the phone ringing interrupted her musing. It was Charlie.

"So, how did the meeting go?" She'd called him earlier to say she wouldn't be there and asked him to call.

As Charlie filled her in on what had transpired, she reached her hand out to blindly feel for the chair and then sat down. Her heart sank at his words.

•   •   •

Charlotte's hand shook as she gripped the phone in her hand. She leaned back in the chair and digested the news from Charlie.

Jenn wanted to close the school. Shut it down. Forever.

How could she do that?

She dialed Jenn's home number.

"Hello?"

She breathed a sigh of relief when Robert answered. She knew Jenn probably hadn't made it home yet, but she wasn't sure how long after the meeting Charlie had called.

"Robert, we need to talk. Jenn approached her committee tonight with the idea of shutting down the school."

There was silence on the other end. Did that mean he knew of her plan? He didn't condone it, did he?

"If you knew about this, why didn't you at least warn me? I knew she said some things to Samantha, but I didn't think she would take it this far."

"I didn't know." Robert's voice held a faraway note to it.

"You didn't know?" She had a hard time believing that. Robert knew everything that happened in this town; that's why he made such a great business partner for her. They worked well as a team.

"No, Charlotte. I didn't. Jenn just drove up; let me talk to her." He hung up on her.

Charlotte sat there in shock. How could Jenn do this to her? Didn't she understand the harm closing their school would do to the town? To the teachers and to the parents? Was she so lost in her grief that she couldn't see past her own anger and sorrow?

Part of her wanted to talk to her friend directly, but there seemed to be a wide schism between them, and she was afraid facing this issue head-on would completely separate them.

Time drifted past, and yet Charlotte didn't move. This betrayal hit her hard. How could Jenn do this to her, especially without talking to her about it first? Didn't she realize Jordan would lose his job? That the teachers they called friends wouldn't have an income and would have to move? That it would destroy their town?

A wet nose nuzzled her hand, and she automatically began to pet Buster. She glanced up to see Jordan standing there, a puzzled look on his face.

"What's wrong?"

She shook her head. How did she even explain this to him?

She thought she'd have heard back from Robert by now, telling her she was overreacting and Jenn didn't actually mean what Charlie had said. But he hadn't. The phone had remained silent.

"Charlotte, what's wrong?" Jordan stood at her side and reached for the phone that rested in her hand still.

When he squatted down beside her, she almost started to cry. She pushed back the tears and gave her head a small shake. She needed to figure this out and stop being so emotional about it.

"They're going to close the school." That didn't come out right, but it was all she could think of to say. They were going to close the school, or at least try. What if they did? What if Jenn spoke to enough people who agreed with her flawed logic?

"Who's going to close the school?" Jordan pulled out the chair beside her. Sweat beads covered his skin from his run, and she could tell he was out of breath. He must have pushed himself.

"Charlotte? Who is going to close the school?"

Forcing herself to focus, Charlotte looked him in the eye. "Jenn."

Jordan laughed. "You honestly believe that? Robert would never let her."

She shook her head. "She went to the committee about it."

"Okay," he sighed. "I doubt the committee will do anything about it. I'm surprised Rob didn't stop her."

"He didn't know."

Jordan reached for her hand, stood up, and pulled her up with him. "Then there's nothing to worry about."

There was a lot to worry about.

"Give her a call tomorrow, and have your girls' chat you two usually do over coffee and chocolate. Find out where her head is at, and see how you can help turn it around." Jordan placed a kiss on the top of her head and then released her.

"Jordan, it's not that simple."

He smiled at her. "It is that simple. You're best friends. You'll figure it out. And I'm sure you'll talk with Robert tomorrow and find out what is going on. We have our school board meeting later this week. Why don't you suggest an impromptu meeting with some of the members before then?"

"So you're not worried?" Her question stopped him in the doorway. How could he be so nonchalant about this?

"I'm not worried." He bent down and patted Buster's head. "Now, if it were anyone else, that's a different story."

"Why?" She knew Jenn. Once she set her mind to something, she didn't let go. If she wanted the school closed, she'd find a way to make it happen.

"Because I trust Robert."

"I don't understand." She trusted Robert as well, but Jenn was her own person, and there was only so much that Robert could do.

"Honey, if you weren't mayor of our small town, Robert would be."

Flabbergasted at his statement, there wasn't much left to say, so she watched him head downstairs to have a shower after his run.

Robert as mayor? While she'd often joked about that with Rob, this was the first time Jordan had ever said anything. Did he think she should step down after this session? She'd planned on running again. She'd even talked it over with Robert, and he'd confirmed he would support her for another term. But did Jordan know something she didn't? Or was she just being overly paranoid right now and reading into things too much?

' She poured herself a glass of wine and headed into her office. She needed to calm herself down and focus on getting ready for Monday. She'd promised some things to Julia today, things she'd meant to talk to Jordan about, but that would have to wait till she was in the office and had her morning meeting with Sheila.

She sat down at her desk and turned on her computer and noticed her phone vibrated.

We need to talk. The message was from Robert.

What's up? Anxiety filled her as she texted him back. She cracked her fingers while she awaited his reply.

Tomorrow.

Tomorrow. So much for calming down.

CHAPTER FIFTEEN

JULIA

Julia grabbed a rag and began the slow process of shining her coffee table so that it gleamed. Earlier she'd cleaned it and thrown away old wrappers, magazines, and tissues she'd left lying there. She'd already gotten rid of the thick layer of dust, but now she slowly rubbed the rag around in circles to bring out the sheen in the wood. She'd fallen in love with this table a few years ago while hunting around at a flea market just south of them. At first glimpse it had been covered in black paint, but there was something there, beneath the layers, that spoke to her.

After hours of scraping the paint off and restoring it back to the original wood, it didn't take much for Julia to realize she'd found something priceless. Her whole house was furnished with similar pieces: antique dressers, tables, stands, and knickknacks.

Her arms ached from the repeated circular motion, but she welcomed the pain. It provided a distraction from her thoughts. When she was finished, she set the arrangement from Paige and Camille in the center of the table and fingered the flowers. She was thankful for their friendship, despite how she'd kept them at bay.

She didn't want their association with her, their friendship, to hurt them businesswise.

The bouquet made her smile, and for one moment, one very brief moment, she forgot.

The knock at the door startled her. She crossed the room and peeked through her curtains to see who it was.

"Julia Berry, you open that door right this instant," Lacie demanded. Her arms were full of bags, and she blew out a piece of stray hair that hung over her eyes.

Julia unlocked the door and stepped to the side. When Lacie set the bags down, Julia should have been prepared for the fierce hug she received, but she wasn't. She staggered against the pressure of Lacie's arms around her.

"Happy birthday," Lacie said before she kissed her cheek and gave her an extra squeeze.

"I'm sorry about this morning," Julia said.

Lacie waved away her apology. "Don't worry about it. As soon as I saw your note on the back door I knew you wanted to be left alone today. But"—she bent down and grabbed the bags—"if you thought your little note would keep me away all day, you should have used different wording." She carried the bags into the kitchen and put them down on the table.

"I thought *birthday wishes=sleep* said it all." Julia followed after her. The other day Lacie had asked her what she wanted for her birthday, and when Julia couldn't come up with an answer, she was told to sleep on it. So she did and realized there was one thing she'd always wanted for her birthday but never got—to sleep in.

Her other wish, she'd been afraid to confess, but somehow Charlotte had already known.

"I've been by a few times today, but you weren't around." Lacie pulled out containers along with some wrapped presents.

"Charlotte came by." Her throat constricted as she took in the presents and the cake with her name on it.

"That's for me?" Tears gathered and she wiped them away.

"Of course it is! Kylie helped to make it and decorate it. She wanted to come, but I wasn't sure . . ." Her voice trailed off, and Julia knew why.

"It was really nice of her. Please tell her that." The last time she'd seen either Kylie or Liam, Lacie's two remaining children, Liam had been quick to tell her he didn't like her anymore, and then Kylie had run out of the room in tears.

"I will." She handed her a small wrapped gift. "This is from Liam."

Julia reached for the gift and held it in her hands as if it were the most precious thing in the world to her. In that moment, she wished Liam and Kylie were here, for her to say thank you. She unwrapped the gift, and the tears couldn't be contained then. It was a layered heart made out of multicolored construction paper and glued together. The hearts were all different sizes, and in the middle was a hand-drawn cake.

"Can I bring them next time?" Lacie asked.

Julia nodded her head.

"So you let Charlotte in but not me? I'm not sure if I should be offended or . . ."

Julia shrugged. "She caught me off guard. And she carried flowers."

The look Lacie gave her was priceless. "Paige and Camille have brought flowers, and you refused to open the door," she pointed out.

"I know." She pulled out a chair and sat down.

"Okay, then." Lacie grabbed two plates from the cupboard, a cutting knife, and forks.

"Should I sing?" she asked as she placed a candle in the middle of the cake.

"Please don't." She loved her friend, but Lacie had the voice of a crow when it came to singing.

Lacie winked at her and lit the candle.

Julia stared at the flame, slightly mesmerized by its flickering light. She could hear Gabe's voice, from when he was little, singing "Happy Birthday" to her and then blowing the candle out for her.

It was their *thing*. Gabe always blew out her candles. He would sing her the birthday song, squeeze her hand while she made her wish, and then blow out her candle, always in a rush so that she wouldn't get to it first. She'd laugh and place a kiss on his cheek and he'd smile, his cheeks bright red from the exertion before she cut into the cake.

She had no wishes to make this year.

"Do you need help?" A teasing smile graced Lacie's face, and Julia shook her head.

She bent down, and with a slight puff from her lips, she blew out the candle.

"What did you do today?" Lacie asked while she took a knife and laid the cut piece on a plate.

"Charlotte took me"—she swallowed—"to the cemetery. To see Gabriel. Or not to see, but to spend time with him," she clarified.

Lacie touched her arm briefly. "I'm glad."

"It was nice." Julia nodded. "I've been afraid to go there."

"Why?"

She shrugged. Did she really need to explain why she stayed away from the cemetery?

"You're allowed to grieve for your son, Julia."

"So is everyone else. In peace."

Lacie grunted, and Julia knew it was in frustration. They'd had this conversation plenty of times in the past.

"I would have taken you."

"I know." Julia gave her a small smile.

"So why let Charlotte take you when I've offered plenty of times?"

Julia bowed her head over her cake, slid her fork into the layers, and sighed.

"Because, Lacie. Charlotte wasn't there to mourn her own child. A child my son killed." It was hard to say the words, to hear them. But they needed to be said.

Lacie didn't respond, but then, Julia didn't really expect her to. This was another topic of conversation they'd had over and over. A guilt Julia couldn't relinquish. A fact Lacie lived with daily. It amazed her that Lacie could still be friends with her. She wondered if this was Lacie's way of proving she could forgive, that she was "doing the Lord's work." She knew Lacie would say no and defend the bond they'd had for years, but there had to be a small part of her friend that hated her.

There had to be.

"Aren't you wondering about all these other gifts?" Lacie forced a smile into her voice; Julia could hear it. "They're from everyone at your store." She held one out to her, but Julia didn't reach for it.

"They didn't have to." She hadn't been able to think about her store, the Treasure Chest. She knew she needed to—it was her only source of income—but who would want to buy, let alone sell, the items in her shop now?

"They wanted to." Lacie pushed a gift into Julia's hands.

Julia set it down, not ready to open it or any of the others. Lacie sighed, ate a few more bites of her cake before she laid the plate down on the table, and gathered her purse.

"I love you, Julia. I wish you would believe that. And I'm not the only one. Yes, there are a lot of hurting people in this town, but it's not because of you." A weariness set in Lacie's gaze, and Julia knew there had to be some hesitation there.

"I love you too, Lacie."

"Happy birthday," her friend said. She gave her a hug and then left, leaving Julia to sit there, at the table, alone once again.

She needed to get used to this. Being alone. No matter what her friend said, no matter what Charlotte did . . . in her heart, she knew. She knew she was to blame. How could she not be? It was her job, as Gabriel's mother, to raise him right.

CHAPTER SIXTEEN

JENNIFER

The insistent knock on the bathroom door was beyond irritating. Why couldn't Robert just leave her alone? She'd made it very obvious that she didn't want to talk to him.

When she walked through their front door last night, the look on his face told her he'd already heard about what she'd proposed at the committee meeting. Before he could say a word, she told him she didn't want to talk about it, poured herself a glass of wine, grabbed the bottle, and headed up to the spare bedroom where she promptly locked the door.

Robert had stood on the other side of the door and attempted to talk to her, but she turned the volume up on the television and ignored him. It was childish, she knew that, but she was already humiliated, and she didn't need a lecture from her husband.

Besides, she had a lot to think about. Merille's confession that she wasn't alone, that a group of other parents felt the same way, left her in an emotional tailspin. She'd made Merille a promise to meet with her to discuss the idea more. The woman had been cagey last night on the sidewalk, as if fearful of who would see them talking. But why? No one had been around, and it had been late.

"Jenn, we need to talk."

It was the first official Monday of summer, which meant he should have left first thing to go shoot a round of golf at the club-house. It was his routine. A round of golf before heading into work.

The pounding was giving her a headache.

"For Pete's sake, Jenn. This is childish. I'll take the door off if I need to. Just unlock it and talk to me." Weariness with a hint of annoyance filled his voice. She took a step toward the door.

"I don't want a lecture," she said.

"I don't plan on giving one. How about just a conversation?"

"I'm serious, Robert."

"So am I. Charity's gone to Amanda's, so it's just us. I'll be downstairs."

Charity was gone? Did Robert plan that, or was it something the girls had just decided on the fly?

She listened to Robert's footsteps fade out of their room before she unlocked the door and opened it.

Her hair was twisted in a loose bun, and she threw on some yoga pants and a loose T-shirt. She had hardly slept last night, and it showed with the bags beneath her eyes.

She'd done a lot of thinking last night. Somewhere around three in the morning she realized that she didn't regret saying what she'd said nor did she believe it to be wrong.

Yes, there were major ramifications for closing the school, but there were also benefits. Stillwater Public School needed a face-lift, a major update. The student body had outgrown the classrooms, and the school had been in discussion for years about bringing in trailers to create extra classrooms.

Why not build a new school? The city owned plenty of land. The community center didn't have enough outdoor space—they could fix that by creating a memorial park or sports area on the grounds where the school now stood.

By building a new school, the school could increase in size and offer more for its families. Yes, it would be expensive, but if there's one thing Jenn knew how to do, it was fund-raise. And with the recent media attention, raising the money wouldn't be an issue.

She realized it would take time, but weren't their children worth it?

Somehow she had to make people realize they needed to shelter their children more, protect them, and forcing them to spend eight hours a day in a place where their friends were murdered before their eyes was wrong.

And if what Merille said were true, then she wasn't as alone in this as she'd thought. *If.* She needed to find out the truth of Merille's words first.

With renewed belief in herself, Jenn made her way downstairs and found Robert holding a plastic bag.

"What are you doing?"

She watched as he grabbed one of the many floral arrangements in their living room and dropped it in the bag.

"It's time we cleaned up."

One after another, Robert emptied all the vases and baskets and threw the flowers, dead or alive, into the bag. Jenn stood at the bottom of the steps, unable to move.

"Why?"

"It's time, don't you think?" He went to gather the cards lying in groups and was about to dump them in the bag before she stopped him.

"Stop." Until now she'd ignored each and every card, not wanting to see them, to read them, or to remember. "Not those. I haven't
. . . I'll put them away for later."

He held them out to her, and she was finally able to move. Her hand trembled as she reached for the multitude of cards, but her grasp was firm when she grabbed them.

She looked around for a spot to place them, somewhere that was out of the way, and spotted a square box beneath an end table. She knelt down and opened the box and found some Lego pieces that belonged to Bobby. Her eyes filled with tears as she placed the envelopes on top of the toys.

When she stood, Robert was behind her and he offered to help her up, but she ignored his hand and pretended she didn't see it.

She headed into the kitchen to pour herself a coffee while he went into the garage and left the bag there.

While he was gone, she brought out the bottle of Baileys and poured some of the liquid gold into her cup before placing it back in the fridge. She wasn't planning on going anywhere this morning, so it's not as if she were doing anything wrong, and yet, she knew if Charity were here, she probably wouldn't have added the liqueur to her coffee.

"Are you ready to talk?" Robert grabbed his mug that sat on the corner of the island and crossed the kitchen to the screen door. "I thought we could sit outside."

Without a word, Jenn followed him and made her way to her favorite chair. She drew her feet up beneath her and looked out over the bay. The crystal-blue water was tranquil today. A few clouds drifted in the sky, and the sound of birds as they flew along the shoreline searching for food filled the air.

"I love this view," she said quietly. She drank in the beauty, letting it fill up her soul with its peacefulness. She needed that today.

She needed the calm, the sliver of hope that all would be well. She held on to that idea.

"I missed you last night."

When Jenn looked at her husband, she was shocked at what she saw. His gaze was steady on the lighthouse that was to their right, across the bay, but his face was haggard. He looked as if he'd aged overnight. The gray was more pronounced on his sideburns, the worry lines on his forehead more visible, and he looked . . . tired.

"I'm sorry." The words were automatic, without thought. And she was sorry. Sorry she'd acted so childish last night by avoiding him, for not facing him when she should have.

"I realized something in the middle of the night." Robert let out a long sigh, his shoulders dropping with the action. "Somehow, in all of this, we lost our way. We've been trying to dig ourselves out of this . . . grave . . . we were thrown into, but instead of doing it together, we've been struggling on our own."

Jenn recoiled at his choice of words.

"I'm sorry I wasn't there for you . . . yesterday." Robert adjusted himself in the chair, angling his legs toward her. He set his hand on the arm of his chair, palm up, as if waiting to see if she would extend her own hand toward him.

She tightened her grip on her mug and looked away from him.

Robert sighed, "Charity told me about the Andersons."

Jenn wrinkled her nose at the memory but didn't say anything. What else had Charity told him? Did she mention her episode by the harbor?

"I thought maybe I'd talk to Shawn and explain that things will be different now."

"Why?" Jenn shook her head. Why would things be different? Robert was the one who insisted that things remain the way they had been in the past, that they put up a brave front for the returning summer families. He was the reason she was still doing the damn baskets.

"Because I was wrong."

Jenn sat there in silence. The sound of the waves as they washed up on the shoreline below them soothed her. Robert was admitting he was wrong. What had happened? Something must have for him to have this change of heart.

"I . . . I didn't want to admit our lives had changed and things would be different. But they are. We have a huge hole in our family, and all I've done is ignore it, hoping that somehow, someday, the hole would disappear. I didn't want what happened to us to affect the families who come here each summer."

"You placed those people ahead of your own family. It's nothing new, Robert. It's what you've always done."

She watched him out of the corner of her eye and had a tiny sliver of satisfaction when she saw her words had hit him hard. Sometimes the truth hurt.

"I'm trying to protect my family; at least, I thought I was."

"How?" This time she did turn toward him, but in anger. "Were you protecting us when you made that deal with the reporters? The one where they could come to our son's funeral as long as they left all of the other families alone during theirs? Was it okay for you to exploit your son's death like that?" Her words boiled over in fury. Her fingers began to tingle from the tight grip she held on the cup, and she forced herself to place the cup down on the side table.

"That's not . . . it wasn't . . ." He shook his head as he visibly struggled for words.

"It was like that. It's been like that, time and time again. Not once have you thought about what Charity or I were going through. You're as bad as Charlotte. She can't seem to take off the mayor persona and be the friend that I need right now. Everything is about this town and the *other* families. Every family but your own."

She could read in his eyes everything Robert wanted to say but couldn't. Everything. Guilt. Shame. Acceptance. Agreement. Grief. It all washed over him as he listened to what she had to say. *Finally* listened to what she had to say.

"I'm sorry." His voice was low and clouded with emotion. "I didn't think. I didn't . . . I let you down. I let Charity down, and I'm so sorry. Instead of being here for you . . . all I've done is push you away. Charity prefers to spend time at Amanda's house rather than here and you . . ."

"And I, what?"

"You're drinking more than normal lately. I don't think I've ever seen you go through so many bottles of Baileys or drink so much wine."

She bristled at his words and knew from the wary look in his eyes that what he'd wanted to say was something much harsher.

"Are you saying you think I have a drinking problem?"

He shook his head, a little too slowly.

"Then what, exactly?" There was a little voice inside her head that told her challenging him wasn't a wise move on her part. That if she let it go, then the issue would dissipate.

"We all handle grief differently," he began.

"And you think I'm using alcohol to . . ."

"To numb yourself."

She couldn't argue with that.

"Listen, I'm sorry. Forget I said anything, okay? I blame myself. If I had been there for you . . . but I wasn't. I'm going to change that. Starting now. You don't have to be alone in this. You don't have to numb yourself anymore." His eyes reddened. "I'm here. I'm here now."

The words of forgiveness that she knew he wanted—needed—
to hear were on the cusp of her tongue, but she couldn't say them.
Saying it and meaning it were two different things. For the past
month she'd been pressed to place her grief behind her and pretend
that all was right in her life, in their town, and she couldn't do it
anymore. It was tearing her up inside to the point where she didn't
even recognize herself anymore.

"Do you even miss him?" she asked.

"Of course I do." His voice broke. "How could you doubt that?"

"Because you don't talk about him." The anger that consumed
her dissipated as tears gathered in her eyes. "When was the last time
you visited his grave?" She could probably guess the answer to that.

He shook his head. "I'm not . . . I can't . . . I'm not ready to say
good-bye." He wiped away a tear that slid down his cheek. "Not like
that. Not yet."

"So you accuse me of pretending that he's not gone, and yet you
do the same thing?"

Robert shrugged. "I'm not pretending. I'm just . . ." He took a
deep breath. "I want to make sure everyone else is okay before I let
myself grieve."

"Why?" Didn't he realize she needed him to grieve with her?
She needed to know he understood.

Robert closed his eyes and leaned his head back against the seat.
"Because I'm afraid that once I start to grieve, I'd never stop. I'd lose
myself, my way, and then I'd be letting you and Charity down. I'd
be letting Bobby down."

At his words, Jenn's heart melted, and she reached her hand
across and touched him.

"About last night . . ." She struggled for the words to use, to
make him understand. "It was the look in your eyes when I first got
home—"

"You needed me to understand and didn't think I would. Right?" He entwined his fingers with hers, tentative at first, and then squeezed. "I wouldn't have. Not then."

So what changed? She must have said that out loud, because he nodded.

"Like I said, I did a lot of thinking. I realized I'm not the man you need right now, that I probably haven't been for a while. I don't blame you for running from me last night and ignoring me."

The weight of his words, the way his gaze trailed from her to the water, made her pause. Something else was going on. The sudden change, in one night, all because she acted like a child, didn't make sense.

"I might not agree with your decision to want to close the school, but the fact you didn't think you could trust me with your thoughts, your feelings . . . that says a lot. Almost too much."

He turned to look at her.

"I want you to always trust me. To know that I have your back. The way I handled your response to Samantha's question Friday was wrong, and I'm sorry."

Jenn didn't know how to respond. Her husband apologizing wasn't something she was used to.

"Robert, how I behaved yesterday was . . . childish. I knew that, but my pride got in the way." She pulled her hand away from his. "But it doesn't change how I feel. By keeping the school open, it's like we're denying the vile acts that happened there. The school should be closed. I know it's not something that can happen in the short term, and I realize the complications of what it means, I do. The idea has been tossed around of expanding the school. Well, why don't we just build a new one? I know the council already decided against this, but think about it. We can use the space the school is on now as a recreation area and build somewhere else. Start fresh.

Show the children of our community that they are important to us."
Passion filled her as she spoke her ideas. It could work, she knew
it. It was a viable solution, and if Robert agreed, then that's all she
needed.

But the doubt on his face, the uncertainty in his gaze, told her
otherwise.

"Just think about it, okay?" She swung her legs out and stood.
"I think I'm going to head to the cemetery." She waited for him to
offer to come, but he just sat there.

"Robert?"

He gave his head a small shake and stood with her. "Would you
like some company?"

She searched his eyes. "Are you sure you want to come?"

"I think today, of all days, is the right time to go." He picked
up both their cups and held them in his hand. He stared into her
cup a lot longer than necessary. "You're right, I've been avoiding
going there."

Jenn didn't understand what was going on with her husband,
didn't understand why this sudden change, especially after her
behavior yesterday and early this morning, but she wasn't going to
argue. She wasn't sure how long it would last or what the angle was,
but she'd take it.

CHAPTER SEVENTEEN

CHARLOTTE

On Monday morning Charlotte waited for word from Robert, making her delay heading into the office, but there was nothing other than a text he sent after nine saying he would talk with her Tuesday.

She'd had nightmares last night of their town losing hope, of families who moved away. In her dream she walked the length of Main Street and only a few die-hard shops were still open, but many others had brown wrapping paper covering their windows with "For Sale" signs taped to the windows.

She'd woken up and had to splash water on her face. She couldn't understand how Jordan was so . . . blasé about this, nor could she believe how much it shook her.

She refused to be a failure, to fail this town, when they needed a strong leader.

"Charlotte?" Sheila nudged the office door open and carried in a tray of coffees from Gina's. "Sam will be here shortly. She's just outside on her phone." Sheila set down the coffees on Charlotte's desk and then picked up the stack of signed papers she'd placed in Charlotte's box earlier.

Charlotte headed over to her large bay window and pulled the curtain aside. Samantha was below, by the water fountain, pacing back and forth, her free hand waving wildly in the air as she talked on her cell phone.

"It's a pretty heated discussion." Sheila stood beside her and looked out.

"Any ideas what she's talking about?"

"You mean, did I eavesdrop?"

Charlotte shrugged.

"Something about a new story line she wants to pursue. I take it she's supposed to head back home, but she wants to stay longer." Sheila shook her head. "Just what we need. I can't wait until everyone will leave this town alone."

Sheila's outburst surprised Charlotte. "I thought you liked Samantha."

"As a person, she's fine." Sheila's lips pursed as she took another look out the window before she stepped away.

"But as a reporter?"

Sheila glanced back, her gaze frosty. "Not sure how much help all these reporters have been for our community. Frankly, I'm surprised you let them all stay as long as they have."

"And this is the first you're saying something? Sheila, I'm surprised." Charlotte frowned. "I've never known you to hold back before."

"I've said it many times; you just never listened." Sheila paused as she picked up her coffee. "What's so different about Samantha?"

Charlotte let the drape she'd held drift back into place. "She seems to care about this town more than the others."

Sheila nodded. "Which is why I like her as a person. Did you know she's been heading over to the retirement home and helping some of the older folks write letters and such to their families?"

"Really?"

"She started off by asking for stories from when they were younger, stories of Stillwater in general, but then it progressed. I guess Dorothea mentioned that some of the residents needed help, and the next thing you know, Samantha comes in with stationery and envelopes and offers to write letters for people." Sheila shrugged. "She's got a good heart. I just wish she'd stop telling others about our lives." Sheila opened the office door and was about to close it behind her when Charlotte stopped her.

"What if she started to share the right kind of stories, though? The ones that helped us, as a community?"

Sheila stepped back into the room, closed the door behind her, and leaned against it. "What kind of stories?"

All she'd told Sheila earlier was that Sam was coming for a meeting. She wasn't sure if she should share the reason or wait and see if anything came of the discussion. She shouldn't have doubted Sheila, though; she was always her strongest ally and conspirator.

"About Julia. She used the analogy that Julia is the black sheep in our *family*"—Charlotte made air quotes with her fingers—"and with everything that has been going on lately, it made me realize it was true." She caught the look on Sheila's face, how she was about to disagree, so she stopped her. "No, think about it. If the vandalism was happening to anyone else in town, there would have been an outrage. When someone is sick, we bring them food. When they get bad news, we surround them with love. If they lose a job, someone steps up and finds them another one. But we've basically ignored Julia."

"Well, it's about time," Sheila said.

"Excuse me?"

"She's not ignored. A few of us have tried to be there for Julia. I send over a crew to clean up the mess in her yard and repaint her house. Lacie brings her food. Others stop by on a daily basis and offer our help, even though she ignores us."

Charlotte was left speechless. She had no idea that so many people had rallied behind Julia already. How could she have been left in the dark like this?

"You've been so focused on everyone else. Don't beat yourself up over it." It was as if Sheila knew exactly what she'd been thinking.

"There must be more that we can do, though, right?" Suddenly, Charlotte felt like her idea paled in comparison to what Sheila and Lacie and others had already been doing.

"Of course there is." Sheila opened the door slightly. "You think Sam can help?"

Charlotte nodded. "Why not? She can at least help to change the media portrayal of Julia, right?"

"Not everyone hates her, you know." Sheila opened the door wider. Samantha was climbing up the stairs to her office.

"Enough do." Charlotte remembered the hateful words spray-painted on the side of Julia's home.

"Let me know how I can help." Sheila held the door open for Samantha and then closed it behind her.

Samantha held up a bag and smiled, but Charlotte could tell it was forced.

"Are you sure you want to talk over coffee and pastry?" Charlotte checked her watch. "It's almost lunchtime. We could go down to the pub if you'd like. You look like you could use something stronger than caffeine."

Samantha dropped the bag from Sweet Bakes on her desk. "Fred's?"

Charlotte nodded. Fred's Tavern was the only pub in town, but it would serve their needs. A table in the corner offered privacy when required, and Charlotte had held many meetings there in the past.

Samantha headed back to the door. "Let's go," she said.

Charlotte picked up her purse and shook her head. Considering Sam's enthusiasm to go to the pub, she could only assume the phone call she'd had outside hadn't gone too well.

She knew Sheila thought the same thing when she told her their plans. Sheila reminded Charlotte of her two o'clock appointment with Arnold Lewery, and Charlotte promised to send a text if she were to run late. Arnold and the paper could wait, but she didn't think Samantha could.

So far, nothing had gone according to schedule today.

· · ·

The moment they stepped into Fred's, Samantha's tense body relaxed and Charlotte was amazed to see the transformation. It was as if the quiet bar soothed her soul.

Fred's was a town icon. It had first opened in 1921, and while it had been updated throughout the years, it still looked similar to the earlier images that decorated its walls. The tables and bar were heritage in design, thick wood slabs made to withstand time, and although the chairs were updated every decade or so, they remained similar in design, black and padded. Fred was the fourth son to own the iconic pub, and everyone knew it would one day pass down to his own son, Fred Jr., who worked with him today at the bar.

"Mayor." Senior raised a glass at Charlotte as they made their way to the back booth. Sam took the side that faced the front entrance and took her phone out of her jeans pocket and placed it in her purse.

"Sam, beer or wine?" Charlotte set her purse down beside her and folded her hands together.

"Whiskey chaser. Please." The *please* was obviously an afterthought as Sam called out.

Charlotte's brow rose. Well, then . . .

"I'll have whatever's on tap, Fred. Thanks."

Charlotte grabbed a napkin and wiped down their table that was covered in peanut casings, while Sam reached for the wicker basket that was half filled with the nuts.

"Doesn't that gross you out?" Charlotte asked.

Sam's hand hovered over the basket. "What?"

"Reaching into a bowl of peanuts, a bowl that other people put their hands in before you? Hands that might not have been washed before eating said peanuts." The idea gave her the wiggles. She'd once read an article about the level of bacteria in a pile of shelled peanuts and had never been tempted again.

"Seriously?" Sam grabbed a handful of shells and dropped them in front of her on the table. "Live a little, Mayor. There's no fun in always being cautious." She began the process of cracking open the nuts and popping them into her mouth, one at a time.

Charlotte altered her gaze so she didn't have to watch and breathed in relief as Fred made his way toward them with their drinks on a tray along with a fresh basket of peanuts. Fred always brought her a new basket, with peanuts straight out of the bag, no bare hands involved. He switched out the basket left on their table with the new one and then handed them their drinks. Samantha didn't even wait. She gulped her whiskey in one shot and then drank half the glass of beer before Charlotte had even taken a sip.

"Rough day?" Charlotte asked as Sam wiped her mouth and sat back.

"Just a little."

"Want to talk about it?" Charlotte drank some more of her own beer.

"Is this our version of kiss and tell?" Samantha winked at her before she held her hand up and whistled to Fred for another drink. He nodded at her and mumbled beneath his breath, loud enough for them to hear, about those "dang city reporters" who needed to learn proper manners.

"Tell you what. I'll go first." Charlotte stared down at her hands for a moment before she stared Samantha in the eyes. "My best friend is trying to destroy this town, and my husband just laughs at my concerns."

Sam opened her mouth and then closed it. She looked like she was weighing her words, deciding what to say and what to hold back.

"My boss threatened to fire me if I don't drag my sorry behind back to work. I have one week to decide. Meanwhile I'm officially now on unpaid vacation." She raised her glass up as if for a toast but then put it back down again.

"Why don't you want to leave?"

"There are more stories to be told of Stillwater." Sam stared out toward the front door. "Which brings us to the point of this meeting. Once we order." She reached for the menus Fred had left and scanned the items.

Charlotte already knew what she was having.

Fred ambled over, picked up Sam's empty glasses, and set down two new ones.

"The regular?" he said to Charlotte. She nodded.

"City girl? What's your craving today?"

Sam scowled at Fred and then pointed to the fish and chips on the menu. "These are fresh, right? You catch them yourself? You don't buy farmed and frozen, right?"

"What's with the million questions when you come in? This is a pub. You drink and eat and maybe leave here with a smile on your face. You don't ask me questions about the food when the answers are right in front of your eyes." Fred frowned before he took off in a huff to the back door that led into the kitchen.

"What was that?" Charlotte asked.

Samantha smiled. "The first few times I came in I'd let him pick something for me to eat. He made a comment one time about the fact I'm a reporter who doesn't care about the details or even know how to ask a few simple questions. So since then, I read the menu and ask him questions. He acts all annoyed, but deep down he's not. Notice the sign out front when we came in?"

Charlotte shook her head, not sure where this was going.

"'What's your craving?' I like to come in and tell him what I'm craving and challenge him to provide it."

Charlotte laughed. She could only imagine the grumblings Fred did with Samantha around. It was good for him. "You're baiting a bear, you know that, right?"

Sam shrugged. "Sure, if you consider him a teddy bear."

Charlotte almost spit out her beer at that and ended up having to wipe her mouth with her napkin.

"Teddy bear is not how I would describe Fred. Opinionated. Grumpy. Stubborn. But teddy bear? Not the Fred I know." Charlotte thought about the multiple bar fights Fred had broken up. That nose of his had more curves than the Oregon coastline.

"Your talk with your boss didn't have anything to do with our conversation yesterday, did it?" Charlotte brought the topic back to hand. She was intrigued as to why Sam would stay in Stillwater when she was told to head back home.

Sam grunted. "His only goal is the story. If the story isn't there, then he'll send me out to where another one is. Except, I think there's still enough interest to warrant a longer stay." She must have caught the way Charlotte winced. "Sorry. I know the last thing you want is to continually be front-page news, but with all the doom and gloom the media preaches, wouldn't it be nice for the silver lining to show through?"

"We have enough silver linings. And we certainly don't need them to be plastered all over the media." Charlotte shrugged. "Sorry. I understand it's your job, and compared to the other reporters who were here, you are my favorite, but there comes a time . . ."

Sam waved her hands. "No apologies needed. I understand, I do."

"So you're sticking around because . . ."

A guarded look crossed Samantha's face. "Let's just say I have unfinished business to take care of."

"In Stillwater?"

Sam nodded. "Don't ask, okay? Let's talk about Julia instead. I've got a week before I need to return back home, so let's do what we can while I'm here."

Charlotte reached for her purse and pulled out her notebook, thumbing through the pages until she found the one she'd scribbled some notes in early this morning after Robert canceled their meeting. Some of the items were redundant after Sheila's insightful talk, but there were other ideas that held some merit to them.

"Do you have some ideas?" Charlotte asked, her pen ready.

Sam nodded. "I do." A soft smile spread across her face as she brought out her own notebook and flipped it open.

"First thing on the list is Fred."

Charlotte's brow creased. "Fred?" What did Fred have to do with helping Julia?

"Mayor, what do you think I've been doing as I meet people in this town? Just eat their food, buy their items, and annoy the hell out of them as I pepper them with questions?"

"I should know you better than that by now." Charlotte chuckled at herself. Interested to know how Fred played such a key part to helping Julia, Charlotte waited for Samantha to continue.

Except she didn't. Fred joined them with their plates and gave what Charlotte could only label as a stink eye to Samantha. She laughed when Sam winked at Fred and then patted the seat beside her, an indication for him to sit down.

"I've got work to do," Fred grumbled, and yet he sat.

"I was about to tell our mayor here your great plan to help Julia, but I thought maybe you'd like to tell her yourself?"

Charlotte sat there, amazed, as Fred's cheeks blazed red and his gaze suddenly ended up on the table. Her amazement didn't end there, however.

She sat there, open mouthed, while Fred outlined his idea, and she finally understood why Samantha called him a teddy bear.

.   .   .

Feeling lighter than she had in ages, Charlotte waved good-bye to both Fred and Samantha, who was now seated at the bar, and headed back toward the town hall.

She had just enough time to make it back to her office to meet with Arnold and discuss with him her ideas, ideas that both Sam and Fred thought would work. She couldn't believe she'd been so blind to what was happening around her.

Blinded to the way members of her community felt about what had happened when Gabriel Berry took a gun into the public school and opened fire. Blinded to how certain families were coping with their grief. Blinded to how others were obviously *not* coping.

She had a feeling the graffiti on Julia's home would stop. Fred was going to take care of that by having a stern talk with Trevor, the man responsible for the public desecration of Julia's home. Samantha was going to use her skill with words to convince others in the community of how they needed to group together, as a unit, and help each other heal, while reminding them it wasn't acceptable to shun someone who would never have turned them away. And Charlotte . . . well, Charlotte would do what she did best: ensure this town continued to move forward.

She adjusted her purse on her shoulder and waved as she caught sight of Charity and her best friend, Amanda, as they headed straight for her.

An idea bloomed.

She stopped the girls and made small talk with them, her intent to find out what their plans were for the rest of the afternoon.

"How would you girls like to earn some money this afternoon?"

From the way their eyes brightened, she knew she had their attention.

"Come with me, then." She didn't even bother to try to keep the smile off her face as they walked toward the Treasure Chest, Julia's store. She fished out a key from her purse, one she'd snagged from Julia yesterday with the excuse that she wanted to look in on it. It had surprised her when Julia handed it over no questions asked.

Treasure Chest was Julia's passion. She always said it was her small way of helping others in the community—through buying and selling their handicrafts. During the summer and Christmas months, her store was one of the most successful ones in town, so it was sad to see it boarded up and closed, especially now. How could

Julia pay her bills if her store wasn't producing any income? How could those who sold their items through her store help make ends meet if no one could buy them?

Well, Charlotte had an idea, and it all started with these girls.

CHAPTER EIGHTEEN

JENNIFER

With it being a beautiful day, it shouldn't have surprised Jenn that they weren't alone in the cemetery. Over in the far corner the landscapers were cutting the grass, trimming the hedges, and working in the gardens while visitors strolled through the walkways.

She couldn't understand how people could find peace at a cemetery. What was so peaceful about gazing upon countless headstones and white crosses? What was so beautiful about the gardens along the pathways or the shelter of trees that surrounded the area?

There was no peace here. Not for her.

Hand in hand, Jenn and Robert walked alongside each other as they made their way to the bench by Bobby's grave. She sank down on the seat while Robert went over to the white cross and squatted down on his legs. His lips moved, but she couldn't hear what was said and she turned her gaze, to give father and son some privacy.

She searched for the other white crosses that marked the graves of the victims from the school shooting and counted in her head the number. Too many. There had been twelve deaths, twelve lives snuffed out unnecessarily, taken against their will. There were more

white crosses than that in this cemetery, but she knew twelve of
them belonged to the victims of Gabriel Berry. She didn't count his
own marker as one. What had Julia been thinking, to bury her son
here?

So she would have a place to visit. The thought brushed her mind,
but she ignored it, as best she could. She didn't want to desecrate
Bobby's memory or ruin their time here by thinking of his murder.
The anger that simmered deep inside her bubbled, the thought of
Gabe and Julia like a flame. She squashed it down because now
wasn't the time or the place.

"Did you bring these?" Robert startled her as he sat down
beside her. She shifted to increase the distance between them. She
didn't want to be touched, not right now. She glanced down at the
plastic car in his hand and shook her head.

"Where were they?" They were similar to the ones she'd seen
yesterday by the boat dock. Who was leaving them?

"There." Robert pointed to the small pile of toy cars, trucks,
and even a boat at the base of the cross.

Her lips tightened. Who was doing this? She looked around her
and found similar toys on other grave sites, some with small dolls,
others with stuffed animals or plastic figurines.

"Someone is leaving toys on the graves," she said quietly. But
who? Who would do that? A parent? A teacher? Maybe it was Jordan. But if so, why hadn't he told the parents?

"I think it's nice. A gesture not many would consider. Bobby
wouldn't have liked all the flowers, anyway. This is more his style."
Robert played with the car, his body hunched over as his fingers
pushed the tiny wheels till they spun.

"I don't like it."

"Why?"

Jenn shrugged. "It's weird, creepy almost. This is our son's grave, and yet these aren't our toys, or even Bobby's toys. Who would bring them . . ." Her voice drifted off as it hit her.

"She did it," Jenn spat out. "As if this could make up for what he did." The thought made her want to grab every single toy, not only on Bobby's grave, but on every other grave in the cemetery and throw them out. Or better yet, throw them at her, through her windows, against her house. How dare she do this? How dare she think she could make up for what her son did?

Jenn's fingers clenched until her nails bit into the skin on her palms.

"No, no, it wasn't Julia," Robert shook his head and reached for her hands, covering her fists with his. "These aren't from Julia, trust me. The woman has been holed up in her home, afraid to come out. She wouldn't do this."

Jenn breathed in through her nose and out her mouth, all in an attempt to calm her racing heart. She was sure Robert was right, but if it wasn't Julia, then who? Who would leave toys on the graves of the children?

"I'll look into it. Maybe talk with Charlotte or the town maintenance manager and see if they know anything." He turned the car over in his hands. "The question, though, is what do we do with these?"

"They're on every grave, Robert. Of all those who died with Bobby."

Robert's head shot up, and he looked around. He stood and turned, not saying anything as he looked around them.

"All of them?"

Jenn nodded.

Robert sat back down on the bench and sighed. He rubbed his chin but didn't say anything. Jenn made a mental note to ask Charlotte about the toys being left.

"If you want to head to the office, I'll stay here a bit longer."

But he shook his head and reached for her hand.

"There's no place I'd rather be than here. I'll admit, it's not a place I see myself coming to often, but it's good to be here, to sit close to our son."

Jenn linked her fingers with his, her anger from earlier ebbing away. "It's not really a place I enjoy coming to either. I prefer to go sit on the beach or out on the cliff by the lighthouse."

"But that's not where Bobby is."

"He's not here either, is he? Not really." His body was here, but she didn't want to think about her son lying there, in his coffin. She just . . . couldn't.

"Did you want to go down to the beach then? We could park at the lighthouse and walk down one of the trails."

The heaviness that had filled her pores earlier lightened. She leaned her head on Robert's shoulder for a brief moment before she stood up. "That would be nice."

She wasn't sure what had happened between yesterday and today, but whatever it was, she would take it. With Robert beside her, maybe she could get through this and find a way to climb out of this pit she was in.

She let go of Robert's hand for a moment and went to stand by Bobby's grave. She lifted her fingers to her lips, placed a small kiss there, and then touched the white cross. "I love you, baby." She wanted to say more, needed to say more, but not here.

Robert waited for her, and she was suddenly very thankful he was there. More than she thought or even expected she would be.

. . .

Time slipped by as Jenn sat beside Robert on the beach. They just sat there, without words to break the peace between them, and it was a time Jenn would forever hold close to her heart. It was as if her heart was slowly healing. They watched the water lap along the shore, the seagulls dive into the water for fish, and the families play down the beach, far enough away to not intrude.

It wasn't until Robert's stomach grumbled that they left the beach. Holding hands, they made their way back up the rough path toward the lighthouse.

"Is that Blake?" Robert had his hand shielding his eyes from the sun and hesitated. He waved at the man who stood on top of the long winding pathway toward the lighthouse. "We should stop in and see how he is. It's been a while."

Jenn grunted as she almost tripped over a rock in her path. Robert's hand steadied her, and they climbed the rest of the way up.

There was a small shop and shed on the grounds beside the lighthouse. It was a nice tourist area for people to stop, buy items at the unique gift shop, and take photos of the historic lighthouse. The view of the water was breathtaking, especially during sunrise or sunset.

The owner of the gift shop was Blake Casser, and he reminded her of a grizzly old biker, even though he was younger than Jenn by a few years. Blake had led a rough life, and that roughness had rubbed off on him.

At the crest of the hill, Blake stood there with two water bottles, and he threw them their way. Thankfully, Robert was a good catch because Jenn flinched. They both opened the bottles and drank. They should have brought their own but hadn't anticipated staying on the beach or the long climb in the sun.

"It's been a while," Robert said after he almost emptied his bottle.

"You know where I live," Blake almost growled.

"In the middle of work?"

Jenn kept quiet. She never really had a good read on Blake, other than he scared her. She wasn't sure why.

Blake shrugged, and the movement caught Jenn's attention. It looked as if there were butterflies or dragonflies on his arm. She peered closer.

"They're not real. Damn near look it, though." Blake stepped closer and held out his arm to her.

"They do," she said. She was amazed at the art on his arm. She wasn't someone who loved the idea of a tattoo, but she knew an artist's touch when she saw it. These looked like a 3-D design.

"A buddy came to visit during the winter and used my arm as a canvas." Blake's voice grated, like sandpaper being scraped against a rock. Robert had told her it was due to an accident he'd been in years ago, and Jenn believed him, based on the scars that covered Blake's throat. She wondered why he'd never covered them up with tattoos.

"Figured you've been busy since I haven't seen you around." Robert relaxed his stance, and Jenn knew he was in the mood to chat. She wasn't, but that was okay. She loved Blake's work and wouldn't mind taking a look around his shop while the boys talked.

"Yeah, I've been working on a few projects." He stuck his hands in his pants pockets. "I've been meaning to talk to you about them." He glanced back toward his shop.

"Are they in there?" Jenn asked. She took a few steps toward the shop, but Blake stepped in her way.

"I'm not quite ready for you to see them. Not yet."

Jenn glanced back at Robert, who shrugged.

"All right then. Is it just us you don't want seeing your work or everyone?"

Blake didn't reply, just stood there. Jenn felt a sudden need to leave, so she gestured to Robert that she was heading back to the car.

"Thanks for the water, Blake," she called over her shoulder. She noticed Robert had moved closer to him, and the two were talking.

While Blake was never overly friendly, she'd never been stopped from entering his shop either. He created the most beautiful designs out of sand glass, and she even had a few pieces in her home that she'd bought. What could he be working on that she couldn't see?

Minutes later Robert made his way over to their SUV and opened the door.

"He's working on a new statue and isn't ready for us to see it. I guess he's doing something for Bobby that we will recognize." He drummed his fingers on the steering wheel.

"Like what?"

Robert shook his head. "Not sure. We're going to meet down at the pub later, and he'll fill me in." He turned the SUV on. "What would you like to do now? Go for an early dinner, head to the club, or go home?"

"If you want to drop me off, I don't mind if you head into work. Besides, Charity will probably be home soon." She couldn't believe they'd spent the day together, like they had, and without any work interruptions. Earlier, he'd turned his ringer off and not once had he checked his phone for messages or returned calls, even though she knew he'd probably received at least half a dozen by now. With summer homeowners returning, Robert was normally the first person they called. He took care of many of their summer family homes, maintained their yards, let housekeepers in, etc.

"She's having a sleepover with Amanda." Robert gave her a small smile as he drove down Pelican Street. He reached for her hand. She really couldn't remember a time, other than during the funerals, that they'd held hands or even touched as much as they had today.

"She is? Why didn't anyone tell me?"

Robert gave her a pointed look, as if to remind her she'd spent the morning in hiding.

"Why don't we go for an early dinner at Fred's then and be home in time to watch the sunset?" That and sunrise were her favorite times of the day. She loved to sit out on the deck with a glass of wine, wrap a blanket around her, and think.

Once Robert pulled into his parking space behind his office, Jenn was prepared for him to head inside and was once again surprised when he took her hand and guided her to the sidewalk and then down the street.

"Don't you need to go in?" She slowed her steps as they approached the front door.

"Not today," he said as he pulled her along.

The feelings inside Jenn ranged all over the place, much like her emotions the past few days. Parts of her wanted to soak in this attention from Robert, letting it permeate her soul and heart, but then another part of her whispered to ignore the attention, warning it would be gone by morning and she'd need to shelter her heart once again. In their marriage, they'd had more downs than ups, enough of them for her to realize it wasn't worth staying. She thought about the separation papers in her desk drawer, about how hard the decision had been to take that step, knowing that she would be the one responsible for tearing her family apart. But then she focused on the way Robert kept holding her hand, his grip tight, and the sense of rightness to his touch.

"I'll understand if you need to do some work tonight in your office."

"I don't need to work all the time, you know. It's okay for me to take a day off here and there. I haven't done it enough, but this summer, I think I might. Brenda is competent enough to handle matters for me. Let's take a look at our calendar tonight and plan some getaways, just you and me and maybe some with Charity too." Robert squeezed her hand three times, an old reminder of the way they used to be when they were first married. Three squeezes meant *I love you.*

She smiled up at him to let him know she understood, but she didn't squeeze his hand back. When was the last time she'd told him she loved him? Really and honestly loved him? She couldn't remember.

"Robert, I . . ." She caught sight of the Treasure Chest and couldn't believe what she saw.

The last time she'd seen the store, the windows had been covered in brown craft paper. It was closed. Should still be closed. And yet, the paper was down, the windows open for all to see, and there were even displays being set up in the front.

"Hey, Treasure Chest will be opening up again. That's great."

Was that excitement and satisfaction she heard in Robert's voice?

"I didn't think Julia was ready to get back to her store, but this is exactly what our town needs," he continued.

Jenn remained quiet. She doubted they would ever feel the same way about Julia, but that's not what bothered her the most. It was what she saw in the store that caught her attention.

"Is that Charity?" She stepped closer and peered into the store. It was hard to see, the way the sun was shining on the window, but she could swear both Charity and Amanda were inside.

"I couldn't imagine why she'd be in there," Robert said, but he too peered in through the window before he went to the door and pushed it in.

Jenn followed after him and wrinkled her nose. The store had a musky odor to it, an overwhelming smell of potpourri.

"Yeah, sorry, Mom. We had the door opened before to air the place out, but people thought that meant the store was open."

"What are you doing in here?"

"Cleaning . . ." She held up the dust rag in her hand and smiled.

"Why?" She could conceive no good reason for her daughter to be in this store, *this store of all places*, and cleaning.

"Oh, Mayor Stone asked us to," Amanda answered.

Jenn glanced down at the girl, who sat on the floor with a clipboard in her lap.

"Asked you to what?" Jenn had a feeling she wasn't going to like the answer. Why would Charlotte ask her daughter to do something for Julia Berry?

"To help get the store ready to open. She even offered us jobs if we wanted to work here. Cool, huh?"

It was all Jenn could do not to scowl at the girl.

"I think it's nice of you girls to be in here and helping. If you're almost done, why don't you come down and join us at Fred's, and I'll treat you to one of his double-fudge brownie sundaes." Robert nudged Jenn and gave a small shake of his head. She knew that gesture. He wanted her to keep quiet.

"I think you're done now, aren't you?" She didn't care what he wanted.

"Sure," Amanda piped up. "We were just talking about making brownies tonight, but this is a better idea."

Jenn smiled in satisfaction when Charity laid her dust rag down and wiped her hands. She nodded at her mom and held her hand out to Amanda to pull her up off the floor.

"We'll just put everything away and then drop the key off with Mayor Stone. We'll meet you there?"

Jenn shook her head and was about to tell them they could give her the key and she would speak to Charlotte on her own, but Robert rushed in and said it was a good idea. He pulled her out of the store and down the sidewalk, not speaking, until they were at the street corner waiting for the light to change.

"You need to calm down," he said to her.

"I am calm." She knew her face wore a cool facade, and yet inside she was seething.

"Really? Is that why your whole body is vibrating?"

"I'm not . . ." She couldn't finish the sentence, couldn't deny something, when it was true. She was upset. She was more than upset. She was livid. How dare Charlotte ask her daughter, *her* daughter, to help out in *that woman's* store.

"She should have asked us." She turned to him. "She should have asked. Doesn't she understand?"

"No, she probably doesn't. How can she? She's not a parent. Yes, she should have asked us first, but how about we look at this in a different way?"

The light turned green, and they walked across the street. Robert kept his grip on her hand despite her insistent tugging.

"This will be good for Charity. Something to keep her occupied this summer. I'm sure it won't be a lot of hours, but enough. It's good for her."

Jenn's lips thinned, and it took all her strength not to say something. She needed time. Time to think before she said anything.

Time and maybe a drink. She wasn't sure how long the girls would be before they joined them, but since they were already at Fred's, the drink couldn't come soon enough.

CHAPTER NINETEEN

CHARLOTTE

Charlotte powered off her computer thankful that the day was over. Jordan was on his way to pick her up and take her out for dinner. He had a craving for Fred's fish and chips; even though she'd been there for lunch, Charlotte wasn't going to complain.

She'd spent the afternoon with Arnold, and while it took a while to convince him to give her idea a try, she managed to make a miracle occur.

She reached for her phone, just as it began to vibrate on her desk, sure that it was Jordan saying he was outside.

She was wrong.

Don't you think you should have asked first?

The text was from Jenn. Charlotte racked her brain to figure out what she'd done wrong this time. Then it hit her. But why would she be so upset about the girls cleaning up the store?

Didn't think it would be an issue, she texted back.

It is. A big one. I'd appreciate you asking me first, as her mother. And as a friend. Or so I thought.

What? Charlotte leaned back in her chair and hesitated before she wrote back. She started to type back, *I'm sorry*, but stopped. What did she have to apologize for?

A horn blared outside and she rose. It was probably Jordan. A quick look outside confirmed he was there. She pulled the curtain aside and waved before she reached for her purse.

Can I call you later? she wrote instead.

Now wasn't the time to deal with this. And knowing the way Jenn had been acting lately, anything she wrote in a text would probably be taken the wrong way.

Fine.

Charlotte's brow rose as she imagined Jenn's voice saying that. She would have her haughty look, the one that said she could not care less what happened but you knew she really did care.

She turned her office lights off, locked her door behind her, and walked down the steps toward the main floor. Muffled voices could be heard in one of the meeting rooms below. She didn't remember there being a meeting on the calendar today. Charlotte's steps slowed as she made it to the bottom of the stairs.

"Either that woman leaves, or we do. I mean it."

She knew that voice. Trevor Blackstone.

"No. I won't calm down. Take your hand off me. Until she's gone, I'm taking my family with me on the road. Where I'll know they are safe."

Charlotte's grip on the handrail tightened. Trevor was a scary man when he was angry. He wasn't often in town—he was a truck driver who did long-haul trips—but when he was, he was either at Fred's drunk as a skunk or at home terrorizing his poor wife. She couldn't imagine what being on the road with him would be like.

She headed toward the closed door to see if there was anything she could do when the door swung open. If she hadn't stepped back in time, it would have hit her.

"Merille." Charlotte reached out her hand to the timid woman who trailed after her husband, their youngest child on her hip. Merille barely glanced up, but she did give a small shake to her head.

"Let's go, Merille," Trevor barked as he grabbed her arm and pulled her along.

"Trevor, wait," she called out.

Trevor stopped at the main doors and looked at her. A shiver of fear shimmied down Charlotte's spine at the hatred in his black eyes. "What could you possibly say to make up for your worthlessness as a mayor?"

Before Charlotte could think of how to reply, he pushed open the door and pulled Merille out alone with him. Charlotte just stood there, in shock.

"One day, that man's anger is going to go too far."

Charlotte blinked and tore her gaze from the door and noticed Pastor Scott beside her.

"So that was you he was yelling at."

"I hope it was okay we came in here to talk? I figured it would be better to discuss his feelings in here rather than outside where everyone would have heard him."

Charlotte waved away his concern. "Of course. These doors are always open, you know that. What happened?"

"I noticed him standing on the corner by Julia's house and suggested he walk away. With everything that has been going on lately . . . well, you never know what could be going through that man's head."

"Thank you for doing that."

The main door to the building opened, and Jordan walked in.

"Everything okay? Trevor looked pissed off when he left here."

"He wants Julia to be run out of town," Scott replied.

Jordan's brows rose as he stood beside Charlotte and placed his arm across her shoulders.

Scott shrugged. "Unfortunately, the mother has taken on the sins of her son, whether it's deserved or not. She's got an uphill battle when there shouldn't be one." He glanced at his watch. "I need to head over to the church for bible study." He smiled at them and then winked. "You know, you two should come one night. It's a marriage group."

Charlotte dug her elbow into Jordan's side when he snorted.

"I'll take that as a *not today* then, shall I?"

"Maybe some other time, Scott. Thanks for the invite, though. Say hi to Lacie for me."

"Oh, she's not going to be there." Scott's voice trembled for a moment before he smiled. "But I'll tell her when I get home."

"Everything okay?"

Scott nodded. "She's just going to take some time . . . away from the church for a bit."

This surprised Charlotte. Lacie taking time away from the church? That was like . . . taking the chocolate out of her croissants . . . just not possible.

"She didn't say anything to me about it, though." Charlotte realized how that sounded after she said it. As if Lacie should have told her first. "Sorry, I didn't mean it that way."

"No, it's okay. It's something she's been mulling over since . . . well, since the funerals, to be honest. I think today was the day she woke up and decided it was time to put herself first. I ask a lot of her. This town asks a lot of her."

Jordan reached out and placed a hand on Scott's shoulder. "We also ask a lot from you. How are you handling things?"

It was as if a mask dropped over Scott's face. One moment there was raw honesty in his eyes and then next, a false sense of peace and happiness. "I'm fine. But thanks for asking. Now, I should really get to the church. Talk to you later."

They stood there as Scott retreated from them. He lifted his hand in a brief wave as the door closed behind him, and they waved back.

"That was weird," Charlotte and Jordan both said in unison.

"I can't believe Lacie is stepping back from the church."

"I'm surprised Scott hasn't done it yet." Jordan placed his hand on the small of her back and urged her toward the main door.

"Why's that?" They climbed down the front steps and made their way to the sidewalk.

"When has the man stopped? He conducted all the funerals, including his own son's, and I'm sure his door has been left open for anyone who needs counseling. Have they even had time to grieve themselves? Not once have I seen him crack under the strain. So it makes you wonder . . ."

"Wonder what?"

"What will happen when he does crack? Who's there for him? I mean, Jenn has you . . . who does Lacie have? Who does Scott have to go to when he needs to cry or get angry or question why God would let something like that happen?"

"That's a good question. I need to do something . . ."

"Why you? It's not your job to take care of everyone in this town, you know, as much as you try."

They had arrived at Fred's Tavern, and Jordan pulled open the thick wood door for her.

"I mean it, Charlotte. It's not your job. You need to let it go."

"I can't. I can't let it go." As hard as she tried, as much as she wanted to, it was her job. A job she'd been doing poorly, she now realized.

Evidence of how poor was right in front of her as her best friend glared at her.

. . .

"Did you know they'd be here?" Jordan murmured to her.

Robert stood up and waved at them. When Jordan waved back, Robert indicated the two free chairs at their table.

"Nope." Charlotte had yet to mention Jenn's angry texts.

"Hey! You should have told us you guys were coming here." Robert pushed his beer across the table and then switched seats, so he was beside Jenn instead of across from her.

Charlotte forced a smile as she took the now empty seat across from Jenn and pushed the basket of peanuts toward the boys. She eyed the drink in front of Jenn and decided to order the same thing.

"How are you guys?" Jordan and Robert slapped one another's backs before they sat down. Jordan leaned over and placed his arm around the back of Charlotte's chair.

Robert glanced over at Jenn, then back to Jordan, and gave a weak smile. "Good. We ran into the girls at the Treasure Chest. They should be here soon for ice cream."

"Oh good." Charlotte smiled, then looked at Jenn. "I ran into them on the street earlier, and they looked bored. I'm sorry. I should have asked you before I had them help dust off shelves. I didn't think."

"No, you didn't, and yes, you should have." Disdain dripped from Jenn's voice.

Was this what she was so upset about? Okay, if she'd thought about it more, maybe having Charity help clean Julia's store wasn't her brightest idea, but . . .

"Stop. Whatever you are thinking, stop," Jenn muttered.

"I'm just trying to figure out where I erred."

Robert leaned forward and planted his elbows on the table. "Any interactions between our family and Julia should really be our decision, don't you think?"

Charlotte sat back and caught the surprise that flashed across Jenn's face.

"Right . . . of course," Charlotte stammered. This was different. Any other time, Robert had been one of Julia's loudest supporters. In fact, he'd been the one to mention the loss to Julia's income if her store remained closed. "You're right. Absolutely. I haven't been thinking—"

Jordan rested his hand on her shoulder and squeezed. "No, you have been thinking." He corrected her. "Of this town, of the businesses, and of the residual effects of the tailspin we've all been in. You are looking at the big picture, and you don't have to apologize for that."

Charlotte didn't know what to say to that, but she was glad for the way her husband came to her rescue. Thankfully, she didn't have to say anything as Fred came over with a fresh basket of peanuts and drinks.

"Fancy seeing you here," Fred teased as he set the basket down in front of her. "Let me guess, your man here was in the mood for my fish and you couldn't say no." He winked as he placed their drinks in front of them.

"Ordering for me now?" She eyed the beer questioningly.

"On the house. Drink up."

Charlotte did as ordered. When she set the beer down, she leaned forward and reached across the table to touch Jenn's cold fingers.

"Are we going to be okay?"

Jenn only shrugged, but Charlotte wasn't going to give up.

"I've been a jerk. I tend to get so caught up in my passion for this town that I forget about my friends. I—" She stopped as Jordan's hand touched her shoulder and squeezed. She smiled at him in thanks.

"Sometimes, your passion for this town overshadows everything else in your life," Jenn said.

Charlotte nodded. "You're right. This isn't the first time you've mentioned this to me."

"But it should be the last time I have to say it when it comes to my children." Jenn's lips narrowed. "You know how I feel about Julia." Charlotte was going to say something, but Jenn held up her hand. "Right or wrong, it's how I feel. Asking my daughter to help clean *that* store . . . that wasn't okay. And asking her to work there during the summer . . . honestly, Char, what were you thinking?"

This piece of information threw Charlotte for a loop. Work there? She wouldn't have asked the girls to do that. For one, they weren't old enough, not legally. Second, it was not her place to hire people like that. No, Julia had people to help run the store; they just needed to get it up and running first.

That's when it all started to make sense: why Jenn sent her those angry texts and why she was so cold right now toward her.

"I didn't offer them a job, Jenn. I promise." She looked from Jenn to Robert. She saw him visibly relax at her words. The tenseness in her shoulders from the moment they walked in began to lessen.

"Is that what the kids think? Is that the reason for the cold shoulder we've got since we sat down?" Jordan asked. Charlotte was grateful for his question, for his willingness to stand beside her and offer clarity to the situation.

"Well, I wouldn't say we've been giving you the cold shoulder," Robert hedged. A slight flush crept along his neckline and upward to his cheeks.

"Are you saying it's not true?" Jenn leaned forward, her elbows now on the table.

Charlotte nodded. "I promise. But I'm sorry they took it that way." She turned to Robert. "You said they're coming here for ice cream?" At Robert's nod, she glanced at Jordan. "Let me clear up the confusion then, when they get here, okay?"

Jenn nodded, and Charlotte blew out a sigh of relief.

"Have you-all made up yet?" Fred appeared at their table with plates of food balanced in his hands and on his forearms. "This food's about to grow cold."

"We"—Charlotte pointed to herself and Jordan—"didn't order yet." She eyed the plates of food.

Fred just gave her a look. The gruff look said *shut up and eat.*

"Since when did you become a mind reader?" she asked. She never was one for taking hints.

"The only thing school-man here orders is the fish. You, you were already here so you weren't gonna order the beef dip again. Doesn't take a genius to figure folks out in this town, especially when they come here enough."

Fred set down a plate with fried chicken and double-dipped french fries. Charlotte almost groaned in delight. It had been a while since she last had Fred's fried chicken, and with the delicious aroma wafting upward, she was glad he knew her like he did. She took in a deep breath and then smiled at him.

He shrugged his broad shoulders before he set down the other plates. Charlotte eyed the three plates of fish and chips and shook her head.

"What? It's the special." Robert grinned before grabbing his fork and slicing into the crunchy skin of his fish.

They ate in silence, and Charlotte was almost able to tune out the voices and music that surrounded them. Fred's was a popular hangout for not only the regular town folks but also for the summer families. Families were welcome to come in with their kids until eight o'clock. After that, Fred kicked them all out. Everyone knew the schedule, and those who were only interested in coming in to drink and dance knew to wait until after the families left.

Fred's Tavern equaled Fred's rules.

A comfortable silence hung over the table, and Charlotte grew to hope that the awkwardness of earlier had left.

"Sorry about the texts," Jenn mumbled as she dipped a french fry into a small container of mayo. Charlotte smiled.

"No harm, no foul," she said. "I'm just glad we were able to clear up the misunderstanding." She leaned back, unable to finish the food on her plate. She eyed the door just as Charity and Amanda made their way in.

"Just in time for dessert," she said as she pushed her plate away. "Why don't I take the girls to a separate booth and have a chat."

"What are you going to say?" Robert wiped his mouth with his napkin.

Charlotte thought for a moment. "What if I presented another option to them, to make up for whatever big summer plans they concocted this afternoon."

"Like what?" Wariness crossed Jenn's features.

"I think we still need volunteers for the Teddy Bear Picnics."

Each week two Teddy Bear Picnics were held on the North Beach during the summer. One for the younger children, toddlers and up, and the second for the school-aged kids up to grade three. They were a huge enticement for families and would help to keep the girls occupied.

"That would be okay." Jenn nodded her agreement.

"Great. And then once their ice cream arrives, maybe we can talk about Julia." Charlotte let the bomb drop as she pushed her chair away and waved to the girls.

As she walked away, she could see the confusion mixed in with irritation swirl around her friend. Jordan's brow arched when she looked his way, but she only smiled.

She didn't need Jenn to agree with her idea, but she did need her friend to understand what she was trying to do. Keeping her in the dark wouldn't work. It would only create more confusion and misunderstandings like today. And Jenn's friendship meant too much to her to ruin it. No, she would gently explain her plan of action and why she felt it was so important, even though she knew it meant a careful tightrope walk across a very narrow line—not only with her friend, but with others who lived in Stillwater Bay.

CHAPTER TWENTY

JENNIFER

Hands on her hips, Jenn took stock of her back patio and frowned. It was time for a change. There was nothing wrong with the furniture. The paint still looked good from last fall when she'd given the wicker a fresh coat, but maybe if she rearranged the furniture and bought new throw cushions, that would help.

She also needed some flowerpots, preferably with live flowers. She couldn't believe Robert hadn't said anything yet about their lackluster garden this year. Maybe she should hire Paige to come in and revitalize it for her.

She toed a planter to the side of the house and then began the process of rearranging the furniture. She loved to sit in the large half chair she'd picked up a few years ago, but it always faced the side, so she had to sit at an angle to watch the sunset over the water most nights. Maybe she should move it to where their love seat sat instead.

Her body was full of nervous energy, and she needed to do something, anything, before she lost it. Robert was inside making some tea, but they'd barely spoken a word since they left Fred's.

By the time Robert nudged open the patio door with two cups of tea in hand, Jenn had moved the furniture around a couple times, unsure of the arrangement. Normally, their patio set was centered around hosting parties, but since this year's calendar was basically empty of their usual barbecues and picnics, there was no reason not to change things around. If Jenn's favorite thing to do on her back deck was to watch the sun rise or set over the water, then that's what the focus of the furniture arrangement would be.

Robert hesitated for a brief moment as he viewed the change but wisely kept quiet. He handed her a mug of tea before he sat in the love seat that was now at a slight angle and patted the seat beside him. Jenn had planned to sit in her seat, which now faced the water directly, but settled down beside her husband instead.

"Doing okay?"

She shrugged. She'd been fine up until they found Charity in Julia's shop. Then everything had gone downhill from there. For a brief moment during dinner she thought maybe things would change, that maybe Charlotte had finally listened to her, but she'd been proven wrong. Again.

She was at a loss. Now, of all times, she needed her friend. Yes, Charlotte had been there for her in those first few weeks when the pain was so intense she wasn't sure how she could survive another minute, let alone get through a day. But the grief doesn't end that quickly. The heartache doesn't heal that fast. The memories linger and hit at the least expected moments. When everyone else had gone on with their lives, that's when she needed her friend the most.

Was it wrong for her to expect Charlotte to realize that? Was it wrong of her to expect her best friend to place her own life on hold? Probably. But yet, it's what she needed.

"I seem to be alone with my feelings." Jenn noticed a lone seagull flying overhead.

"You're not." Robert's fingers rested on her knee as if unsure his touch would be welcomed.

"You can honestly say you feel the same way toward Julia as I do?" The challenge was in her voice despite her quiet tone.

"No, in that I don't." Robert hesitated.

She just waited. Either she was alone or not.

"But I understand why you feel the way you do," he sighed, as if the admission was too heavy to bear.

"I don't understand." She turned to face him better. "Why you don't feel the same way. What is it about that woman that has you championing her?"

Robert shook his head, but Jenn caught the haunted look on his face. A look that had become familiar to her whenever Julia was mentioned.

"Have you tried to place yourself in her shoes? Just once?" Robert asked her.

Jenn shook her head. "Why would I? We don't have a child who would ever consider taking another's life. We didn't have a child who acted out all his life, who was a bad seed—"

"He was not a bad seed." Steel determination filled Robert's voice as he interrupted her. "He was a sad boy. A lonely child. A child full of anger and hurt. But Julia's not to blame."

"She's not?" Of course she was. Gabriel clearly needed help. They all knew it. They all tried, in one form or another. Most of the men in their community had tried to be a good influence, to help him, but it hadn't been enough. Julia should have done more. She should have seen more. She should have stopped her son.

She should never have had a gun in the house that he could access. Ever.

"She did everything she could for Gabe."

"Obviously not enough."

"Was that her fault? She did everything she could with what resources she had. You know that. We all know that. It's why we all pitched in to help when we could." Robert pushed himself up from his seat and almost slammed his mug down on the table in front of them.

"Damn it, Jenn. You were the one who encouraged me to be a mentor to the boy, to help him pull through whatever he was going through, remember that? What were the words you used? Be a *father figure*?" His fingers air quoted around those words.

She remembered. She remembered calling Julia a friend once. She remembered sitting with her night after night at Gina's, drinking coffee, sharing stories about raising their kids, and offering help and advice. She remembered Gabriel being a boy everyone wanted to help, but no one thought was fixable or even redeemable.

But they'd taken the view of "It takes a village to raise a child" to heart. And look where it had got them.

That was probably what hurt the most.

"I don't think anything could have helped that boy. God knows we tried. Look where it got us."

Robert's head dropped to his chest, his eyes squeezed shut as he stood there.

"You'll never forgive him or her, will you?"

She only shook her head. The words didn't need to be said.

"I stand by what I said earlier, to Charlotte." Robert lifted his head and stared at her; a fire of determination lit his face. His words were a challenge, but she didn't care.

"Do what you need to do. Just don't expect me to support you." She pushed her shoulders back and tore her gaze away from his. She stared out at the swirl of clouds that appeared out of nowhere. "Not in this."

Storm clouds rolled in off the bay, a visual display of visceral emotions, similar to what brewed inside Jenn. The rolling clouds were an array of purples and blues, with the light wisps being swallowed up as the wind picked up. Jenn shivered as a draft of cool air swirled around her.

"Storm is coming in," Robert muttered as he stepped away from her and down the steps onto their lawn. Jenn followed him, a reminder of the days when they used to come out and watch the storms roll in off the bay in past years.

After a few moments, Robert turned to her. "Just promise me that whatever is happening right now, it won't destroy us."

Jenn stared at him. Pure honesty shone in his eyes, so pure that it hurt to see. Destroy them? It would tear them apart.

"I found the papers, Jenn. The ones in your desk."

His words hung heavy between them.

"I'm not ready to give up on us. I don't think you are either, otherwise you wouldn't have hidden them in there for so long."

He stepped toward her. She stepped back.

"I wasn't going to tell you that I found them. But . . . I want to be honest with you"—he turned his back and stared out into the bay—"and I don't want to lose you." He turned back to her, and she saw the tears in his eyes. "Please, Jenn, please promise me that we can work through this?"

She shook her head, unable to promise him anything. She didn't see how they could survive this if he publicly supported Julia, something Charlotte hadn't asked them to do, but he'd volunteered for anyway at Fred's.

Even Jordan had been caught off guard.

When Charlotte had returned to their table after speaking with the girls, a grim determination had settled over her.

"I am going to do something, but I want you to be aware of it first. I'm not asking you to help; I'm not even asking for your support. But I don't want you to be caught unaware when you see things in the paper or hear me talking about it to others."

The moment Charlotte said those words, Jenn knew. She knew it had to do with Julia, and she knew she didn't want to hear any of it. She couldn't. She wasn't sure how she would handle the news so she stood up to leave, but Robert grabbed her hand and urged her to sit back down.

While Charlotte spoke, Jenn sat there, dumbfounded. Part of her admired Charlotte for what she was about to attempt, but another part of her couldn't believe the audacity of her friend.

When Robert thanked Charlotte for telling them, Jenn sat there in silence. Charlotte became a stranger to her in those moments, a stranger she wasn't sure she wanted to be associated with. But it was the words Robert said that took her breath away.

"I'll support you. Whatever you need," Robert said.

His words seemed to shock everyone at the table. When she could, Jenn stood up, brushed Robert's hand off of her arm, and walked out of the tavern. She'd continued to walk up the street and across the bridge until Robert pulled alongside of her and waited for her to get in.

Now, as they stood there in their backyard, she tried to make sense of why Robert would support Julia.

"Jenn, please . . ." His voice broke as he shook his head and reached out to her.

"You . . . you can't ask this of me. You can't. You might be able to forgive her, move past what happened, but don't ask me to. Please." She bowed her head. "I can't forgive her. I just can't."

"I'm not asking you to."

She stared at him as if he were a stranger. Of course he was. He might not be saying it outright, but it was what he expected.

Her body shook as she struggled to take everything in. Everything in her life continued to be ripped away from her, as if her soul were being torn into tiny little pieces until there was nothing left of her. She couldn't take any more. She edged backward, one step at a time, until she was far enough away from Robert that he couldn't touch her or even stop her.

"You're asking for the impossible. You expect a miracle when there can't be one. And if there could be, then you're asking for the wrong one. Forgive Julia? Why? Can she turn back time? Can she bring Bobby back? Can she give me my son back?" She shook her head no. "You do this, Robert, and I'm not sure I will be able to forgive you either."

The resignation on his face registered with her before she turned and headed back into the house, each step a nail in the coffin of their marriage. Somehow the gulf between them had widened until whatever foundation they'd had left disintegrated before their eyes. There was nothing left. Nothing for them to rebuild upon, not if he demanded the impossible.

CHAPTER TWENTY-ONE

SAMANTHA

Samantha's pen tapped on the table beside her as she reread her last sentence.

The heart of a town isn't an idea, a purpose or even a mission statement. It's a person.

When she'd first talked with Charlotte about tackling this project, her initial thought was it was a good excuse to extend her stay in Stillwater. But the more she thought of the idea, the more she liked it, and her notebook was full of random notes of what she could do.

Let's remind the people what our town is about. That's what Charlotte had wanted.

Arnold, the editor of the *Stillwater News*, was skeptical, and Sam didn't blame him. This column of hers was meant to remind people that Julia Berry wasn't a monster; she wasn't a horrible, evil person. She was the heart and soul of what this town embodied, or at least, had been.

Charlotte wanted Sam's first article to be centered around Julia, but Arnold disagreed, and Samantha had to agree with him. It was smarter to keep Julia in the background, and yet, always have her there, in each article. Sam's goal was to focus on those around Julia, keeping her to the sidelines for as long as possible until it became evident that the real heart of the town was Julia. Or at least, she was part of it.

Arnold had given her a list of people to interview. There were those names she'd expected to see on the list: Anne Marie, the baker from Sweet Bakes; Fred Gibbons from Fred's Tavern; Shelley Peterson, her landlady. There were also others that she really hadn't gotten to know very well during her stay, like Dorothea Peters, the manager of the retirement home, or Blake Casser, the glassworker.

Arnold had numbers beside each name listed, fifteen in total. That was four months of articles with Julia's being the very last one. Four months where she could stay in this town and soak in the peace she needed. She knew Alex wanted her home and would tell her she could write these on her own time, that she didn't need to stay here until Thanksgiving . . . but she did.

"How about I refill your cup with some hot water?" Shelley appeared at her side with a teapot in hand.

Sam smiled. Before coming to Stillwater, coffee with an extra shot of espresso was her go-to beverage of choice during the day, but somehow, Shelley had managed to switch her over to tea in the afternoons.

"What are you working on?" Shelley set the hot pot down on a tea cozy and then sat down across from her at the dining room table.

Sam toyed with her pen, twirling it in circles. "Arnold asked me to head up a new column for the paper."

"Arnold?"

Sam nodded.

"Arnold isn't known for his . . . generosity when it comes to columns in the paper. My husband used to write for him off and on."

Samantha leaned forward and rested her elbows on the table. "Really? You never mentioned this during our talks about him."

Shelley shrugged. "George was a lot of things. Being a writer was just one part." A soft smile played with her lips, and Samantha knew she was lost to memories. It happened every time her late husband was brought up.

She reread what she'd written and knew immediately whom her first article would be about.

"Shelley." She waited a few seconds for the woman to look at her. "I'm going to be writing a series of articles about the people in this town, and I'd like my first article to be about you. Would that be okay?"

Shelley placed her hand over her heart as her eyes widened. "Me? Why would you want to write about me?"

"Because I think you're an important part of whom this town is, and I'd like to help refocus people on what makes this town so family oriented."

Understanding covered Shelley's gaze. "Of course. Just promise me one thing?"

The doorbell rang, and Shelley pushed her chair back.

"Who's that?" Sam said as she watched her head toward the front door. Shelley knew with the upcoming weekend that her bed-and-breakfast would be filling with guests, and in fact, all but one of her rooms were already booked.

"Don't share any of my recipes," Shelley called over her shoulder. Sam smiled. No, she wouldn't share any recipes. It was something Shelley had made her promise when she first arrived, to never divulge any information regarding her baking. Apparently she made a few closely guarded dishes, ones that normally won contests, and she took great pride in the fact they were well-kept secrets.

Instead of new guests, it was Blake Casser who walked in. She was about to raise her hand in greeting but caught the steel look in his eyes.

"I heard what you're up to, and we need to talk." Blake stood beside her, his massive arms crossed over his equally massive chest, and he glared down at her.

Sam shrunk back a little. The man had intimidation down pat, that's for sure. She had to remind herself she'd dealt with men like him before, men who liked to push women around and who thought their muscles held more sway than her words, and she stood up, forcing her chair to squeak backward and him to take a step back.

"So talk."

The room was silent. Shelley stood there, not saying a word. But there was a hint of a smile, a hint of something Samantha knew she didn't want any part of. She'd been warned by Charlotte that her landlady was quite the matchmaker in town.

"If this is going to be done right, then we need to work together."

"This?" Sam asked. How did he know what *this* was, and who had blabbed?

Right then her cell phone rang and she knew by the ringtone it was Alex, her editor. She contemplated not answering, but she'd already ignored his calls the past three days.

"How do some tea and cookies sound?" Shelley stepped forward and placed her hand on Blake's arm.

Sam smiled in gratitude as she grabbed her phone and made her way out of the room. She didn't need anyone listening in.

"Alex," she answered.

"It's about time you picked up. I'm about to drive out there tomorrow to drag you home."

"Please don't," she said.

"Too bad. I need you here."

"I mean it, Alex. Don't come. I'm not ready to come back yet."

Alex groaned. "Ready or not, you need to come back. And don't tell me there's still a story here. If you haven't been able to dig up anything on the principal by now, then the story is cold."

Sam wrinkled her nose in disgust. Jordan Stone. There was something about him, something that still didn't sit right. He was next on her list, and it would be a great excuse to try to dig deeper into his story of what had happened that day. But Alex was right. Jordan Stone wasn't enough to keep her there.

"Fine," she said. Her gut churned as she said the word before really thinking about her answer.

"Fine? What do you mean, fine? Fine you'll come home, or fine you're taking time off?"

"I want the summer."

"The summer?" Alex sputtered. She'd caught him off guard, and that was good. He might be open to her suggestion.

"You don't have to worry about my column. I'll fill it with some special pieces I'm writing. But give me the summer. I need it, Alex. I've seen too much, done too much. I just need time."

"Time for what? Time to relax? Then let me talk to my friend who has a time-share in Mexico. Heck, I'll even come with you and bring some of your friends that you seem to have forgotten about."

She shook her head. "No, Alex. That's not . . . ," she sighed deeply. She didn't need this guilt trip from him.

She glanced behind her and caught Blake watching her. Her cheeks flushed, and she turned her attention back to the wall in front of her.

"You have a life here, Sam. Or did you forget that?" His voice softened and Sam could picture him, sitting there in his office, his elbows resting on his knees while his shoulders sloped. Alex was small and lean, unlike the man behind her whose gaze bored holes into her back.

"I know. I just . . . give me the summer, okay?" She didn't know how to explain this to him. They'd been friends for so long, but she doubted he would understand why she had to stay here. "I'll take unpaid leave. Whatever it takes. I just can't come back yet, okay?"

She didn't even wait for him to respond. She hit the button to end the call, stowed her phone in her pocket, and then turned around.

Both Blake and Shelley stood there, watching her. Shelley was concerned; she could see the worry lines etched on her face. But Blake . . . well, he looked like he'd just eaten a rotten mushroom but was too manly to spit it out.

"Looks like I've got the summer off," she said. "I hope you haven't booked my room yet."

"You're staying?" Blake spat the words out.

"Is that a problem?"

Blake grumbled something beneath his breath before he stormed past her and let the wooden screen door slap behind him.

"Oh dear," Shelley mumbled.

"What did I miss? If I need to find someplace else to stay . . ." She really didn't want to have to leave Seaglass; she loved it here.

"Oh no." Shelley waved her hand dismissively. "And don't you worry none about that boy. He'll be back. Now, where were we?"

Sam sat back down at the table, reached for her tea, and winked at Shelley.

"I think you were about to spill the recipe for your strawberry-cream muffins."

CHAPTER TWENTY-TWO

CHARLOTTE

Charlotte nursed her mug of coffee between her hands as she sat on her back deck steps and waited for Jordan to return from his morning jog.

She was mentally preparing herself for today. It was their first Teddy Bear Picnic of the summer, starting the first Wednesday of July and then every week until end of August, and Charlotte was more than a bit nervous. For one, she didn't normally do this . . . help with the picnics, and two, she wasn't all that sure of the turn-out. The online registration had fallen to the wayside this year, and it hadn't been until late last night when she'd received an e-mail from one of the parent volunteers that Charlotte realized the registration link had never officially opened.

She couldn't believe no one had noticed it.

She was jittery, and sitting here was almost torture. Where was Jordan, and why wasn't he back by now? He'd said it would only be a short run as he'd offered to help her this morning. But a short run for her meant jogging on the spot.

Would there be enough kids today? Did she have enough volunteers? What if there were too many helpers? What if there weren't enough? What if the kids hated the activities she'd put together? What if it all flopped?

Lost in her thoughts, she didn't see or hear Jordan until he squatted down in front of her.

"Hey, I thought you would be dressed by now."

"I was waiting for you." She put her hand out to pat their dog on the head. She wrinkled her nose in disgust when her hand met wet fur. "In the water, again?"

Jordan shrugged. "He's a natural, what can I say."

"He's not coming in the house like this." The last time they left their dog in the house alone while he was wet, she'd had to wipe down their walls and clean the carpet.

"Why don't we bring him? He'd love it, and I'm sure the kids would too."

Charlotte was about to say no until she realized it was a good idea.

"We're taking your Jeep then."

Her husband nodded before he headed into the house. "Go get dressed. I'll meet you in the Jeep."

She followed him inside and then made her way up to their room while he went down to have his shower. Should she wear a sundress, shorts, or capris? Why was this so difficult for her? Ever since she woke up, she'd been struggling with every little thought, every small decision. This wasn't like her.

She was still standing there when Jordan came up.

"Capris," he said as if he could read her mind. It probably wasn't difficult since she stood there with a sundress in one hand and capris in the other.

"What's going on? You seem . . . off somewhat. You okay?" He sat down on their bed and pulled on his jeans. She eyed his body with appreciation before she nodded and then shook her head.

"I'm not sure." She shrugged before hanging the dress back up in her closet. She looked over the multitude of tops and sighed.

"This one." Jordan reached for a blue top with a scooped neckline. He then reached for a cream tank top off her shelf and handed it to her.

Charlotte shook her head. Here she was, a grown woman, and her husband had to dress her today.

"I don't know what's wrong, but my world feels off-kilter."

Jordan squeezed her shoulder before he pulled a shirt off a hanger for himself. He chose a deep blue, a complementary color to her outfit.

"You've had a rough week. Maybe it's all just catching up to you." His fingers hesitated as he buttoned up his shirt. "Why don't we go for a drive later? Maybe along the coast, and do some second-hand store shopping?"

Charlotte smiled at the idea. They used to take off on weekends and do that, something to get away from their jobs, their commitments. She used to love those weekends and looked forward to them, but it had been a while, years actually, since they'd done that.

"I'm not sure." Could they actually get away? Was now a good time to do so? The fair started tomorrow . . .

Jordan reached for her hand and tugged her backward until she rested against his chest. They stood in front of their full-length mirror, and Charlotte looked at them, together. She wasn't really familiar with this sight. Any intimacy between them had petered off until they were more like comfortable roommates instead of husband and wife.

"You've put committees in place to ensure everything is going ahead smoothly, so trust them, okay? This isn't our first summer fair; this town knows what they are doing. Besides, we'll only be gone for a few hours." When she hesitated, he placed a soft kiss on the back of her head. "We need this, Charlotte."

How could she say no?

"Maybe all you need is time away to get a fresh perspective while we drive. You always did find inspiration that way."

Which was true. The more she mulled over the idea, the more she liked it.

"Just think on it, okay? We can ask Gina to put together a basket lunch and take it with us. We can be back before it's dark."

She saw the hope in his gaze and the feel of his arms around her felt warm, right. It had been too long and maybe . . . maybe this would be good for them. Not just for her, but for them.

"Okay." She nodded in agreement. "Let's do it." She turned around and tilted her head up for a kiss. "Let me tell Sheila so she can field all my calls."

"Thank you." The relief in Jordan's gaze was noticeable. "I've been meaning to mention it for a while, but it was never the right time."

Charlotte searched his gaze, suddenly nervous. Why was going away so important to him?

"Maybe our problem is we don't know how to make time," Charlotte said quietly.

She saw the answer in his face and knew he didn't need to reply. Time wasn't their only problem. Their marriage had been placed on the back burner for a long time. Her position as mayor and his role as principal was paramount in their lives. Who they were as individuals was so tightly meshed into their careers that the line was blurred.

Just as Jenn had said. Sometimes she didn't know when to stop being the mayor and start being a friend.

One afternoon away from it all wasn't going to solve all their problems. But it would be a nice distraction.

•   •   •

Charlotte dusted the sand from the top of the picnic table before she unfolded the plastic tablecloth and spread it out. Her hands shook, and she mentally scolded herself for being silly. There was no reason to be nervous. Everything was going to turn out just fine.

Ever since she'd agreed to their afternoon getaway trip, Jordan couldn't contain his smile or laughter. Even now, when he was supposed to be up here helping to spread out the food and art supplies, he was down by the water, throwing a ball out for their dog to fetch. Around him gathered some small children. She hoped they were here to take part in the picnic.

Ten minutes ago, Amanda and Charity had arrived and were placing blankets down on the sand, stations where they would host activities for the kids. Having them here and having Jordan help eased the nervous jitters but not completely.

"Stop being so silly," she muttered to herself. Place her in a room with adults, and she was fine. But with children, that was a different story. Especially these children. She wanted today to be a happy day for them, a day they could look back on with happiness. It was the first official day of summer for Stillwater, and she wanted it to be perfect.

"Excuse me, is this where the Teddy Bear Picnic is taking place?"

Charlotte looked up and found a couple standing in front of her with their daughter, a little girl who carried a stuffed bear in her arms.

"Sure is. I'm Charlotte." She stretched out her hand and shook first the mother's hand and then the father's.

"This is Hayley." The mother, Debbie, had her arm around her daughter's shoulders. "We were up at the lighthouse and noticed a flyer. Are we able to join in? I'd love to help if possible."

Charlotte smiled. "Of course, that would be lovely. We're about to get started." She bent down until she was eye level with Hayley. "Do you see that man down by the water with the dog? That's my husband and our school principal. And that's my dog, Buster. Why don't you go and give him a pet? Be careful, though; I think he's a bit wet." She caught the sparkle of interest in Hayley's eyes at the mention of Buster and was glad Jordan had thought to bring him down with them.

"She was so excited when we found out about these picnics," Debbie mentioned as they turned to watch as Hayley's dad led her down to the water.

"She'll have a great time. It's something we do every week during the summer for the little ones. Are you just passing through, or will you be staying here for a bit?"

"We're here for the fair actually, staying at the bed-and-breakfast. We went up to the lighthouse to watch the sunrise, and that's when we saw the notice."

Charlotte smiled. "Did Shelley tell you how she came up with the name for her bed-and-breakfast?"

•   •   •

The story was probably one of Charlotte's favorites. Every store in Stillwater Bay had a name that was unique, not only to the town, but for themselves as well. Shelley's place was one such example.

Years ago, after losing her husband to cancer, Shelley decided to turn their century-old home into a bed-and-breakfast. After months of construction and redecorating, just before she was about to officially open, she realized she needed a name but couldn't think of anything that held any sort of meaning. One of their dreams, as a couple while her husband was still well, had been to operate a bed-and-breakfast, so she wanted the name to be special and have meaning.

At first, she'd called it Stillwater B&B and welcomed her first guests. Word spread about her quaint rooms and sweet service, and her calendar quickly booked up. She kept the name Stillwater B&B for over a year but had a basket on her front reception desk where customers could give name suggestions. She decided to choose a winner on the anniversary of her husband's passing.

That night, she sat on her front porch with the basket beside her and went through all the name submissions. There were some good ideas, but nothing stood out to her. Shelley had a small party planned for the following day to announce the new name, so she knew she had to pick one, but unfortunately, nothing sounded right. Just as she was about to head inside, a motorcycle drew up along her front walkway. There was only one man in town who rode a Harley, but Shelley wasn't sure why Blake Casser would be coming to her place, this late at night.

He held a package in his hands, tightly wrapped in plastic, but looked a tad bit uncomfortable as he stood on her porch.

"It's a bit late for a visit, isn't it?" Shelley eyed the package in his hands.

"Afraid word will spread?" A twitch of a smile played with Blake's lips.

Shelley didn't say anything, but she couldn't hold back the laughter. Blake was a special one in her eyes. He was a badly scarred man with a hole in his heart, and she loved him like a son.

"Will you be here tomorrow?" She'd sent him an invite, knowing full well he wouldn't show. He never did. It was rare for Blake to leave the lighthouse. It was his sanctuary, he said.

"I'm not one for crowds," Blake hedged before he sat down beside her. He still held the package in his hands.

"Then I'll expect you for dinner." She didn't leave any opening for him to disagree. Besides, she knew he wouldn't pass on a home-cooked meal. He rarely did. She had him over at least once a week for the past few years. They kept one another company.

"Have you picked a name yet?" He eyed the basket she'd set down on the ground.

"I can't seem to. Nothing fits," Shelley sighed. "I don't know what to do."

"Maybe this will help." Blake handed over the package.

Shelley carefully lifted off the tape and unwound the mounds of packaging and gasped when she saw what he'd brought her. Tears filled her eyes, and she was at a loss for words.

Blake had given her a sand-glass sculpture he'd made, but it was unlike anything she'd ever seen. It was in the shape of a heart that encased a smaller shard of glass inside. It was beautiful. A heart within a heart.

"How did you do this?" She outlined the edges of the smaller heart within the glass with her finger. It looked like a bubble had formed inside the sand glass, a bubble in the shape of a heart.

"This was all Mother Nature. I just smoothed the edges a bit to give it more of a defined look. I thought of you and George the moment I saw it."

Shelley could only nod. Her throat swelled as she struggled to hold back her emotions. George used to love working with Blake in his shop; it had been the only thing that kept him going those last few months before the cancer took hold and he couldn't do anything without too much pain.

"He used to say to me, 'She's my heart.' He talked about wanting to create something for you, something that would show you this, but nothing seemed right."

She shook her head. "I knew. I always knew. Because he was mine as well." The tears slipped down her face, and she wiped them away with the palm of her hand. "This is beautiful."

"Is the name okay?" Blake's voice hesitated a little.

Shelley glanced up at him in confusion. "Name?"

He pointed to the bottom of the heart. Shaped in a square and etched onto the glass were the words *Seaglass B&B.*

"Seaglass." The name rolled on her lips and resonated in her heart.

George used to tell her that the color of her eyes while they made love reminded him of sea glass, capturing the way the water would be absolutely still and perfect. He used to tease her that he could stare into her eyes forever and remain perfectly happy.

It was perfect.

Shelley squeezed Blake's hand, unable to express in words how she felt. To have this gift, the night before the anniversary of George's death, meant the world to her.

•   •   •

Charlotte always got misty-eyed when she told Shelley's story and was pleased to see that it affected Debbie the same way.

"I'll have to ask her when we go back if I can see the statue."

"She'd love that. And be sure to take a drive up to the light-house. The artist still lives there and has a wonderful collection. I have some of his sculptures in my home and office."

"Mayor Stone?"

Charlotte glanced over to where she heard her name being called. Charity waved at her and Charlotte waved back. "Guess it's time to start. Feel free to join us, or if you'd like, relax on the beach and watch us having fun with our teddy bears."

She made her way down to the water and was almost instantly surrounded by small children. She looked around for little Ellie but didn't see her. She squashed down the disappointment and focused on the children that were there, all with their teddy bears and stuffed animals.

"Are we ready to have some fun?" The tingling sensation of cautiousness still hovered, but she ignored it. After all, what did she have to fear? These were just children. Small children with cute stuffed animals who wanted to have fun.

What could go wrong?

CHAPTER TWENTY-THREE

JENNIFER

When Jenn received a text from an unknown number to meet a group of *like-minded individuals* down at South Beach, she was a little skeptical.

She knew practically everyone in town and had most of their numbers in her phone.

And what did *like-minded individuals* even mean?

Every time she went to hit the delete button on that message she stopped, for some unknown reason. It was a puzzle, and puzzles had always fascinated her.

She'd found, throughout the years, that her first thought was always the right or closest one, even though she'd spend hours thinking of other possible scenarios for situations. So her first conclusion in this instance was that the text was about the school and the *like-minded* part had to do with that group Merille mentioned.

Really, what else could there be?

She really didn't have time to deal with any of this today, though. The Stillwater Fair started this week. The Teddy Bear Picnic was going on right now down at the beach with activities to follow throughout the day until the fair's kickoff Thursday night with a parade and fireworks. Baskets and boxes of items filled her kitchen counter, ready to be packed in her SUV and taken downtown. She didn't have time to meet anyone at the beach . . . except, a part of her really wanted to.

The garage door slammed shut, and Robert's footsteps thudded loudly on their floor.

"How much more?"

Jenn glanced at the remaining boxes on the counter and shrugged.

Robert shook his head before he picked up more boxes and made his way to the door again, muttering to himself along the way.

"Need help?" She probably should have gone and opened the door for him. It was the least she could have done. She hadn't asked for his help today, figuring that he would want to keep his distance from her after last night, but once again, he'd proven her wrong.

After their talk last night, Jenn had gone to have a long soak in the tub. She knew Robert was vegged out in front of the television in their bedroom, as she could hear the low drone over the water jets. When she'd gotten out, he'd already fallen asleep, so she headed downstairs, poured herself a glass of white wine, and read a book. It wasn't until almost two o'clock in the morning when she realized the time and crawled her way up the stairs and into bed.

She was back to looking at that text message when Robert came back in.

"Everything okay?"

She closed the screen and placed the phone in her pocket. She still wasn't sure what to do with it, but if she somehow ended up at South Beach in time for the meeting, then she would go.

"Everything's fine. Someone wants to get together if I have time, that's all."

Robert grabbed the remaining box while Jenn collected the bags. "Oh yeah? Who's that? Charlotte?"

Jenn shook her head. "I imagine she's too busy with the Teddy Bear Picnic today."

She followed him out to the garage and couldn't believe how full the back of the SUV was.

"What all are you bringing anyway?" Robert shut the truck door, and they hopped inside.

"Just the usual for my booth on the grounds." As part of the official welcoming committee, Jenn always manned the welcome booth, one of the first booths people saw as they walked onto the grounds. Normally she loved setting up the booth and being front and center when people walked in; in fact, it was probably her favorite part of the whole weekend, but this year she'd asked others to take care of it for her. She planned to oversee its setup and ensure they maintained enough giveaway bags for everyone who entered the grounds, but she didn't want to be there to meet people. Not this year.

"I don't remember you having this much last year."

"It's the same as last year. I just decided to bundle it all up instead of making repeat trips like in previous years. I won't be around as much, so I'd rather the booth have more items than not enough."

Robert reached his hand across for hers.

"I'm glad you're not doing it this year. We've never really enjoyed it as a family, all together. Actually"—he looked at her before turning his attention back to the road—"we never even enjoyed it as a couple. We should this year."

"How?"

"Just the two of us. Like when we were younger." He squeezed her hand.

Like when they were younger. That brought back a lot of memories. They would spend the day walking the grounds, going on the rides, and playing the games until he'd won her the largest stuffed animal around. They would walk from one beach to the other, sometimes going out on the water in the small boats people rented out for the day. They were so in love back then, wrapped up in one another. It had been a good time for them.

"What about Charity?"

"No doubt she'll be too embarrassed to hang out with us and will be off having fun with Amanda and their friends. Let her make memories of her own. She needs them." He paused. "We all do."

Jenn swallowed hard. Building new memories meant a life without Bobby. She knew she had to accept that, but she didn't want to.

She bit her lip from the sudden roller coaster of emotions that hit her and stared out the passenger window.

"Jenn?" Robert squeezed her hand again.

"Bobby loved the fair. He would have been tall enough to go on most of the rides himself this year. He was so looking forward to that." Her voice caught as a sharp knife stabbed her heart.

"Bobby loved life. He would want us to love it too."

There was silence between them as they made their way down Second Street Bridge.

"I'm sorry," Jenn said as she broke the silence. This time she squeezed her husband's hand.

"We'll just take it a moment at a time, okay?"

Jenn nodded. "Okay."

The scene in the parking lot at the community center was alive with activity. Robert edged his way to the sidelines, where the sparse parking area was allocated for booth holders.

"It's like a zoo in here," he muttered.

By not using the school grounds this year, space was limited. The midway rides and booths took up the majority of space.

"Are you sure your welcome booth was to be set up in here? I thought you said some were going to be on South Beach."

Jenn glanced down at her list where she'd written everything down. Everything but where her booth was to be located.

She glanced over at the midway and then back at Robert with a sheepish grin on her face.

"Would you believe me if I said I can't remember?"

The look he gave her said no. She racked her brain trying to remember what she'd been told. Normally her booth was at the school, where all the families visited for the kid activities. She remembered someone mentioning that her booth should be set up in the midway near the community center because most people would stop there first this year since the South Beach venue was a last-minute addition.

But it made more sense for her to be at South Beach instead. Right?

"Why don't you text whoever is manning the booth this year," Robert suggested.

A quick intake of air, a shake of her head, and her fingers started to tingle.

"Hey, hey, it's okay." Robert reached across and pulled her into his arms.

She felt like such a fool. She was about to have a panic attack over something so small.

She rested against his shoulder for a moment before she pulled away.

"Let's go down to the beach." She gave him a small smile, as if to confirm she was okay, while inside she was shaking like a leaf.

Maybe it was the growing crowds or the plethora of rides within the midway. Maybe it was the signage everywhere she looked . . . but whatever it was, it was throwing her off.

This would be their first Stillwater Fair without Bobby. The first one where he wouldn't be holding on to her hand as they walked through the midway, where she wouldn't take a photo of the painting on his face, where they wouldn't share a cone of cotton candy together.

She wasn't the only one feeling this way either. She could see it in the eyes of parents who walked down Main Street as they drove past. They could dress it up all they wanted, decorate the town with streamers and balloons, but the grief was still there. Still palpable. Heavy. Dense like the fog over the bay in the early morning.

· · ·

Both Shelley and Anne Marie stood by the entrance from the South Beach parking area and waved when Jenn noticed them. Robert was at the back of the SUV, getting ready to unload.

"We weren't sure if you got lost or something." Shelley smiled while she gave Jenn a hug. She then waved to a group of teenagers who stood around in a circle.

"We've rounded up some helpers for the day."

"I thought you'd be at your store today." Jenn handed Anne Marie a bag.

"I needed a break. The shop has been busy all morning. When I saw Shelley here, I figured maybe I could help." She gave Jenn a hug.

"Anne Marie," Robert said as he grabbed boxes from the trunk and handed them to the teens.

"So nice to see you, big brother," Anne Marie said. "We were starting to wonder when you'd show up."

"I forgot we were down here. We went to the community center first," Jenn explained.

This brought a puzzled glance from both Anne Marie and Shelley.

"But it was your idea to put the booth here."

"My fault," Robert butted in before Jenn could say anything. "I wanted to check something out at the center first."

Thank you, she mouthed to him when Shelley wasn't looking. Anne Marie caught it, though, and smiled.

"Robert, we need some help with setting up the booth, if you wouldn't mind?" Shelley stopped in front of where their booth lay in pieces on the sand.

"I tried to get it started but . . ." Anne Marie set her stack of boxes down on an empty picnic table.

"Since when did you know how to pick up a tool?"

"Since my brother decided to ignore my requests for help when things broke down in my shop."

"That's why you call someone for help."

"I did." Anne Marie stuck her tongue out at him.

"A professional." Robert shook his head in disgust and turned his back on her.

"I thought you were. At least, that's what you claim to be on your business cards."

Robert rolled his eyes and stared up into the sky. Jenn knew what he was doing. He was mentally counting to ten.

Jenn set her bags down and looked around, needing to ignore the sibling rivalry. If the two could last one minute without getting into an argument or a showdown on who was right and who was wrong, she'd be surprised.

Ever since their parents had passed away, things had never been the same between Robert and Anne Marie. Jenn knew there was a lot of hurt festering between them over the care their parents had received in the retirement home before their deaths. Anne Marie felt they'd been neglected, but Robert swore they received the best care possible, because that was what he'd paid for.

This side of the tiny island was really beautiful. It was one of her favorite spots to walk. Up to the left, on the cliffs, the top portion of their home was visible from down here. On one side of the sidewalk was the sand that led out to the bay. Playground structures, picnic tables, and assembled booths stood on the other side of the sidewalk. The setup didn't look too crowded, and it seemed like early-morning walkers were enjoying the booths as they strolled along the pathway.

She knew Charity should be around here, as she was helping with the Teddy Bear Picnics. Jenn scanned the beach and saw, down the beach to her left, a group of children and blankets spread out on the sand.

Off to her right, down a way, was a group of people standing together. Someone from the group waved, and Jenn looked around her to see whom they were waving to.

Then she remembered the text she'd gotten this morning.

When she noticed a figure break away from the group and walk her way, Jenn turned to her husband, his sister, and Shelley.

"I'm going to grab some coffee from the shack down the beach. Would you like one?"

"An extra large." Robert was down on his knees trying to figure out how to put the booth together.

"Please." Anne Marie nudged Robert with her foot.

He scowled at her but said *please*, nonetheless.

"A tea would be great," Shelley said. "I should probably stay here and help since I'm the one responsible for it being in such disarray."

"Anne Marie?" Jenn asked.

"I'm good, thank you, though."

She made her way down the beach, her feet pushing into the sand with each step. It would have been easier for her to walk on the pathway, as her shoes were filling up with sand, but she loved the way her feet sank down and the feel of the scratchiness of the sand against her toes as it seeped into her shoes with each step.

"I wasn't sure if you were coming." Merille met her halfway.

"I wasn't sure if I was going to."

She followed Merille to the others. There were five others in the group. The conversation halted at her arrival. No one said a word as they all looked at her, and Jenn felt more than a little self-conscious. She crossed her arms and looked each person in the eye. All the families here had lost a child thanks to Gabriel Berry. The underlying theme that bound them together was that they understood the pain of death. Of a child's death.

In those first few moments, Jenn should have been made to feel welcome. After all, her own child had died. She was a parent who knew their pain, shared it even. So why did she feel alienated in a group that should count her as one of their own?

She stood there, on the outskirts, and waited for someone to step back and allow her an opening. All it would take was a slight shuffle, a step back, and there would be room for her, but no one moved. Merille stood a bit off to the side to allow her to at least see everyone, but it wasn't much.

"What's she doing here?" Trevor Blackstone, Merille's husband, sneered over at Jenn.

"I invited her," Merille said. She lowered her gaze to the sand at her husband's expression for a moment before she looked over at Jenn and gave her a half smile.

"Why?"

"Why not?" Jenn responded to Trevor. She'd never liked him. Abrupt and brusque, he carried a chip on his shoulder. He stood there, his legs spread wide and his arms crossed over his wide frame, making his biceps bulge and his tattoos more prominent.

"Not sure how our conversation has anything to do with you." He gave her a dismissive glance.

"Depends on what the conversation is about, doesn't it? If you're talking about what needs to happen to the school in the upcoming year, then I might have an idea or two."

"I told you she understood." Merille nudged her husband with her elbow.

"Is this everyone?" Jenn asked.

Besides Merille and Trevor, Julie and Frank were there—they'd lost their daughter—as well as Sarah, a divorced mother of three. None of her children were school-aged yet, she didn't think. Why was she here?

This couldn't be it. Surely. From the way Merille had made it sound, there had to be more families involved.

"Is this not enough?" Trevor growled.

Jenn couldn't help herself from taking a step back in response. Merille and Trevor were best friends with Frank and Julie. Frank was a truck driver, just like Trevor. Which meant he was rarely home. She'd never had much interaction with Julie, so she wasn't sure what she was like, but from how she stood there, timid and unwilling to even smile at her, Jenn doubted her voice would be powerful enough to accomplish anything. Which meant this group was being led by Trevor and Frank, two bullies who preferred threats and domination to logical thinking.

Seeing them standing there left a sour taste in Jenn's mouth. She shook her head at Merille. "Sorry, I thought . . . I expected . . . not this." She turned to leave, but a hand on her arm stopped her.

"Give us a chance, please? We need you."

"We don't need her. We're doing fine on our own. That whore will leave town soon enough and—"

"Excuse me?" Jenn couldn't believe what she was hearing. "You're the one defacing Julia's home?"

Trevor shrugged, but she caught the smug look on his face. "She's not welcome here."

"That doesn't give you the right to be a bully."

"You're defending her?" Trevor stood right in front of her, his chest puffed out and his face inches from her own.

"So what, you're going to start bullying me now?" She turned to look down the beach to where Robert waited for her. What was she doing here?

"You gonna call for your hubby to beat me up?" Trevor snorted before he turned his back on her.

So she was dismissed?

"Stop it, please. Trevor, this isn't helping. We need Jennifer to be on our side. We need her help," Merille spoke up. Jenn read the hope and desperation in Merille's face, but she knew she wasn't the answer.

"I don't think you need me, not for this. If you were serious about doing something in regard to the school . . . then maybe. But I'm not going to be part of some bullying tactic. Stillwater doesn't need a vengeance committee."

"This isn't about vengeance."

Jenn heard the desperation in Merille's voice.

"I think it is."

"No. You know what the issue here is?" Trevor jerked Merille away from her. "You're just too sissy to stand up to your mayor friend and husband, aren't you?" Trevor spat in the sand.

Angry words formed on Jenn's tongue, but she swallowed them. The anger within this group was viral, she could feel it. And she didn't need to surround herself with it. Not when she had her own anger and grief to deal with.

"No, Trevor, I'm not. But our grief shouldn't dictate what happens in this town." She couldn't believe those words came out of her mouth.

She backed away from the group and made her way to the shack for the coffee she'd promised Robert and Shelley. She thought about the very strange moment back there and tried to wrap her head around it.

First, it wasn't what she had expected at all. She knew the support group that met at the church was quite large. Not only were the families of the twelve victims encouraged to come, but so were their friends, coworkers, teachers . . . basically anyone who needed help to process the horrific acts. When Merille had said there was a group, she naively assumed that meant most of those who attended the support group. Had even gotten her hopes up that maybe she wasn't just speaking from grief and anger but from a logical viewpoint.

She should have known better.

While she placed her order and waited for the hot drinks, Jenn took in her surroundings. It had only been a month since the shooting, since the lives of ten children and two teachers were taken. She never expected to be alone in her turmoil, and yet, there were children all around her, playing on the beach, on the swings and slides and jungle gyms . . . and they were all happy. Their laughter joined in with the cries of the seagulls hoping for some free food until it became a cacophony of noise.

If she were to compare those children to herself . . . she knew she'd come up short. She had to remind herself all the time to live in the moment. She couldn't even remember the last time she'd laughed, really laughed, with happiness. If she were being honest, she would admit she wasn't sure if she would ever laugh again. The grief was still too heavy, too fresh, in her mind.

She noticed Trevor and Frank's small group had disbanded and were heading her way. She reached for her beverages that were now ready and placed them in a Styrofoam tray. She managed to catch Merille's gaze before they passed her. The woman's eyes were dulled, her gaze distant, as if she saw through Jenn without really noticing her.

She understood Merille's pain. Recognized the emotional numbness in her gaze. And it scared her.

She didn't want to be like that. It wasn't what Bobby would want. It wasn't what Charity needed.

It also wasn't who Jenn wanted to be. This realization awoke something inside of her. Something that she'd long since buried and didn't believe was possible.

Hope.

CHAPTER TWENTY-FOUR

CHARLOTTE

Charlotte waved to Ellie and Lauren as they left with a new teddy bear clutched tight in Ellie's arms. They'd arrived late, but Lauren looked a little better this morning, so hopefully that meant she'd gotten plenty of rest yesterday. Ellie had given Charlotte a long hug and thanked her for *the bestest day ever* before leaving.

The beach was filling up with booths and copious amounts of children and balloons. She bent down and scooped out the edges of a blanket buried in the sand and began the process of shaking the blanket, careful to stand behind it so the wind didn't blow all the sand back at her.

"That went well." Jordan stood beside her and attached Buster's leash to his collar.

"Surprisingly."

Jordan nudged her playfully. "You were great with the kids. I bet you got more hugs from them than the other girls did."

"That's because I was the one handing out free teddy bears." She tossed the blanket to Jordan and waved good-bye to Charity and Amanda as they headed down the beach.

Their help today had saved the Teddy Bear Picnic from becoming a disaster. While Charlotte had felt overwhelmed, the girls took it all in stride, able to change up the schedule to keep all the kids under control, even to the point of creating new games that the kids seemed to love.

"Oh, to have the energy of a teenager back again," Jordan sighed. He placed the blanket in a large plastic bag they'd brought with them and then stretched, his arms raised high above his head. "I could go for a nap right about now."

"We don't have time for naps, not today. Help me load all this up in the shed over there, and then we can walk down the pathway and see how things are going." She pointed to the shed that was reserved for these events. They kept almost everything in there, from dry snacks and juice boxes to extra teddy bears, games, and blankets . . . anything to help them with the summer activities planned by the town.

The first booth they stopped at was the welcome booth, set up at the crossroads of where all the pathways met. Prime location since everyone would walk by it.

Shelley offered a platter of minimuffins to them as they approached.

"These look delicious," Charlotte said. She winked at Shelley, who smiled back. When Charlotte had stopped by the bed-and-breakfast to pick up Ellie, she'd sampled some of these muffins, baked that morning by all the girls who'd stayed for the sleepover.

"This is the best welcome present a man could get," Jordan said as he took a muffin and popped it in his mouth.

Shelley pointed to the Tupperware containers of muffins at her feet. "I hope others feel the same way, otherwise you'll need to come by later and take the extras home."

Jordan eyed the containers and rubbed his hands together. "I promise to spread the word about how"—he coughed and covered his mouth—"disgusting these muffins are." He winked at Shelley before plopping another muffin into his mouth.

"Have you seen Jenn and Robert?" Charlotte had noticed them earlier.

"They went down the pathway. Robert mentioned something about seeing if others needed a hand putting their booths together and Jenn went with him."

"She's not manning the booth today?" This surprised Charlotte.

Shelley shook her head. "No. I offered to take care of it this year."

Shelley offered the platter to others who walked by, giving them a smile as it was evident they didn't want to stop. Charlotte thought about how Jenn would have stopped them anyway and asked them questions to make them feel welcome. Her presence at the booth would be missed by those out-of-town guests returning for the fair.

"Did you know about the ceremony for this afternoon?" Shelley asked.

"What ceremony?" There were no scheduled events at the fair.

Shelley pinched her lips but couldn't help the smile from growing on her face. She grabbed a flyer off the booth's table and handed it to them.

"I knew it was a secret, but I wasn't sure if anyone had mentioned it to you today or not. Wouldn't want you to miss it, considering you're the guests of honor."

"Guests of . . . what are you talking about?" Charlotte read the sheet that was in Jordan's hands. She couldn't believe what she was reading. A special ceremony to honor the victims of the Stillwater Public School shooting and the heroes of Stillwater Bay.

"Heroes?" Jordan's voice caught as he read the word out loud. "What heroes?" His hands shook as he held the paper tight in his grasp.

"Why, you two, of course."

Jordan's face blanched. His mouth opened and closed, but no words came out.

"Jordan?" Charlotte touched his icy cold hands, concerned.

He cleared his throat and thrust the paper at Charlotte. "I wish they wouldn't do that. I really wish . . . I have to go. Excuse me for a moment."

Befuddled, Charlotte stood there and watched her husband jog toward the beach bathrooms, but instead of going into the men's area, he disappeared around the corner to where the cottage homes were located.

"Is he okay?" Shelley asked.

Charlotte shook her head. She had no idea. Anytime anyone attempted to praise Jordan for how he'd handled the school shooting, he seemed to get cold and distant before he tried to focus the attention on others who had helped as well. Charlotte thought he was just being modest. But now . . . now she was worried.

Jordan really hadn't gone for any type of counseling, not on his own. Maybe he needed to. Had something happened she didn't know about? Was there more to the story than what he'd told her?

"I'm sure he's fine. He doesn't really like when the attention is on him." Charlotte stared off and tried to figure out where he would have gone.

"Which is why no one wanted to say anything. We all know how he feels, and yet, we need to do this. As a community. I hope you'll let us." Shelley gave a light tap to Charlotte's arm before she turned and offered her tray of muffins to more passersby.

There were only a few places Jordan would go in this area, but Charlotte couldn't think of one good reason why he would go to any of them. Not today and not right now. But she followed after him, smiling in greeting to those she passed along the way, the flyer still clutched tight in her hand.

She didn't mind that the town wanted to do this. It was nice of them. And she had a feeling, from what was on the flyer, that it was more about remembering as a community rather than focusing on Jordan or even herself. Besides, others in this small town had also stepped up to help carry the load. No doubt they would be honored as well. So why was Jordan so spooked?

She rounded the corner of the bathroom stalls, but there was still no sign of Jordan so she continued on, following the path that circled to the back of the cottages.

The area was empty and quiet. Each cottage had a hedge for shelter and privacy, so she couldn't see inside. Jordan had either continued down this path or stopped in at Julia's, but that didn't make sense if he had. He'd expressed no interest in helping Julia out personally. He backed her on this crusade to remind the community that Julia was more than just the killer's mother, but he'd already told her not to expect much else from him.

Which is why, when she saw the top of his head over the hedge leading into Julia's backyard, she was surprised.

"Jordan?" Charlotte pushed open the unlocked gate.

Crying, Julia sat there, on one of her chairs with her feet propped up on the small table. Jordan stood beside her, his hand on her shoulder, but she couldn't see his face.

"Charlotte, I . . ." Jordan gazed at her, helpless, and she knew he'd been crying as well.

For some reason, she couldn't move. It's not that she didn't want to but that she couldn't. There was something more here, something more than just a man finding a woman crying.

So she forced her legs to move, turn around, and walk back the way she'd come. She heard her name being called but ignored it, afraid to listen to anything Jordan would say.

Why was he there? It's possible he ran into Julia, right? Maybe she was standing outside, away from her backyard, tempted to join in on the festivities, but couldn't. Maybe Jordan had said something that affected her or both of them.

So many thoughts ran through her head, so many ideas, scenarios. All she needed to do was stop and listen to him, but she was too scared. Why?

He caught up with her and grabbed for her arm. She stopped but waited for him to speak first.

"I'm sorry I ran."

"Why?"

When he didn't say anything, she turned and faced him. "Why, Jordan? Why did you run? It's a small ceremony, not even focused on us. Why?"

His Adam's apple bobbed as he swallowed and looked beyond her. "I don't know."

Like she believed that.

"Looks like we won't be able to go for a drive after all. If you need to head back to the house, go ahead. I'll just walk around town and visit with people. Do my rounds."

"What about Julia?" There was desperation in his red-rimmed eyes.

"What about her?"

This seemed to take Jordan off guard. "I thought . . . I just thought you'd want to be with her, spend time with her. Maybe coax her out of her home for a bit?"

She shook her head. That would be the last thing she'd want to do today of all days. Not when her town was full of tourists. When Julia finally felt safe enough to leave her home, it would be on a quiet day, when she could walk down to her shop and not be worried about having eggs thrown at her.

"Why were you in her backyard?"

"What?"

"Julia's backyard. Why did you go there? Of all the places you could have gone . . . why Julia's?"

Jordan bit his lip and looked away from her.

"Jordan?" She didn't think it was a very difficult question. He ran and stopped at Julia's. A woman he refused to talk about or see since the school shooting.

"I don't know."

"What do you mean, you don't know?"

He shrugged. "I just . . . I just stopped and went in."

He still wouldn't look at her.

"You just went in. Into the backyard of a woman you don't even like? I'm sorry . . . I'm having a hard time believing that."

He didn't reply.

"There's a lot you don't know about today, it seems. You don't know why the ceremony bothers you, why you ran, and now why you stopped at Julia's place."

She cocked her head and tried to read him but couldn't. He was completely shut off from her.

"Should I be worried?"

He shook his head.

"Great. That answers a lot." She tapped her foot on the ground. "So now what?"

"What do you mean?"

Charlotte squeezed the bridge of her nose and struggled to remain calm. He was hiding something from her, something about Julia, which didn't make sense at all. But there was a ceremony this afternoon they needed to be at and a fair going on, meaning her town was full of visitors. As much as it bothered her to know Julia was in her backyard crying, she couldn't focus on her today.

God, that made her seem so cold.

"I want to go visit Julia's shop and see how things are."

Jordan sighed. His lips thinned, and she knew he wanted to say something but held himself back.

"I'll go with you. If we can't run away, then we can at least stay together." He reached for her hand but hesitated, as if unsure.

"You'll come to the ceremony then? It won't be all that bad. And it looks like there is some sort of reveal happening."

There it was, that glazed look in his eyes. The same look he always got when someone mentioned how heroic he'd been that day.

That expression he had in his eyes when she'd met him at the school, outside by an ambulance. He'd stood there, dazed, as he stared blankly about him. The moment he called her, she dropped everything and rushed up to the school. All he'd said on the phone was "He had a gun. He had a gun." She'd had no idea who carried the gun or what had happened, but she cried the moment she saw him standing there, a blanket wrapped around his shoulders. She flung her arms around him and held him close, shocked to find his body shaking. Once she knew he wasn't shot, she put everything aside, all her emotions, and did what needed to be done. Comfort those around her, help direct the children that weren't hurt to a safe area, coordinate the teachers to help keep everyone calm.

Jordan just stood there, shell-shocked. She knew something terrifying had happened for him to react that way. It took a good thirty minutes for him to come out of his daze and realize he was needed.

Whatever had happened, whatever it was that he kept secret . . . it still affected him and Charlotte felt helpless.

"What's being revealed?" There was feigned interest in his voice.

Charlotte shrugged. She wasn't going to force the issue with him. "No idea. Just what the flyer says." It was still crumpled in her hand, so she held it out to him.

"You have no idea?" She could tell he didn't believe her, but it was the truth.

"Doesn't that worry you?"

It did. She wouldn't lie. She didn't like being kept in the dark, especially about something like this. But there wasn't much she could do about it, especially after Charlie Monroe had told her to mind her own business anytime she tried to get involved. They'd just have to wait for the ceremony to see what all the fuss and secrecy was about.

They made their way down the path until they hit the sidewalk that led up Main Street. The North Beach should be full of activities as well, as most of the kids' events would be there. From clowns to face painting to turtle races. If they walked slowly and didn't stop to talk to too many people, they might make it there in fifteen minutes. They could spend some time at the beach, talking with families and interacting with the children, something she knew Jordan would love to do, and then they could walk back down to the town hall in time for the ceremony.

It wasn't the afternoon they'd originally planned, but nothing made Charlotte happier than spending time in her town, amongst the people. She'd only agreed to go for the drive for Jordan, because he seemed to need it.

But not her. This is where she got her energy from. This is what invigorated her. The town. The people.

She pushed aside the lingering questions about Jordan and Julia from her mind.

CHAPTER TWENTY-FIVE

JENNIFER

There was a lightness to her heart that surprised her as she walked hand in hand with Robert down Main Street. Maybe it was the air filled with the regular sounds of happy children—screaming, crying, laughing—as they enjoyed the day outdoors with their families. Sounds Jenn hadn't been sure would ever be heard again in this town. Or maybe sounds she knew she'd hear again, but because it meant life was returning back to normal, she hadn't been ready to accept them.

Up ahead was Merlin the Magician, better known as Thomas Woodward, a retired schoolteacher. Every year he dressed up in his magician finery and mesmerized the children of Stillwater with his tricks. A group of boys all stood around him, their hands clasped tight behind their backs, as they watched him do one trick after another.

Jenn recognized those boys. Bobby used to hang out with them. Jenn had hosted their mothers at her house for playdates before the boys were old enough for school. While their children played with Legos or action figures, she'd put on a pot of coffee or opened a bottle of wine, and the moms sat and gossiped about their lives while their children entertained one another.

It had been a while since she last had coffee with them. Once their children were in school, she hadn't felt the need to continue to have them over.

She vaguely remembered them at Bobby's funeral. The women all sat in one section, their families filling up the pews. She distinctly remembered the way they sniffled and held their own child's hand as they came up to her and Robert after the funeral. She also remembered the envy she had experienced watching those mothers with their children. Children who hadn't died that day. Children who had been in the same class as Bobby yet spared.

"That used to be me," Robert said. "I used to beg him to show me, over and over, how he did his tricks. You know what he would tell me?"

Jenn smiled up at him. "A magician never tells, only shows," she answered.

He squeezed her hand. "My poor mom. I would beg her for magic books so I could learn on my own. I would bug Mr. Woodward at recess all the time, trying to show him what I'd learned. And yet, I could never do the tricks properly."

"Never?"

"Never. I was too nervous. He was my idol, way back then."

She nudged him in the side. "He still is," she said. It was true. Robert met with the elderly man once a week up at the clubhouse and drank coffee, talking about golf or the way things used to be. He said he was spending time with him because he was lonely, but Jenn knew otherwise. Robert eventually mentioned issues he was dealing with as a member of the town council or with work, and he took Thomas Woodward's advice more often than not.

"You know, I was hoping maybe Bobby would have developed an interest in magic."

Jenn tilted her head up to look at her husband and noticed his gaze was on his old friend. She wrapped her hand around his arm and squeezed.

"I even bought him his very own magic kit." He cleared his throat. "I'm not too sure what to do with it now."

If it were her, she'd be tempted to keep it. It was bought for her son, and so it would always remain his.

"It's something we'll have to think about, eventually. What to do with his things."

She nodded. They would. One day.

They stood there on the sidewalk, quiet in their thoughts, and waited for the elderly magician to completely mesmerize the children who surrounded him until he sent them on their way.

•   •   •

"That used to be you," Thomas said as he packed away his supplies in his big black magician's bag.

"I was just saying that to Jenn." Robert grinned.

Thomas zipped up his bag, dusted his hands off, and cracked his gnarly and knotted knuckles.

"You were a curious one, that's for sure," he said. "Always bugging me to show you how I did things, and trying to show me your own tricks." He winked. "I did say try, right? I'm not sure you ever got a magic trick right."

Robert laughed, and it was in his laughter that Jenn once more saw that glimmer of hope. She drank it in, glued to the way her husband's eyes lit up and how his laughter infected those around them. People stopped and stared at them, smiles on their faces as they continued on their way.

"Where are you off to now?" Robert asked.

"I thought I'd grab something to drink before the ceremony." Thomas glanced across the street toward where the town hall was located. "That's something I don't want to miss."

"Do you know what's it's about?" Jenn asked. She'd asked Shelley earlier when she caught sight of the flyers, but Shelley had remained tightlipped about it. Considering this was the first she'd heard about the event this afternoon, she was more than a bit curious.

"I do. But don't ask me to tell you. Just be there," Thomas said. He pursed his lips and gave his head a small shake when she was about to ask him another question.

"It's strange that something like this would be arranged without either one of us knowing about it," Robert said.

Thomas shrugged. "You don't always need to be in the know." He picked up his bag and tugged the strap over his arm. "Sometimes it's good to give up control. Good for your soul. You should try it." He tapped the top of his forehead with two fingers and gave a minisalute before he headed down the sidewalk.

They watched him go. No doubt he was headed to find another group of kids at the beach or in the community center parking lot. Jenn tugged at Robert's arm, and they continued their walk.

They came to the intersection of Main Street and Water Avenue, where the town hall was located on one side and the library on the other. A crowd had gathered already in front of the town hall, where a podium had been erected alongside a large covered object.

Charity stood on the outskirts, as if waiting for them, and waved.

Jenn scanned the crowd for Charlotte but didn't see her. She did, however, catch the eye of Lacie and her family, who stood close to the front. Lacie waved and gestured for them to join her, but Jenn shook her head. She was more than happy to stay on the outskirts of the crowd.

"You have nothing to do with this, right?" she asked Robert. Normally he'd be right up there, at the front, preparing to give a speech or to talk with other council members and their families.

"Nothing." He reached into his pants pocket and pulled out his phone. "Hang on a second," he said. He angled his body away from her as he answered his phone.

Jenn stepped closer to Charity and linked her arm through her daughter's. "What do you have planned for the rest of the day?"

Charity held her hand up and waved. "Amanda and I were going to head to the beach for a game of volleyball, if that's okay? Then just hang out at the midway with friends later until the fireworks."

Jenn placed a small kiss on the top of Charity's head. "Sounds like fun." She knew her daughter was itching to hang with her friends. Robert had been right about that. "Go ahead. Will we see you later or . . ."

"Can I sleep over at Amanda's again?" There was a hopeful note in her voice. Jenn nodded in response and was thrilled to have Charity give her a brief hug before she took off to join her friend in the crowd.

Jenn turned to face Robert, to let him know what was going on, but he was still engrossed in his phone call. His face glared a brilliant red, and the muscle in his cheek pulsed. He was angry, and she could tell it was all he could do to keep a tight rein on his emotions. Whom was he talking to?

"No, I will not do that," he said into the phone. He paused. "No, I don't think you understand. What you're asking me to do is not only illegal but . . ." He paused again, but this time Jenn could hear yelling from the other person. Robert pulled the phone away from his ear and grimaced. "I highly doubt you'll find anyone in this town who will take care of this for you." His lips thinned. "No, that won't work for me. I'll call you back next week and arrange something." He jabbed the screen of his phone and jammed it back into his pocket.

"What's going on?" she asked. She reached out to him, but he took a step back, looked around, and realized others had heard his conversation and blanched.

Jenn glared at the people around them and was thankful they all had the decency to turn away from them.

"Robert?"

He groaned. "Nothing I can't handle."

"It was the Robertsons, wasn't it? Was this about Julia again?" She recalled the conversation she'd walked into a few days ago, when he'd told her they wanted the woman evicted from her home.

He nodded. The look on his face told her he didn't want to discuss it, and as much as she wanted to prod, to give him her own opinion, surprisingly, she didn't.

"You'll figure it out. I'm sure Charlotte would love to help if you told her." That was all she said.

He gave her a half smile before he placed his arm around her, and they edged closer to the crowd. Charlie Monroe, another town council member and head of the fair committee, took the stage and reached for the microphone. He tapped it a few times, and everyone in the crowd winced at the loud shriek from the speakers.

"Hello, everyone. You can hear me okay?" he asked.

"More than we want to," yelled a voice from the middle of the crowd. People around them laughed and Charlie grinned. He was known for having a loud mouth and not being afraid to speak his mind—anywhere, anytime—and it didn't matter the place.

"Very funny, Dick. Very funny. On behalf of . . . well, on behalf of the members of this town, I want to thank everyone for being here. This weekend we're celebrating the vibrancy of our town, but we also need to take the time to remember the loss we've all experienced as well. Sometimes it's easy to get lost in that grief, but, as our good pastor here said"—he pointed toward Pastor Scott Helman at the front of the crowd—"a little bit of happiness does our soul good. So today, we want to help bring that happiness if we can." He walked closer to the covered object and fingered the large sheet. "Did you know we have an artist in this town? Sometimes we tend to forget him, as he tends to hibernate up at the lighthouse throughout the year, and unless you venture up that way, he's a bit easy to miss. He's a quiet man"—he coughed to hide his smile—"but has a way of making a statement with his hands and mind."

Charlie looked out over the crowd and pointed to Blake Casser before he beckoned him up to the stage.

"As a town, we wanted there to be a way to remember the lives that were lost last month in a way that would be memorable and befitting of who they were. Most of those who died were children, but we lost a few good teachers as well." Charlie wiped at the tears that trickled down his cheek.

Jenn grasped on to Robert's hand.

Charlie handed the microphone to Blake, who scowled at him but took it from his hand.

"Sometimes words aren't enough. And sometimes they are too much. You all know I'm not a fan of platitudes . . . and I won't say something that's not true. Being sorry can't replace the hugs you would get from your children if they were still alive. Sympathy can't fill the void in your hearts. I know this. But I also know that sometimes, we need something tangible to remember . . . to remember they were real and they did make a difference." He scuffled his feet a bit before he gathered the hem of the cover and then paused.

"This is nowhere near what is in my heart for each and every one of you, but I hope when you see it, whether today or a year from now, it will bring a smile to your face and joy to your heart." He handed the microphone back to Charlie and then, with a pull from his arms, uncovered the large sculpture.

Jenn gasped along with everyone else in the crowd. She covered her mouth with her fist to hold back the sobs that racked her body.

The statue was amazing. Even from this distance, Jenn could see that somehow Blake had managed to meld together sand glass into the shape of a heart. But it was what was inside the heart that stole her breath. Out of glass, Blake had etched out what looked to be the names of all those who died on that fateful day. Jenn wanted to get closer, to see for herself if she were right. She wanted to see Bobby's name there, forever remembered. She must have tried to move forward because Robert's arms tightened around her and held her back.

"Wait. Let's just wait," he murmured into her ear.

"For those who can't see, I created a wreath of sea glass in the shape of a heart. Inside this heart is a pane of glass I blew myself with the date and name of each person—whether child or adult— who lost their life. They will never be forgotten." Blake cleared his throat before he stepped back.

Charlie pulled out a handkerchief and mopped his face. He glanced over at the crowd and pointed to someone, but Jenn couldn't see to whom.

"We also wanted to honor some heroes in the crowd, but apparently they're too shy to come up. Many more lives would have been lost that day if it wasn't for the smart thinking of our principal and teachers. Without them . . . well, my granddaughter wouldn't be here." He cleared this throat.

Jenn ducked her head. Yes, those teachers protected the lives of many, but they missed some. She watched parents pull their children closer and noticed some of the teachers in the crowd who were surrounded by loved ones.

Yes, they were heroes. Even though her son hadn't been protected, her daughter was still alive. She had to remember that. She needed to remember that.

"Principal Stone, it was due to your bravery and dedication to protecting our children that more lives were not lost. This town can't thank you, or the wonder team of teachers and staff at Stillwater Public, enough. Same with our mayor. The way you took charge afterward, how you handled the press and stepped in to ensure this town survived through those first few days and then weeks . . . well, I know you won't come up so we can thank you properly"—Charlie frowned at them—"but I hope that this little piece set at the bottom of this amazing tribute tells you how we feel about you."

Charlie knelt down and pulled off the cloth covering the black marble base. There was an etching on there that couldn't be seen, so Charlie read it out.

"For the bravery, dedication, and love you have provided, Stillwater Bay will never forget those who stepped forward to protect our own. Even in death."

Jenn couldn't stop the tears from falling then. *Even in death.* She knew that was meant to honor the two teachers who'd been shot to death as they stood in front of their students.

Charlie was right. The way Jordan and Charlotte had stepped up . . . it was not only heroic but . . . life changing. Jenn felt guilty for lambasting her friend for not caring and placing the needs of the town ahead of everything else.

It was Jordan who'd caught Gabriel Berry's attention and stopped the spree of bullets from killing more lives.

It was Charlotte who had taken charge when everyone else couldn't.

And it was Jenn who'd pushed her friend away, not realizing just how wrong she'd been.

"I need to find Charlotte," she said to Robert.

"Why?"

"I just do." Jenn pushed her husband's arms away and made her way through the crowd. She found Charlotte, standing next to Lacie.

Jenn stood in front of her friend and placed her arms around her, giving her a tight hug. She squeezed, not wanting to let go, and was relieved when Charlotte's arms encircled her.

"I'm so sorry," Jenn whispered into her friend's ear.

Charlotte strengthened her embrace. "You have nothing to apologize for. Nothing."

"Thank you," she said. She turned and reached for Jordan's hand and squeezed it. "Thank you," she repeated.

Jordan's face was pasty white, and his pupils were dilated. She wasn't even sure he'd heard her; it looked like he was struggling to contain a panic attack.

"Jordan?"

He moistened his lips and blinked a few times before he was able to respond.

"Please don't. Don't thank me. Please," he croaked. His jaw tensed, and he wouldn't look her in the eye. Charlotte mouthed *don't* to Jenn, asking her to leave whatever was happening alone.

But she couldn't. It didn't feel right. Except . . . somehow she knew if she pushed Jordan, he'd fall apart. She could see it in his eyes. His hands were fisted together, and his skin was clammy. Why? What was wrong with him?

"You need to get it together; people are coming." Charlotte laid her hand on her husband's shoulder, and from the way her fingers went white, Jenn knew the grip was tight.

It took a few seconds, but the look on Jordan's face changed. Gone was the panic-stricken man somehow affected by the ceremony, and the principal this town knew and loved returned. His body became erect, his shoulders pushed back, and a slight smile appeared. He still didn't look at Jenn but instead focused on Charlie, who had stepped down to talk with him.

"Is everything okay?" Jenn asked Charlotte.

Charlotte watched her husband, concern evident from the way she studied him. "I don't know. I just . . . I don't know."

Lacie stepped up and linked her arms through both Jenn's and Charlotte's.

"I don't know about you girls, but I could use some girlfriend time. Obviously not today, but how about this weekend? Does Sunday work? We can grab Shelley and maybe head to that inn just down the coast and go for brunch?"

"On a Sunday?" Jenn asked.

"Yes. On a Sunday. I don't want to be here when Scott leaves for the church. Please?" She glanced over her shoulder at her family. "Run away with me, even if it's only for a few hours?" she pleaded.

The pleading did it for Jenn. Something was happening to Lacie, something that went beyond just the regular issues of a pastor's wife. Over the past month, Jenn had been so lost in her own grief, she'd forgotten that there were others around her experiencing the same loss. She'd been so angry with Robert for making her wear a mask that she'd forgotten she wasn't the only one in the public eye who had to pretend they were okay.

"It's a date." Jenn didn't wait to see what Charlotte would say.

Relief swept over Lacie's features. "Thank you," she said. "Thank you." She turned back to her husband, who had called her name.

Robert stood a few feet away from Jenn and waved. She waved back. She saw a brief glimpse of what their future could be as long as they stayed united, as a team. But could they?

She sure hoped so.

CHAPTER TWENTY-SIX

CHARLOTTE

Jordan paced the length of Charlotte's office multiple times before he managed to calm down. Charlotte waited at the little table she had in her office and watched him.

Truth be told, she was actually a little nervous.

He'd bolted from the crowd after the unveiling of the amazing statue up to her office once people started to come their way. He'd managed to shake a few hands and make small talk with a few individuals, but that had been it. He'd left her standing there, with no explanation or excuses, until the crowd had thinned enough that she felt she could check up on him.

"I can't do this anymore," Jordan muttered. He ran his fingers through his hair, messing it up even more than it already had been, and dropped into the seat opposite of her.

"Can't do what?"

He wouldn't look her in the eye; instead, he dropped his head into his hands and leaned over until he was bent over his knees.

"Jordan, talk to me. Please." She scooted to the edge of her chair and placed her hand on his knee.

"I can't do this. I can't. It's eating away at me, and I feel like I'm about to lose myself." He raised his head and his bloodshot eyes alarmed her. Her hand squeezed his knee involuntarily.

"Jordan," she said, her voice firm and full of authority, "I need you to focus. Tell me what is going on."

He stared at her before he sat up straight and placed his hands in his lap.

"This isn't something you can fix. It's not."

"Not if you won't let me try." She saw a tiny glimmer of hope in his eyes at her words.

He stood up and went to the window, pulling aside the curtains to look down at the street below.

"I'm not who they think I am."

That didn't make sense to her. "Who are you then?"

He was silent for a few minutes. She wasn't sure he was going to respond, but then she heard the words she never thought she'd ever hear from him.

"I'm a coward."

"No you're not." She couldn't believe he'd even say that. If there was one thing Jordan was not, it was a coward.

"I am. I didn't save anyone's life, and in fact, I may have been more responsible for their deaths than I thought."

This time Charlotte was the one to stand.

"What are you talking about? Of course you're not responsible. Didn't you hear them today? You saved lives. It was you, Jordan, who stopped Gabe Berry in the end. You."

Jordan crossed his arms over his chest as if hugging himself.

"No." He swallowed hard. "I lied to you. I lied to the police . . . to everyone. I wasn't there." A pained look crossed his face. "I wasn't there to talk down Gabe. Not at first, anyway."

"Then where were you?"

She couldn't imagine what he had to say could be as horrible as he was making it out to be. Had he been in a classroom trying to calm the students? Had he been in the office protecting his staff? Where could he have been that was so horrible?

"I was hiding."

Charlotte let out the breath she held in. Okay, that wasn't so bad. She would have hid as well once she heard the first gunshot.

Jordan looked out the window, his palm touching the glass.

"I'm not a hero. I'm a coward. A coward who hid in his office closet the moment he heard the first gunshot." His palm slid down the glass, leaving streak marks. Charlotte concentrated on the lines of those marks, knowing they would be forever marked in her memory. "I hid. I didn't rush out and help any of the students find a safe place. I didn't barricade a classroom door so no one would come out. I didn't face down Gabe and attempt to calm him down." His voice hitched, and in that moment, Charlotte saw him as a weak man.

"But . . . you did see Gabe? You told me you did. You were there when he killed himself. You told me . . ." Her voice trailed off, suddenly unsure if anything he'd told her had been the truth or not.

A movement to her left caught her eye, close to the door that was partially closed. It had been closed, right?

"Wait," she said. She got up and went to close the door, but first, she opened it slightly and listened. A low murmur of voices echoed off the walls below as people gathered. Had someone come up to her office and heard Jordan's confession? She hoped not. Oh God, she hoped not.

"I don't want to hear any more," she said once the door was closed. She breathed in deep, her thoughts overloaded as she thought of what to do next. Now was not the time for her husband to bare his soul. Not here and certainly not now. Not when they needed to leave and join those crowds.

"But . . ." Jordan slumped against the wall. "I need to tell you. I need to tell you the truth."

"No." She held up her hand to stop him. "What you need is to man up. If you need to have a nervous breakdown, fine. But not here. Go home, have a long shower, and try to relax. I'll join you later, and we can talk." She grabbed her purse and slung it over her shoulder. "Right now, to this town, you are a hero, and I refuse to let you change that."

"But I need . . . I need to tell you about Gabe. About what he said."

She shook her head. Hearing this was not what she needed. How dare he do this to her now with everyone below. Why couldn't he have trusted her in the beginning? He should have told her the truth then, whatever the truth was, and they could have dealt with it together. But now . . . to unload on her now . . . in the middle of the town fair and after the ceremony? No. She couldn't do this. Not now.

"What I need is for you to get your act together. When we walk out of this office, I need you to be the principal everyone believes you to be. That's it. You need to smile and look calm and go home. I'll see you later, and we can figure out what to do next."

"But you don't know—"

"Jordan, I swear, if you tell me now, I will lose it. Right now you will pull yourself together and act as if nothing is wrong. Tonight you can tell me, and we will figure out how to fix it. Whatever it is. But not now." She stopped him from saying more. She wanted to know what had him so freaked out, but not here. After a moment, she held out her hand and waited for him to take it.

She knew that whatever he was about to tell her, it would change their lives forever. She knew it, deep in her heart. She wasn't sure why today was the catalyst for Jordan's change of heart, but it had obviously been too much for him.

She thought about how he'd run earlier at the first mention of the ceremony and how she'd found him in Julia's backyard with tears in his eyes. Something had happened in those few moments, something he hadn't wanted her to know. Her teeth ground together as she struggled to focus. She pushed every other thought out of her head as Jordan clasped her hand and they walked out of her office.

A round of applause broke out as they made their way down the stairs, and Charlotte squeezed her husband's hand while plastering a smile on her face. She wasn't sure why people were down there, waiting for them, clapping for them. But when she saw little Ellie Thomlin standing at the bottom of the steps holding a bouquet of flowers in front of her, she knew.

She knew the moment Jordan noticed Ellie. His hand shook in her grip, and he almost tripped.

"Ellie, honey." Charlotte bent down until she rested on her heels once they hit the bottom of the stairs. Jordan stood there, at her side, frozen. "These are beautiful," she said to the little girl.

"For you and Principal Stone." Ellie held out the bouquet, and Charlotte took them from her hands before offering them up to Jordan. Once he took them, Charlotte held out her arms and hugged the little girl tight.

"Thank you," she said to Ellie.

Charlotte nudged Jordan with her elbow in his knee, and he bent down with a grunt.

"These are very pretty, Ellie. Did you pick them out yourself?" he asked her. His voice was wooden, but Ellie wouldn't notice.

"Mommy helped." Ellie glanced up at her mom. "I wanted to say thank you for saving me." Her lips trembled at the words.

Charlotte blinked away tears that gathered in her eyes, and she knew Lauren, Ellie's mom, did the same.

Jordan shook his head before he took Ellie's hands in his own. He cleared his throat a few times before he could respond.

"Oh Ellie." He bit his lip and glanced at Charlotte out of the corner of his eye. "I'm not a hero. You are. I know you didn't think I noticed, but I saw how you were there for your friends, giving them hugs and telling them everything would be okay. I saw you, Ellie Thomlin. For what you did afterward, how you helped your friends and the way you help your mom every day, to me, you're the real hero."

Jordan leaned forward and placed a gentle kiss on Ellie's forehead before he stood up and reached for Charlotte's hand. Then, just before they went to walk out of the building, he handed the flowers to Charlotte and reached for Ellie's hand.

"What do you say us heroes go get an ice cream cone?" he asked Ellie.

The smile on Ellie's face, the way Lauren's shoulders relaxed, and the forced ease in Jordan's voice told Charlotte everything would be okay. For now.

Like Jenn, she held on to this moment and prayed it would last.

CHAPTER TWENTY-SEVEN

JENNIFER

The crowd from the ceremony slowly dispersed, Jenn and Robert amongst them. They didn't say much as they walked mindlessly down the sidewalk and across the street. Jenn felt a little overwhelmed and was attempting to let it all soak in.

Up ahead was Still Blooming, and Paige was outside handing flowers to people as they walked by.

"I'm sorry I haven't bought you flowers in a while," Robert said.

Jenn rolled her eyes. "It's not like we haven't had enough flowers in our house, Robert."

"Yeah, I know." He shrugged. "But none of them are from me."

Every week Robert used to bring her home a bouquet of flowers she would place in an antique water jug they'd picked up years ago at a garage sale.

"Maybe you can start again," she suggested. She'd never said it, but she'd gotten so used to him bringing flowers home that the meaning had been lost. One more thing she'd taken for granted in their marriage.

"I think I will." He leaned down and placed a kiss on her lips.

"All right you two, that's enough," Paige teased. She held out a bright-orange gerbera to Jenn.

"These are beautiful." Jenn loved the vibrancy of the flower.

"It's my last orange, but your daughter asked me to specifically keep it for you." Paige set the basket she'd held in the crook of her arm down on the stool beside her and gave Jenn a hug.

"She did?" Robert asked. "We just left her at the town hall."

"I think she took off with Amanda," Jenn said. She didn't remember saying good-bye to Charity or seeing her leave, but no doubt the kids had their own plans for the day. She would have liked to spend more time with her today, especially after the ceremony.

"The girls just stepped inside there." Paige pointed to the Treasure Chest, which Jenn hadn't noticed earlier. Its door was held open by a sign letting customers know it was open again.

"She's in there?"

Paige nodded.

Jenn stared through the open doorway to find her daughter, but she wasn't able to see much past the crowds of people inside. Charity wasn't supposed to be in there working; she thought that had all been cleared up.

"Do you want to wait out here for a minute?" she asked Robert. "I want to talk to Charity and find out what's going on." At his nod, she squeezed past two women who were coming out of the store, their arms loaded with bags full of items.

"I was so worried this shop wouldn't be open; this is the highlight of my trip every year," one of the women said as she passed Jenn.

The store was packed. Displays of homemade crafts created by Stillwater artisans and other local vendors filled the tables and walls, and she was amazed at the transformation.

"Hey." Charity appeared in front of her. "I thought you'd still be at the town hall." She dragged Jenn out of the store, with Amanda following after them, and bumped into Julia, who stood outside with Camille, Paige, and Robert.

Julia's eyes widened at Jenn's sharp intake of breath, and then she cast her gaze downward.

Robert stood there, looking slightly awkward and holding the bright-orange gerbera daisy in his hands.

No one said anything. No one really needed to. What was there to say? Was she expected to stand there and create some inane conversation to make the woman feel welcomed? Was she supposed to pretend there was nothing between them?

And yet . . . this was the first time she'd seen Julia since that dreadful day. The first time she'd taken the time to look at her, really look at her.

Julia looked . . . beaten. Her shoulder bones protruded from the back of her shirt, and there were large dark circles beneath her eyes. With her hair pulled back into a ponytail, she looked gaunt. If Jenn didn't know better, she would think Julia was sick, but then she realized Julia was. Sick with grief.

Jenn took a step forward, closer to Julia, and she could feel the panic of everyone around her. They were all unsure of what she was going to do, and she knew instantly they were all there to protect Julia. Against her. Her. That hurt. She swallowed the betrayal from her husband and friends but still didn't say anything. Instead, she waited. Waited to see if Julia would raise her gaze from the pavement and look her in the eye.

Jenn had no idea what she was doing or even what she would say. But she knew she was living in a moment that would change the rest of her life.

Isn't that what moments were all about? Small opportunities to direct the path chosen? To influence decisions and outcomes? To make a stand in how to move forward?

Each moment required a decision. A decision to live or die. She could choose in this moment to start healing or to remain lost in her grief. That's all she'd done up until now—remained fixated on anger and grief. Angry that all the moments she could have spent with her son, watching him grow, had been stolen from her.

Her hand itched to make contact with Julia's face, to slap her and leave a red imprint there, a testimony of her anger. But, she couldn't. She stood there, knowing that it wasn't in her to add any more grief to this woman who'd been destroyed by it.

Maybe it was the way Julia stood there, her shoulders curled forward, her hands clasped too tight in front, expecting to be vilified and doing nothing to stop the barrage of filth Jenn wished to say.

Or maybe it was the sheen of tears in Julia's eyes as she finally looked up, the emptiness in her gaze, or the way she looked through Jenn as if she wasn't worthy of being there.

Or maybe it was the shared grieving of two mothers, that faint glimmer of pain and guilt in Julia's eyes that touched Jenn's heart in a way she hadn't expected.

In that second, Jenn saw Julia not as the monster she'd wished her to be, not the woman who'd given birth to the demon child who murdered her own son, but as a mother who'd lost her own child, a mother who knew there were no second chances and no opportunities to make things right.

She saw the sorrow and anguish in Julia's gaze along with the knowledge that her own child had destroyed the lives of so many. And that look, their shared moment, melted Jenn's cold heart toward the mother in front of her.

Instead of slapping her, she hugged her.

Julia's body was stiff in her embrace, so Jenn tightened her hold. She could feel the sharp points of her spine jutting out from her back, and she knew that unless something changed, Julia wouldn't be with them for much longer. Grief was eating away at her, leaving her as a shell, and Jenn understood why Charlotte had decided to fight for this woman.

"I'm sorry for your loss," Jenn whispered into Julia's ear. She said it softly, so that no one else would hear. Her words were meant from one woman to another. One mother to another. That was all. She wasn't sorry Gabriel Berry was dead. She wasn't sorry he'd taken his own life after he took so many others. But she was sorry that Julia had to experience the grief of losing a child.

That was something no mother was ever prepared to live with.

She pulled back and blinked away the tears in her eyes as she saw the look of amazement and hope in Julia's. She knew Julia was about to say something, and so she stopped her.

"I'm not sure I can ever forgive your son for what he did, but I do know that I have to stop blaming you," Jenn said.

Robert moved to stand beside her, finally, and Charity stood on the other side of her, linking their arms together as a family.

"I will never forgive myself," Julia said. "I certainly don't expect others to."

"You're still loved, Julia." Camille wrapped her arm around Julia's shoulders and held tight. She mouthed *thank you* to Jenn as they stood there.

"I wanted her to see that her store was open and full," Camille said, as if in answer to the question that hung between everyone. "It's time for her to stop hiding."

"Isn't it great," Charity piped up. "And it's full of stuff. So much stuff. But the way people are buying, you're going to have to restock soon." Her teenage daughter burst with overt enthusiasm, as if trying to alleviate the tension between all of them.

"I never expected . . ." Julia choked up as she stared through the open doorway. "I didn't know."

"Of course not, it was supposed to be a surprise." Charity smiled.

"You still have friends in this town, Julia. You're not alone." Camille said the words softly.

Camille led Julia to the door of her store, and Robert led Jenn away from the area, continuing their way down the street.

"I think it's time for ice cream, isn't it? Amanda? Will you join us?" Jenn said. She knew Charity and Robert must both be a tad anxious, unsure of how she would react. But she felt okay. Not fine. Not happy. Just okay. Life continued on, the way it should, by moving forward. One moment of understanding didn't exonerate all the other moments of anger, grief, and sadness. But it did help her to see there was hope ahead.

Jenn kept quiet. She enjoyed the way they walked together, as a family unit. She'd missed this. It had been a long time since they'd been together like this, in public, without the shadow of their loss overhead.

Yes, the memory of Bobby would always be there. But that memory didn't always have to be tinged with sadness, right?

As they walked down the street together, Jenn knew as long as they remained a family, they could get through anything.

And it was that thought that placed a small smile on her face.

STILLWATER DEEP

A STILLWATER BAY NOVEL

CHARLOTTE

Her hands pummeled the punching bag with a steady rhythm. She pushed everything else out of her mind and concentrated only on her timing. Sweat dropped from her forehead, her chest hurt from the workout, and her knuckles cramped up from the constant impact, but she wasn't ready to give up, to give in.

"Will you talk to me, please?"

Jordan appeared in front of her, his hands on both sides of the bag, forcing her to stop. She bent down, her hands gripping her knees, and gulped in air.

"Go. Away," she managed to get out.

"No." His arms dropped from the bag, and he handed her a towel and her bottle of water. "I'm done with you avoiding me."

"Excuse me?" He did not just say that. He had no right. As far as she was concerned, she could and would avoid him as long as she needed to.

Two days ago he'd destroyed her world by sharing a secret she should have known from the beginning.

"We need to talk about this."

She wiped her face and took a long drink of her water before she rolled her shoulders to work out the stiffness. She ignored him, like she'd done for the past two days, and walked past him and up the stairs.

She refilled her water bottle, cut a few slices of cheese, and went up the stairs to their bedroom where she got ready for a cold shower. She knew Jordan had followed her. Knew he wanted to speak to her, needed her to say something to him. But she refused to.

Maybe he'd go away and leave her in peace.

"I'm not going away, Charlotte." Jordan sat down in the armchair in the corner of the room and crossed his legs.

"What do you expect me to say, Jordan? That I forgive you? That I understand why you did what you did? That I find it perfectly okay that you would . . ." She couldn't say it. She just couldn't.

Everything made perfect sense now. Or not. God, no, nothing made sense anymore.

Two days ago when she'd found Jordan in Julia's backyard, both of them crying, she knew something was off. Why would her husband, the man who wanted nothing to do with Julia Berry, be in that woman's backyard, crying with her?

Crying with her. She had seen those tears.

"No. What I did wasn't okay, and I don't want your forgiveness. I don't deserve it."

"Then what is it you need?" Her body shook from unspent emotion.

Back in her office, when Jordan broke down after the ceremony, she'd told him that they'd deal with whatever had happened, together. But she hadn't expected this.

This, she didn't know how to fix.

"I don't know." His voice was full of remorse and rejection. She knew he expected her to do something, to say something that would fix everything, but this . . . was unfixable.

She turned her back on him and walked into their bathroom, locking the door behind her.

She leaned against the wall and stared at herself in the mirror. She'd aged dramatically in the past two days. More wrinkles showed around her eyes and forehead, and the gray hairs had more than doubled.

Yesterday she'd locked herself in her office, and the only thing she'd done was look through old photos of her and Jordan, starting from when they first met. She wasn't sure what she'd expected to find in the images, a clue maybe to the double life her husband led.

When he confessed his duplicity to her, the fact that he'd actually hid in a closet on the day Gabriel Berry came into the Stillwater Public School, she'd thought she could handle it. Okay, so her husband was a coward and not the hero everyone made him out to be. She could handle that. She'd help him keep his secret. Right now, the town didn't need to know he'd placed his own life ahead of his students. That he'd hid at the first sound of gunshots.

She tried very hard not to judge him for that.

But it was afterward. When they were at home, when he'd confessed his deep, dark secret, that her world, the one she'd known, had been destroyed.

How did she fix this?

How could she face Julia again? Look her in the eye and pretend everything was normal between them, that she didn't know of the secret between her and Jordan?

When Charlotte emerged from the shower, Jordan was still there, in the chair, waiting for her.

"All right, Jordan. You want to talk. You want me to open up and tell you how I'm feeling, is that right?" With her back turned toward him, she donned a sundress, pulled her hair back in a pony-tail, and took in a deep breath.

"Yes, that's what I want. That's what I need."

"Need?" She shook her head. "Right now, your needs are the last thing on my mind."

She knew, from this moment on, things would never be the same between them again. Ever. She couldn't leave him. Not now. Not when her town was so fragile and needed her support and strength. She didn't have any extra energy to put toward rebuild-ing her sham of a marriage, and to be honest, she wasn't sure she wanted to.

"Here's what I need. I need you to move out of our bedroom. Sleep in the guest bedroom downstairs or the one up here, I don't care. But you're not welcome here, in my room, in my bed. Not now. I'm not sure if you ever will be again."

Jordan cast his gaze downward but nodded.

"I also want you to start looking for a new position. Somewhere else. I don't care where. It can be in Seattle, Portland, or all the way across the country. I. Don't. Care." She steeled her voice as he lifted his gaze and looked at her with shock. "You won't do it until after the start of the school year, though. This town needs to begin the new school year in September with some normalcy, and you'll con-tinue to play the role of a hero. Do you understand?"

God help him if he didn't.

"Would you give up being mayor?"

She shook her head. She wasn't going to give up anything. Not for him.

"I can't do that, Charlotte. I can't." Jordan wiped at the tears that gathered in his eyes, as the understanding of what she meant hit him and she hardened her heart against him even more.

"You can and you will."

Two days ago, Jordan had destroyed her world by not only admitting to his cowardice but also to a lie he'd lived for years.

His disdain for Julia had been real, but not for the reasons Charlotte had imagined.

He'd known Julia for years. He'd even known Gabriel. Or known of him, before Julia moved to Stillwater Bay.

Jordan was Gabe's absentee father, and the reason Gabe had gone into Stillwater Public with a gun was not because of some psychotic breakdown, but because he'd just found out who his father was.

ABOUT THE AUTHOR

With a passion for storytelling, Steena took her dream of being a full-time writer and made it a reality, writing her first novel while working as a receptionist. She won the National Indie Excellence Book Award in 2012 for her bestselling novel, *Finding Emma*. Steena currently lives in Calgary, Alberta, with her husband, three daughters, and two dogs. She likes to celebrate completing each new novel with chocolate.